CW00418567

South London January 2004

"Don't turn around *Father*".

The voice behind him sent an icy chill down the spine of Billy Kelly. A voice he knew. A voice he could remember only too well. A voice from his past.

This was a voice he wished he could forget and had hoped he would never hear again as long as he lived.

But in all honesty, the way things had played out, that was never going to happen!

The sarcasm in overemphasising the word *"Father"* was particularly chilling. Billy started to turn, had only turned halfway when the voice stopped him.

"I told you not to turn around, I won't tell you again. You turn around again to look at me you slag and I will blow your fucking kneecap out".

Billy felt the barrel of a gun nudge the back of his head. The voice with the familiar London accent ordered him to look away. Billy knew only too well the man standing behind him meant it, they had once been friends, his name was - Jimmy Walsh.

Billy was dressed in a grey Crombie overcoat black trousers and black ankle-high chukka boots, under the coat he wore a white shirt, black waistcoat and the traditional roman collar of a Catholic priest. Billy was not a priest, the disguise had served him well on numerous occasions over the past near twenty years to move around unnoticed and unmolested. It had come as somewhat of a surprise to Billy as to how people reacted to a priest, how men dropped their stares and women smiled with a welcoming *"good morning, Father"*.

On many occasions, the none too holy thoughts that ran through *Father Billy's* mind would certainly have made a nun blush, not to mention the unsuspecting ladies who were offering the greetings.

Billy was stood on the damp grass verge of a newly backfilled grave, floral tributes laid on freshly mounded earth, the ink from the attached condolence cards was smudged and ran in tiny inky blue rivulets, the overnight raindrops still clung to the blades of the lush green grass. The dark cloudy London skies overhead now lent an even more sombre air to the cold grey moss-covered gravestones that stood silently around them. An icy wind blew as the drizzle swirled around and fell to cover everything in a fine mist.

The grave was occupied by Billy's' father who had died eight days previously, and whose funeral had taken place two days earlier.

"I knew this day would come, I always knew you would come back. So I waited, I knew when the old man died you wouldn't stay away, nineteen years, but I knew, I knew you would come back, and here you are back on the old manor. I have to say though old son I thought you would probably have made me wait a bit longer, you must have known I would be expecting you..." Jimmy let the sentence trail.

Manor is London slang for a neighbourhood, all those years ago he had been Billy Kelly street thug, enforcer, gangster. Billy and Jimmy had been the best of friends at that time, attending the same schools since they were five-year-olds. They grew up on the same South London streets where they stole what they needed to survive as a way of life. They were involved in house burglaries, bag snatches and muggings before they had graduated to the more lucrative and violent crimes that came as part of their newfound vocation employed as enforcers for Jack Riordan, a local underworld crime boss. They collected protection money, gambling debts. The extortion of money from drug dealers, known as taxing was another lucrative income stream, they made a good living, Jack Riordan an even better one.

Billy was never able to claim as Jimmy could, that crime was his way out of poverty or an escape route from a dysfunctional family. Billy had had a comfortable upbringing, his father was a responsible man who held down a steady job, his mother also worked full time, and they had given Billy everything they could to show him the love they felt for him. Billy was more a peer pressure excitement junkie, he did what he did because he chose too, and he enjoyed it.

"Back in the old parish, and you dressed as a priest, how ironic Billy" Jimmy laughed at his own joke.

Jimmy Walsh was six feet tall, bright red hair cut in a quarter-inch crop close to his skull, sunken green eyes in an almost perfectly round face, a crooked mouth set almost permanently in a psychopathic half-smirk.

"Hello, Jimmy - how are you? I always knew we would meet again. I just hoped it wasn't going to be in this life" Billy replied nervously not trying to be funny.

Jimmy chuckled at Billy's attempt at mild humour.

"Oh I'm good Billy, now you're back I'm even better. I mean it's been a lucky last twelve months for me. *Monty's pass* wins the Grand National, *Kris Kin* wins the Derby, and *Millwall* - miracle of miracles, get to the FA Cup Final, and now you're back, well - I think my accumulator might have just come up".

"Like I said it's been a long time - *I missed ya*" Jimmy hissed.

"I always wondered how you were. I spent a lot of time thinking about you. Mainly in the early hours of the mornings, as I just lay on my bunk staring at the ceiling, I was always wondering how you were doing Billy? But being behind the door does that for you, you get to wonder about old friends, especially those that put you there". Jimmy said.

"I didn't put you away, and I didn't grass on you, I gave up Riordan, It wasn't like I had any choice was it, Jimmy? We knew that you were going to hang us all out to dry, we knew that you had cut a deal. You were going to save your own skin."

"Really, that's what they told you is it?" Jimmy spat the words out showing his contempt of the very idea that he would have turned on anyone in the firm.

"It was you or us and they were only going to wait for twenty fours hours before they withdrew the offer they had on the table, they wanted you, but we would do if they couldn't get you," Billy said.

"It was Jack Riordan that fitted me up, how could you not see that? How could I tell them Riordan ordered me to do the hit? That would have got me two life sentences, are you really that stupid, Jimmy asked, but you go right ahead and offer up the fact that Jack Riordan gangland boss of the whole of South fucking London ordered the hit"

"I had nothing else to give them. I wasn't going away for fifteen years for Jack Riordan. It was self-preservation Jimmy pure and simple. I told you not to do it, but you didn't listen, Riordan was more important to you than our business, you made that clear".

"Oh that's alright then, I'm glad we cleared all that up, let's have a cup of tea and a catch up then. Ask yourself a question Billy, Jimmy continued, what happened to Riordan, how the fuck do you think he got away?"

"I know what happened to Riordan he was allowed to fly out of the country, he took off for Spain the next day, he knew that he couldn't be extradited from there, Billy replied, they also had Paddy and Tommy too, that's why they needed us - they needed bodies in the dock to give evidence against you. I refused to answer questions about you at the interviews, that's why I gave them Riordan - I wasn't going to give you up to them".

Jimmy tutted and shook his head.

"Not good enough Billy, just not good enough. I knew about Paddy and Tommy, but they were soon gone. I didn't expect much more of the - but you Billy? We were like brothers, you knew that. I heard they gave you a nice little setup Billy, soft time and some readies when you got out, the press made you famous, you're famous you know - but of course, you know - your friends in the press would have told you all about that, the man that put away *"Crazy Jimmy Walsh"* Jimmy said.

"I didn't put you away Jimmy, you put yourself away, I told you not to do as Riordan asked, but as it turned out you were doing deals behind his back, and my back too for that matter *partner* "Billy sneered at the word partner.

The two men Billy referred to as Paddy and Tommy, were Paddy Meehan and Tommy Callaghan. Both men were childhood friends of Billy and Jimmy having grown up together attending the same schools. They had all served as altar boys at their local parish church. That had played for the same boys' football teams and attended the same youth club, Jimmy had actually been Godfather to Paddy's boy.

"Paddy dead, found with two in his head, and what about Tommy? Found face down in his Tenerife swimming pool - his throat cut. Well, that's like moving to Bermondsey Billy, I mean Tenerife, half the firms in London still winter there, how the fuck did he think he was going to get by unnoticed in Tenerife. Fucking mug" Jimmy said.

Jimmy laughed again, as he thought of the stories he had read in the newspapers when both Paddy and Tommy had met their end. It was rumoured that Jimmy had ordered these hits from his prison cell although it hadn't been proven to be true. The underworld was still rife with the rumours. Jimmy had never been accused of the murders, as the perpetrators had never been caught. Billy, though had proved far more elusive, he had really gone dark. Vanished like smoke into a Guy Fawkes nights air.

"Anyway Billy - I'm going to tell you a story, not going anywhere, are you? Jimmy chuckled again.

Jimmy was starting to enjoy himself and Billy knew that was not a good sign, this would not end well one way or the other. Billy was scared, he felt an involuntary shiver run down his spine and knew that it was only partly due to the bitterly cold London morning. His bladder all of a sudden felt full. His mouth was dry. His breathing was heavier than usual, but he was trying his best to control it.

"I know you like telling stories Billy but now you are going to listen to one, don't worry it's a good one, you will like it I promise, or maybe not come to think of it, but I like it and that's what really matters, *innit* Billy". Jimmy cackled again.

Billy wanted to turn around again. His head moved slightly to the left. He felt a sharp pain explode above his right ear as the gun collided against his head. He staggered about three feet to his left.

"I told you to not turn around Billy, are you fucking stupid? Try that again and I will hurt you permanently. The only reason you are still breathing is I haven't told you my story yet". Jimmy seemed to be almost pleading to be heard.

Billy now knew that Jimmy intended to kill him. He listened silently as he felt the warm trickle of blood run down behind his ear. He had once had a hot oil scalp massage from an old girlfriend, strangely that's what he thought of when he felt the trickle of blood, it was the same sensation. Billy had also noticed that when he staggered to his left, he was now standing at the foot of an open grave. It was just staring up at him as if waiting for him to jump in. The walls of the grave forming a perfect rectangle. Billy suddenly felt very claustrophobic!

Jimmy moved, standing directly behind him again.

"Do you remember when we went to Margate Billy? We went there after I got that not guilty for those *Yardies*?

Billy remembered only too well the incident in 1983 that catapulted Jimmy Walsh to legendary status in South London, and firmly put him on the radar of every policeman in the Metropolitan and Greater London areas.

Chapter 2

South London 1983

The press had labelled Jimmy Walsh "*Crazy Jimmy*" during his trial at the Old Bailey in July 983 when he stood trial for the attempted murder of two Jamaican "*Yardie*" gangsters who had broken into Jimmy's house one night to collect an unofficial tax rebate on their contributions.

They had been hired by a London gang from their base in the St. Paul's area of Bristol, they were to carry out an "*extreme punishment*" that was the order. What that actually entailed was open to interpretation. The two men, rumoured to have connections to the notorious *Tivoli Gardens Shower Posse* in Kingston, Jamaica, had broken in through the front door of the small terraced house, this had been a big mistake, had they done their homework they would have known that Jimmy never used this door, he always came and went via the back door leading to an alleyway, which in turn led onto a side street.

The reason being that the hallway was stripped down to the bare wooden floorboards. The floorboards were then removed and four-inch stainless steel nails driven through them. They were then replaced with the nails protruding upwards.

The first three feet of the hallway floorboards were left nail-free to make sure that anyone coming in through the front door in a hurry would have leverage enough to come down on the nails with enough force. The Yardies had come through the door at a rapid pace, guns were drawn as they looked for Jimmy, their feet protected only by the thin rubber soles of their trendy basketball boots. The first Yardie's lead foot came down on the nails, and he felt the explosion of excruciating pain sear through his body, his brain and mind numb, his body twisted as he fell forward screaming in agony, the second Yardie just a footstep behind him tripped over his prone accomplice and fell face-first into the booby-trapped floorboards. The nails puncturing the front of his body and face like a pincushion. The screams of the two men as they lay impaled on the bed of nails were terrible.

Jimmy emerged from the kitchen, the smirk on his face now twisted into a wide-mouthed psychotic grin, aluminium baseball bat in hand. Jimmy proceeded to beat the *Yardies* to a bloody pulp, splitting skin and breaking bones in a ferocious attack.

Jimmy was found not guilty of two attempted murders, and other associated charges and a legend was born. His barrister had argued passionately, and successfully that the two armed men had broken into Jimmy's home to do him harm. It was self-defence. The fact they were incapable of defending themselves at the time of the beatings bore no weight and was irrelevant to the case as they had entered the house armed and uninvited with the intention of killing or maiming Jimmy with malice aforethought. Anything that followed their unlawful entry to the property and subsequent trespass was a consequence of their initial wrongdoing.

Chapter 3

South London 2004

"A long weekend in Margate to celebrate. Margate, nice sea air on the coast, great fish and chips, lousy beer though tasted like piss. Do you remember that pub we were in, that Welsh geezer was the *governor* there, you remember him, Billy, his brother played for the *Yids* ". Jimmy said.

"Yes I remember Jimmy" Billy answered.

"That's what we are going to do is it, reminisce about the old days?"

Billy didn't know where this was going, he thought Jimmy had really lost the plot.

"We could do Billy, but I'm going off at tangents here. I need to focus because it's quite a story. Ok - when you and those other two slags disappeared I had all the chaps looking high and low for you. I mean I got twenty-two years Billy, I had done sixteen of those years by the time I eventually got out - sixteen years of my life".

"I did time too you know, I didn't walk away scot-free, and I didn't do anything," Billy said.

"I was twenty-seven when I went away forty-three when I came out. Best years of my life some might say. I was banged up twenty-three hours a day most days. But you get used to it, I shouldn't complain. I'm getting away from the point again, anyway it only took three months for Tommy to be found. Living it large in Tenerife not even hiding. They did a real number on him you know, they did the old Colombian necktie job on him, Billy, do you know what that is?"

Billy knew only too well, but kept quiet, as Jimmy continued without waiting for an answer.

"It's what the Colombian drug cartels do to grasses, they cut their throat and pull their tongue out through the hole, makes an example of them you see - let everyone know what he was, a grass," Jimmy said, chuckling away as if he was recalling a fond childhood memory of a day out at the seaside.

"The geezer that did it made his woman watch, so she could get the message out also. I bet he cried and begged, you know Billy like a little bitch, he helped put me away and then said he was sorry, tell Jimmy I'm sorry please tell Jimmy I'm sorry, sobbing he was I bet, I wish I had been there, but I saw the photos, good enough I guess fucking mess it made of the pool though, face down he was, claret everywhere and the water - it was like a purple colour. Paint sprayed the word *GRASS* on the floor and my initials, like a signature same as Paddy too".

"Yeah, well I know all this I read it in the papers, same as everyone else, people were talking about nothing else, Billy said, most people thought you were stupid, signing your own work".

Billy felt his blood run cold as he thought about the fear Tommy must have felt at that time, not the brightest of boys and certainly not the bravest. But he loved to play the gangster, and he had too much to say. Probably had himself fingered shooting his mouth off in a bar one-night bragging about his London gangster lifestyle. Billy imagined him begging for his life, crying and pleading with his tormentors, knowing that none of it was going to help him.

"I never did like him, you know Billy, Tommy I mean, never did like him. Always too much to say and to flash, and nothing to back it up."

"Tommy was our friend Jimmy, so was Paddy, and they both backed us up plenty of times, you were Paddy's son's Godfather for fuck's sake"

"They betrayed me" Jimmy screamed in Billy's ear.

Billy almost fell forward into the open grave.

"He didn't like me either. I know that he didn't like me, didn't respect me but he was certainly scared of me, that's for sure very scared indeed, that's why I'm sorry I wasn't there when he died, I would have liked to have seen the look on his face when he first saw me - that would have been a picture Billy"

"How can you talk about this like it's nothing, you murdered our friends Jimmy"

"They were grasses! Anyway that accounted for Tommy, Jimmy continued uninterested in Billy's objections, so then there was Paddy".

"Anyway, Paddy - he was living up in Scotland, Aberdeen to be precise. He was living a nice little life up there apparently, that little blonde wife of his, house, car, yeah thought he was safe away from London, but the world's a small place nowadays Billy, and if you've got chatty relatives, well there you go cover blown".

"Is that what happened then, someone in his family gave him up?"

"It's not like back in the eighties now is it, we didn't have any of this internet stuff to help you track people down then back then, just the old school way, private investigators and grasses. It doesn't take long to find somebody nowadays Billy once you have all those leads to follow, all those friends of friends of friends on the computer, no not long at all, but not like it was then".

"I really don't want to hear this Jimmy, you make it sound like you enjoyed killing them, or at least having them killed because you were still banged up at the time ".

"I don't care what you want to hear Billy, you are going to listen".
Jimmy seemed to be getting more irritated as he spoke.

"Anyway that was Paddy dealt with, two in the head face down on the kitchen floor, he was just about to have a bit of lunch, ham salad it was. They made a couple of sandwiches for the journey back, no point wasting a nice bit of ham - hey Billy. Newspapers said they reckon the killer was back in London the same night.

Guess he didn't like Scotland too much, too fucking cold I bet, haggis, deep-fried mars bars and Iron Bru, hardly *a la carte* is it? That's why he came back so quickly.

I bet it was different in Tenerife before they did for Tommy. I bet he spent about a week there, looking at the girls' tits on the beach no doubt and getting a bit of a tan, but fuck Scotland he must have thought".

Jimmy was laughing again.

"You know something Billy, you keep saying that we were friends. Do you remember when we were growing up, you, me Tommy and Paddy? We were always together; I remember the day we met them. I do remember that they were our friends, but I never cheated or grassed on anyone, you all turned on me Billy - you all turned on me, that's not what friends do" Jimmy said sadly.

Chapter 4

South London The Teenage Years.

Tommy Callaghan and Paddy Meehan had always been friends. They had been inseparable since the age of five when they had first met on their first day of primary school in 1963, at Our Lady of Victories infants school in South Kensington, London.

Tommy was a bit taller than Paddy and treated him like a little brother. The boys lived on the same council estate just two streets apart. By the time they were ten the only neighbourhood that they had known as home, was to be redeveloped. All the families that lived there and called the place home, were to be relocated to a new housing estate in Penge, South London. Tommy and Paddy were very excited when they learned they were being rehoused in the same street just a few doors away from each other.

The move went smoothly and just a few weeks later they found themselves in new homes and a new school. The school they would attend was to be St. Anthony's Catholic Junior school in Anerley, South London. Both Tommy and Paddy were keen Footballers and had both played for their previous schools' teams. They spoke excitedly of the upcoming trials for the school team at St. Anthony's.

The day of the trials duly arrived and both Tommy and Paddy had prepared for the day with their own training routines. They had gone through their drills in the local park. Paddy was a particularly tenacious player making up for in grit and determination, for what he lacked in skill. Tommy was a more elegant player, he had a liking to get on the ball and make things happen with a deft range of passing and an eye for goal. Tommy had always excelled as a footballer and was being considered by a number of professional teams to be offered terms as a future youth player.

About thirty boys had turned up for the trials, all were known to each other as they had attended the school for a few years now, only Tommy and Paddy were new faces.

"Boys, boys, all in here now", Mr Connor, the games master, called the boys to order.

"Most of you probably know the two new lads here to my right, but for those of you who don't know them I would like to introduce to you, Paddy Meehan and Tommy Callaghan."

Tommy and Paddy both smiled shyly as they were introduced, the rest of the boys gave a slightly awkward round of applause after a hefty hand-clapping started by Mr Connor.

"Ok, yellow-bibs, red-bibs, take them alternately. Tommy and Paddy had seen this coming and Paddy slipped back one in line to make sure he was on the same team as Tommy. As Paddy stepped backwards, he accidentally trod on the ankle of the boy behind him, dumping him on the seat of his pants, which caused him to yelp in pain.

"Oi - for fuck's sake mate, what's your game?". The small ginger-haired boy snapped.

A taller boy behind came forward and helped his friend from the ground, where he sat rubbing his ankle.

"Calm down Jimmy, he didn't mean it, he's just trying to get on the same team as his mate is all, ain't that right mate?" Billy Kelly said.

"Yeah, I'm sorry mate, I didn't see you behind me, no harm is done hey?" Paddy said apologetically, reaching down to take Jimmy's other hand and help him to his feet.

"Yeah no problem mate, it's ok nothing broken I reckon," Jimmy said.

The boys regained their positions in the line, strategically placing themselves in positions in the line that would allow them all to be playing on the yellow team.

"Ok - twenty minutes each way - captains pick your starting eleven, let's go", shouted Mr Connor.

The match finished in a two-nil win for the yellow team, both goals coming from Tommy Callaghan. Both Jimmy and Billy were mightily impressed with their new teammates and let them know after the game.

"You are quite a player Tommy," Billy said.

"Thanks, Billy, I enjoyed playing with you both, I hope we all make the team. I reckon we could have a good side here boys," Tommy said.

As the boys arrived home that evening after the football trials, all four of them had felt a certain camaraderie they had never experienced before. Jimmy, in particular, felt that he had made two new friends, not as close as Billy, but he could sense these two guys would be trustworthy and loyal to him, just as Billy was.

As the years passed by they moved up from their junior school to the same secondary school at St. Mary's in Croydon. By the age of fifteen, they had matured into young men and did what all young men tend to do. They discovered girls and they were involved in other things apart from football, such as youth clubs, coffee bars, music, clothes and movies. The problem for the four boys was that all these things were not free. They needed to find the money from somewhere to keep up with all the latest fashions, trends and events of the day, at all the places one would want to be seen, as any self-respecting teenage London boy would have to.

Billy had found a job with the local dairy and would rise every morning at four o'clock, apart from Sunday's. Come rain, sleet or snow Billy would accompany the milkman on his rounds, sometimes even driving the electric milk float on the deserted early morning streets. Billy would be home by seven-thirty in time for breakfast with his parents before going to school. For his labours, he was paid the sum of six pounds, plus tips on collection nights. It was a job which Billy loved.

Jimmy and Paddy had found work delivering the local evening newspapers around the neighbourhood, a job Jimmy found both demeaning and laborious. Jimmy had lasted only one week toiling at this menial task he felt was below him. Jimmy having been paid the princely sum of three pounds for his week's endeavours had decided to protest his disgust at the slave wages paid in the printed press delivery industry by setting fire to three London Evening Standard newsstands, one outside the local train station, one at the bus depot and another at a newsagent on the high street.

Tommy had managed to find a Saturday job at a local shopping mall, through his football contacts, one of the coaches at the youth team Tommy played for was the manager at the shop. Tommy worked as a trainee sales assistant in a menswear shop. Tommy liked the job and was paid ten pounds for the eight-hour day he worked. This was where Jimmy had spotted his first business opportunity. Jimmy had persuaded Tommy to select a number of shirts, jeans and trousers and hang them on the rail closest to the door.

The plan was simple. Jimmy, Billy and Paddy would go into the shop carrying a brand new dustbin. Billy and Paddy would carry the bin holding a handle either side. Jimmy would fill the dustbin with the selected items. They would then proceed to leave the shop with Billy and Paddy now carrying the full dustbin through the security barriers. Just as they were about to leave Jimmy would walk alongside them with a shirt, complete with a security tag, holding the shirt up to the light, the alarm would sound and the barriers would flash. Jimmy, a look of utter shock on his face, would then apologize to the alerted security guard profusely, claiming he just wanted to see what the shirt looked like in the light as Billy and Paddy walked straight out the door with two hundred and fifty pounds' worth of merchandise in the bin. They would then sell their ill-gotten gains for half the price to a local market trader.

This scam worked three times before a stock audit brought tighter security measures, including a new *CCTV* system and extra security guards on the busier weekends. Tommy, however, managed to keep his job and used his very generous family and friends staff discount to help kit out the boys in the latest gear.

This was the start of a long friendship between the four boys that would see them through their teenage years and early twenties. They would remain friends up until that fateful day in North London some years later. The next chapters of their young lives would be filled with violence and tragedy.

Chapter 5

South London 2004

The blood had now stopped running down Billy's neck and had soaked into his white shirt collar turning it almost black. The small cut above his ear had stopped bleeding now. Billy wanted to touch the lump that had formed above his ear but didn't want to risk getting another crack of the gun if he moved. Jimmy continued telling his story.

"But like I just said, you proved more difficult Billy. Gone like you had a magician disappear you! That's why I mentioned Margate because I heard a whisper that you had been seen down there, actually that you had been hanging out down there. So I thought what the fuck would Billy be doing in Margate, anyway, I sent some people down there, they poked around a bit, asked a few of the local faces if they had been seen around, but no, it was nothing apparently a red herring. But you know something kept on telling me to keep looking for you there. You know what, I didn't know what I was looking for, then I remembered those two girls we met there that time. Yeah, because you were a bit sweet on that one girl for a while Billy do you remember her? Do you remember her name, Billy? I even had the boys go back down to Margate again the day after you were released to talk with her, I thought you might have shown up there, but no - if you did, they must have missed you again I reckon".

Jimmy waited as he watched Billy's back stiffen.

"Yes I remember; I remember her name" answered Billy.

"What was it Billy, what was her name?" asked Jimmy.

"It was Simone, what about Simone? Did you hurt her?" Billy asked.

He was dreading hearing the answer to his question.

"Hurt Simone? Why on earth would I hurt her?" Jimmy said.

"After all we were friends, I never hurt my friends you should know that my enemies yes, my friends...never Billy".

Chapter 6

Margate 1983

Simone Dawson was twenty-five years old. Simone had lived her whole life in the Kent seaside town of Margate on the South East coast of England. She was the oldest of two sisters, her younger sibling three years her junior. Simone had attended Hartsdown Academy less than a mile from Margate main British Rail train station and close to her parents' home on Willow Way. Simone had a happy childhood. Her parents were good people and provided a stable and loving family environment for both Simone and her sister, a beautiful home and the nurturing support that most people as parents wish they could, and genuinely believe they have provided for their children.

Simone was a good student and had taken, and passed, her A and O levels in seven subjects. Much to their disappointment, although unspoken, Simone's parents had recoiled in silent horror when she announced she would be attending hairdressing college, as it had always been her dream to own her own salon. Her parents had openly courted the idea of placing and supporting her in the nearby Canterbury University to take a degree of her choosing, however much to their continued chagrin, Simone had made her choice and could not be dissuaded. Her ever-supportive parents conceded and agreed that they would not stand in her way and would indeed help her to set up her small business when she had graduated from her college courses and was ready to enter into the world of full-time employment.

Simone duly enrolled in the college of her choice and set out to prove to everyone she had made the right decision in her vocational pursuits. So the seventeen-year-old Simone followed her dream and put everything she had into making that dream come true, she had given up almost everything to study, she was far from reclusive but preferred to spend her time on more important things like understanding the business side of running a successful venture, spending even more time looking at product range, the latest equipment, the latest methods and fads, fashion, and the interior design of the salon, she could see so very clearly in her mind's eye.

Three years later Simone was ready, she had been an exemplary student and was now a fully qualified hairdresser and beautician. Simone handpicked three other top students from her college colleagues and had offered them the opportunity to rent chairs at the salon she was about to open with her parents' support. She had also offered a full-time position to two young school leavers as receptionists, assistants and general help in the business. The chair renting financial model was a guaranteed income that greatly weighed in favour of the business being a success against the overhead of full-time employees. The salon was about to be the first of its kind on the Margate seafront to offer "the full hairdressing and beautification experience". Simone was not sure if the blue rinse brigade of Thanet were ready for this, but the flyers and posters had to say something, and they were not the primary demographic for the business, the disposable income of the twenty to forty-year-old ladies of the area was.

Simone and her parents could not have been happier the way the first six months of the business had panned out. The salon had built a solid base of loyal core customers and had attracted more than its fair share of free promotional advertising and local media coverage. Simone was a natural marketeer as well as being the perfect PR face of the business. Bubbly, bright, funny and articulate Simone was always prepared to give an impromptu radio interview or to speak to the fashion editor of the local newspapers. It always helped that the interviewer or journalist was a young lady, as a complimentary manicure, pedicure or facial goes a long way to maintaining an ongoing relationship, and was ideal to keep the business at the forefront of the local ladies' minds when selecting their beauty salon of choice. Simone also had a knack for eliciting from her chosen customer base the up-sale of enhanced treatments and products, complimenting her clients continuously whilst waxing lyrical about the latest highlighting, nail treatment or facials could do for such "a natural beauty as yourself".

Understanding that the young ladies that enjoy going to the salon on a regular basis and spend money on their appearance, would also be the same group that spent money on gym memberships to keep their bodies in shape also. Simone had entered into reciprocal arrangements with three local upmarket keep fit establishments to cross-promote their businesses'. Free spa days on offer for ten visits to the salon, and a free day at the salon for a gym membership purchase at the partner gyms. This arrangement was working very well for all, as the gyms were not competition for each other due to their geographical locations and different catchment areas, whereas ladies like a gym to be local to their homes, they are more than happy to travel for their weekly beauty requirements.

All in all, life was good for Simone, but she knew there was something missing. Her social life had improved and she had entertained the dating scene more frequently than the previous years. Simone had dated some local guys on a casual basis but had found herself somewhat empty by the whole experience, the local guys seemed, not unlike herself, very insular and less than cosmopolitan in their life experiences. Simone knew what she was looking for in a man, all the usual things that her friends seemed to like, good looks, confidence, a position in life and a man that knew what he wanted.

Simone wanted something different, she was looking for something more, she wanted the added spice of excitement, she didn't want to settle for a humdrum, run of the mill, middle of the road existence. She wanted a man that made her feel alive and special, a man that gave her own space but wanted to be with her all the time, a man that seemed aloof, dangerous and mysterious, a man that treated her as his personal property but set her free at the same time. But as the old saying goes "be careful what you wish for". One warm Saturday evening in a dive bar on the Margate seafront, not far from her home and business premises, such a man appeared as though heaven-sent and he did walk straight into her life - for Simone Dawson life would never be the same again. That man was Billy Kelly.

*****

Tall, blonde and slender, ivory skin as pale and smooth as alabaster, piercing blue eyes and a smile that could capture a man's heart with one simple glance in his direction. Billy Kelly remembered the first time he had ever seen Simone Dawson. Simone was with a friend in an underground dive bar in Margate. It was late summer or early autumn of 1983.

Simone was standing directly opposite the table occupied by Jimmy, Billy, Tommy, Paddy, and some other members of their party, maybe ten or eleven in total. The boys and some of their associates had come down to the coast to celebrate Jimmy's acquittal in a double attempted murder trial.

There were two guys at the bar doing their best to impress the girls, Simone was having none of it. Billy watched as she pirouetted with the graceful poise of a prima ballerina, removed something from her bag and headed towards the jukebox. Simone dropped coins into the machine and made her choices carefully. The bar was dark and smoky. Billy thought she was beautiful, a real touch of class about her, not the kind of girl he expected to see in such a rough house as this hovel. He wanted to go and speak to her but was reluctant given the way she had brushed off the two guys at the bar. Her friend seemed much more at ease in the company of the two men.

"That's a really nice piece of arse there Billy boy, Jimmy grinned at Billy, catching him staring at Simone, are you thinking of pulling that?"

"I don't think so, she's not the type Jimmy she already stonewalled those two flash fuckers at the bar, I think she just wants to leave, keeps giving her mate the evils"'. Billy said.

"Not the type Billy? Are you having a laugh? Let me at it, I will show what type she is". Jimmy challenged Billy with a crooked grin on his face. The rest of the group laughed and shouted encouragement to Jimmy to show Billy how it was done.

"I never said I wasn't going to try Jimmy, just waiting for the right moment is all".

The thought of Jimmy being embarrassed by a knockback from Simone filled Billy with horror for some inexplicable reason. Then he realized that if that happened Simone would get hurt for sure, and Billy didn't want that. He would rather risk being humiliated himself than see this beautiful woman brutalized by Jimmy.

Billy turned to the group, grabbed an open bottle of champagne from one of the ice buckets on the table and stood up.

"You fucking wankers" he muttered to the group as he turned and marched towards what he imagined was about to be the most horrific put down he was ever likely to have to endure.

The group cheered and whistled as Billy strode towards the bar, his stomach turned somersaults like that of a teenage boy with butterflies when he has been caught by his schoolgirl crush staring at her, for just a split second too long.

Just as Billy approached Simone, her back to him, the unmistakable voice of *Paul Weller* and the music of the *Style Council* filled the bar room with the song *"You're the best thing"*. Billy moved in behind Simone.

"I like this song, did you put this on?

Simone turned at the sound of Billy's voice. She looked him up and down for a second or two, a slight smile on her face.

"Yes I did, I'm glad you approve" she answered.

"Sorry - I just saw you at the jukebox, I'm assuming a classy girl like you has good taste in all things, Billy smiled back and offered his hand for Simone to take, oh I most definitely approve, I'm Billy, very nice to meet you…" Billy let the sentence trail. Simone knew from his accent that Billy was not from the area, he was possibly from London, almost definitely.

"I'm Simone" she looked deep into Billy's eyes as if searching for something more substantial than the usual reason a random stranger is standing in front of her clutching a bottle of champagne in his hand, the usual reason being they thought she would be an easy lay, day trippers looking for a one-night stand. Simone gingerly offered her hand.

Billy took Simone's fingers in his hand, raised it gently to his lips and kissed her knuckles.

"My pleasure Simone, like I said all class - Simone that's a lovely name". Billy looked somewhat embarrassed at his clumsy efforts at chivalry.

Simone's face broke into a smile, then glancing down at the champagne bottle dangling from his hand.

"If that's for me Billy, it would have been so much more romantic if you had actually brought something I could drink it from …!"

Unfazed Billy reached into a box of plastic straws on the bar and removed two, handing one to Simone.

"Cheers Simone," he said as he slid his straw into the neck of the open champagne bottle.

Simone laughed at the way Billy had saved face and inserted her straw into the neck of the bottle. Her eyes softened as they looked at each other, their faces just inches apart as they prepared to drink the champagne. Billy's heart was beating so loud he was sure Simone could hear it.

"Cheers Billy" Simone breathed almost in almost a whisper, as she lowered her pale pink lips to the straw.

For the next three months, Simone and Billy's relationship developed at a rapid pace. Billy drove the seventy miles from London to Margate every weekend and stayed over at least one night. Simone had a small promenade flat just along from Dreamland, Margate's famous amusement park and fairground, situated above her Beauty Salon business.

They loved to just stroll along the beachfront, eating fish and chips at a local chippie. Billy, like most Londoners, was very fond of the rock salmon, or dogfish, to give it its real name. They were almost inseparable for those twelve weeks.

Simone despite her earlier reservations had really fallen for Billy, he had a presence about him, something that made her feel safe, a confidence that she had rarely encountered in her cocooned life on the coast, she guessed it came with him being from the city, she assumed that all men from the city were the same, confident, self-assured and a bit cocky. All the same, Billy was her man and he treated her well. He brought an excitement to her life she had never felt before with her previous boyfriends. Billy was different, different in a way that excited her, made her want to be with him. She didn't really know what he did for work, only that he was part of something that he didn't really want her to be a part of. Something dark, something mysterious, and best of all - something dangerous.

Billy protected their relationship to the point of paranoia.

"I don't want the pressure of London at the weekends, I love being here, I love being here with you, I could see myself living here you know. Just the two of us babe a little cottage on the seafront nice cosy little place. Pull the curtains and shut the world out, leave work behind, leave London behind". Billy looked down shyly when he realized his thoughts were being broadcast out loud and Simone was smiling at his musings.

"Well if you want to I mean I'm not assuming anything or trying to push you into something you don't want, I just err - well I never felt like this before Simone I just want to know if there is a future with you - err if that's a possibility I mean - I mean would you consider me, err I mean it, not it, you know what I mean, you know the cottage thing I mean - it's just …."

Simone put her fingers gently to his lips.

"I know what you mean Billy. I know I feel the same".

Simone's eyes had filled with tears; she had wanted to hear those words from Billy but was never going to pressure him into saying them. They had known each other only three short months, three short months that had been filled with happiness, fun and a closeness she had craved all her life.

Simone was eight weeks pregnant. She hadn't told Billy yet. She wasn't sure how he would react. She knew now, and that knowledge lifted a weight from her heart and mind, knowing that this man she had only known for a few short months wanted her. She now knew that Billy was the real deal, not just along for the fun, he wanted long term stability, he wanted a relationship that was real and going the distance.

The following morning Billy rose at seven-thirty. The peal of the Sunday morning church bells rang out in the distance. Over breakfast of tea and toast, Simone and Billy planned to look for a place the following weekend. Billy was sure he could get down next Thursday night so they could spend Friday and Saturday just looking at places. He told Simone he was sorry that he couldn't stay today but he and Jimmy had an important meeting that morning at eleven o'clock that he couldn't avoid. It was a beautiful early November morning on the coast. The mist rolled in off the English Channel, the sun just peeking through the clouds, it was just cold enough that you needed a sweater, but on a morning like this, the fresh sea air to breathe and a beautiful woman to love, what more could a man want or need.

Billy knew he and Simone had made the right decision. This seemed so right. Simone kissed him on the mouth as he was about to leave, she held him longer than usual, hugged him tighter than usual to her. Billy felt her cling to him and pulled her closer, looking into her eyes he said.

"I will be back before you know it babe, can't wait for Thursday, don't forget to ring those estate agents, we have a lot to do next weekend ".

Billy kissed Simone and walked out of the door at the bottom of the stairs that led to both the salon and the flat.

As he pulled away from the curb Simone mouthed the words "I love you…" to Billy.

Billy mouthed back "I know" to Simone.

A personal joke that had started when Simone first said the words to Billy, and in his shock and awkwardness he just replied: "I know".

Simone smiled and waved him goodbye.

Little did either of them know that on that beautiful early autumn morning, as they waved their farewells that life was about to play the cruelest of tricks on the young lovers - they were never to be together again.

Billy headed straight through Margate town centre towards the motorway. The M2 would take him directly onto the A2 over the Medway bridge some forty-odd miles away, another twenty-five to Blackheath Common down Shooters Hill and into South London, an hour and a half at a leisurely cruise should see him home around 10 am.

Billy had arranged to meet Jimmy in their local pub Bradys' at around ten-thirty, an hour and a half before they officially opened to talk about the meeting that Jimmy had arranged with Jack Riordan. They still occasionally worked for Riordan, not exclusively as they had at one time, as they now had other interests and took on work for selective gangland enterprises, with the blessing of the main man.

They also had their own ventures such as a small security firm that supplied the staff on the doors of pubs and clubs throughout South London. Control the doors and you control the sale of drugs on the premises, this was locked down through a local drug dealer who took all his supplies from Jack Riordan. He had exclusive free rein to sell his wares in all the pubs and clubs of which the firm had access control. This arrangement worked for all parties. Any interlopers caught selling drugs in any of the premises were dealt with in a swift and brutal fashion, after being relieved of any surplus supplies and cash.

Billy didn't know any of the details or indeed what this particular meeting was about. Jimmy had been very tight-lipped about the whole thing; he didn't want word getting out about any of this business.

Jimmy had become more guarded of late, secretive and paranoid. He was very volatile, even more so than usual. His violent outbursts were a concern to everyone, friends and enemies alike, it was a real worry to Billy the way Jimmy had become dependent on using cocaine on an almost hourly basis, sniffing line after line of the white powder to keep himself sharp and alive as he would put it.

Chapter 7

London October 1983

The Park Lane London Intercontinental Hotel lies between Hyde and Green parks in London's West End. The official address is Number 1 Hamilton Place and it stands on the corner of Hyde Park Corner with Park Lane, close to the shopping centre of Knightsbridge and Piccadilly.

The Arch bar at the Intercontinental Park Lane was a particular favorite of Jack Riordan, he had arranged to meet a very important contact there at seven o'clock that evening. Riordan had arrived as usual with his trusted second in command Christy Monaghan, the two men made themselves comfortable at a corner table in the bar and waited for a waiter to take their drinks order. Riordan handed Christy the drinks menu and waited for the response he knew would surely come when he opened it.

Jack Riordan, a man over sixty years of age, tall with and powerfully built with greying hair. He was renowned in his early years for being a tough street fighter and barroom brawler until he realized that he was never going to get rich fighting in bars or on the street. He changed his ways almost overnight to become a respectable businessman in the earthmoving, road building and construction industry. He had always been a hard-working fellow and had thought about branching out into the world on his own to make his fortune, and this he certainly did through sheer hard graft and treating his employees and other contractors fairly and squarely. If Jack Riordan said he will pay you, X, then X is what you got when the job was done. He never tried to welch or change the deal halfway through and had earned a reputation for being a man of his word. He took out a one hundred-thousand-pound loan to buy two used JCB digging machines, two second-hand dumpers and an earthmover. Jack Riordan took his workforce from the local London Irish bars and looked after the boys as if they were his brothers. Jack Riordan was not only a well-respected man, he was a beloved local philanthropist giving generously to local orphanages and the local parish church.

A married man with three daughters he was for the whole world to see a perfect gentleman and a generous benefactor. What the outside world did not see was the darker side of Jack Riordan. The gangland boss who had used his wealth and legitimate businesses to build a criminal empire that stretched far beyond London, he had contacts and business interests in nearly every major city in Britain and Ireland, some even said as far as America, although this seemed highly unlikely given that Jack Riordan had never set foot in the USA or ever planned to. Jack Riordan was an extremely wealthy man. His legitimate businesses saw to that. His illegal activities, on the other hand, made him a dangerously wealthy man. Drugs, weapons and gambling. Jack Riordan had a finger in every pie in every part of South London and beyond and thanks to the earthmoving business he also controlled a ready-made transportation network of forty-tonne trucks to move everything around the country with ease.

It was brilliant who would think of or bother stopping an open back truck loaded with freshly dug earth to look for anything suspicious. This mode of transport for the clandestine distribution of all types of contraband was the brainchild of none other than Jimmy Walsh.

It was almost foolproof, save for any loose talk from anyone in the know. The plan was simple, move whatever needs to be moved from one city to another under the guise of the transportation of sand, roadstone aggregate, tarmac, shingle or ballast.

Jack Riordan had a fleet of trucks and open-backed lorries, what could look more innocent or uninteresting to the authorities than an open-backed or sheeted lorry load of road construction materials, why would anybody suspect this mode of transport was carrying anything other than what was visible to the naked eye?

*****

"*Suffering Jaysus* - have you seen these prices, Jack? What the fuck is this - does Dick *fucking* Turpin own this place? Christy said.

Christy ran his fingers through his shock of thick brown curly hair.

"Would you ever keep the noise down Christy? Do you want people to think you are some kind of riff-raff and you don't belong here - *ya fucking tinker ya*"? Riordan laughed looking at the shock on Christy's face at the prices on the bar list.

"What you pay for here Christy is quality, the beautiful upper-class clientele, and the elegant yet simple ambience - you won't get the likes that fella coming in here and plonking himself down beside you pestering ya for a *few bob*, the fucking miscreant that he is," Riordan said mysteriously.

"What fella?" Christy asked.

"That Jarrett fella comes in sometimes to Bradys', he got himself lifted in the park the other day, trying to shag a cat so he was," Riordan said.

"What!? - Christy looked dumbstruck, "A fucking cat, go on with ya, you're fucking *codding* me on".

"I'm fucking telling you as sure as I'm here, molesting a *moggie* in full view of St. Michael's so he was" Riordan affirmed.

"Didn't the Mother Superior herself call the guards and the queer fella was nicked, scratched to fuck he was, him chasing the cat, the guards chasing himself - like Benny fucking Hill it must have been".

Christy burst out laughing at Riordan's comical description of the episode.

"Jack do you know something…? Christy asked.

"What's that Christy?" Riordan said.

"That Jarrett fella, that's the only bit of *pussy* he will ever have I reckon" Christy roared laughing at his own joke, slapping his thigh for good measure.

"Ah right enough there Christy so you are, the only bit for the next six months that's for fucking sure the dirty bastard so he is," Riordan said, wiping a tear of laughter from his eye.

A smartly dressed waiter came over as the two men had just about finished laughing at the conversation they had just had.

"Good evening gentlemen, what can I get for you tonight?" He asked Riordan and Christy.

"I'm in a good mood tonight young man, give us two large Redbreasts on the rocks," Riordan said.

"Very good sir" the waiter replied and went to fetch the drinks.

"And don't you be gulping this whiskey down like it's the regular fucking *Jamie*, Christy, Riordan said, it's for the more complex and refined palate, so it is".

"Complex and refined palate is it, *la di fucking da* I'm sure" Christy retorted.

"A wonderfully intense flavour so, it has a rich full body, it's aromatic, Riordan continued - but mainly - it's fucking expensive, *so sip ya heathen ya*".

Both men burst out laughing again.

Riordan and Christy were enjoying their drinks, just killing time with small talk when the contact arrived.

Detective Chief Superintendent Graham Simpson was in his fifties and close to retirement. He had served the vast majority of his thirty-eight years in the police force right here in London. He was now based at Stoke Newington police station in North London.

Simpson was impeccably dressed in a black suit with a white shirt and red tie. His perfectly groomed hair and designer glasses seemed to be the perfect accompaniment for his upper-class English accent.

Riordan and Christy both stood up as Simpson approached their table.

"Detective Chief Superintendent, how are you? May I introduce my business associate Christy Monaghan?" Riordan said.

"I'm fine Jack thank you, how's yourself?" Simpson answered.

The three men shook hands and settled down. Simpson ordered a Hendricks gin with tonic. Riordan was not aware of anything other than the usual monthly meeting held between the two men, and the customary pleasant drinks. The reason for Christy's presence was just a formality, a mere introduction for Christy to become a more recognizable face for the Riordan business, and to meet one of Riordan's more influential contacts.

The meeting took on a more sinister note after about ten minutes of the usual small talk.

"Jack, I need to speak frankly about a problem we have" Simpson started.

"We - Graham?" Riordan replied, clearly uncomfortable with the sudden change of topic.

"Yes, Jack - we - I'm sure you must be aware that there was a seizure of drugs on a houseboat in Essex last week, a large consignment of ecstasy pills from Holland. We have someone very much on the inside of that firm Jack" Simpson said.

"And what firm might that be Graham?" Riordan enquired.

"The North London Turks Jack - the Arslan family, your name came up, I didn't realize you were in bed with those people," Simpson said.

"Purely a financial arrangement Graham, nothing more I can assure you," Riordan said.

"Yes indeed, 250K to be exact Jack, 250K from you and another 250K from a Liverpool mob" Simpson looked for any glimmer of Jack knowing this information already, there was none.

"Well as I said Graham this is purely a financial arrangement," Riordan said.

"What is this Mr Simpson? Are you demonstrating your usefulness to us or trying to shake us down?" Christy asked pointedly. Riordan put his hand on Christy's knee to calm him down.

"As I said, Christy, we have a problem, but as always I have a solution. A win-win if you please. I want something, and if you agree to give me what I want, you can get your money back - is that of interest to you?" Simpson said.

"Of course Graham, what exactly is it you want?" Riordan asked.

This was not like Simpson at all. He had never been greedy; he had never strayed outside the parameters of their arrangement before. This must be something personal, or personal for someone important to Simpson. Jack Riordan had paid Graham Simpson well over the years, and Simpson had proved more than useful and very loyal to Riordan.

Simpson took a long drink of the G&T and looked Riordan straight in the eye.

"I want Arda Arslan gone," Simpson said.

"And for this service you will get my quarter of a million back - is that correct Graham"? Riordan asked.

"Yes Jack, that's exactly what we will do, not only the 250K - I will give you the drugs too, less my commission of course, but that will leave the Liverpool mob very angry Jack, can you handle that?" Simpson said as he smiled knowingly.

"I can handle it if I need to handle it Graham, but it won't come to that I'm sure, Riordan said, can I ask why you want him gone? Not that it matters to me, I'm just curious"

"Well the boy has become a bit of a liability, he's started his own enterprise, his father, Mehmet Arslan knows nothing about it. Not only that Jack, but he has also got himself involved with the wife of a prominent politician, who shall remain nameless, and who would rather not have his dirty laundry washed in public, the impact on his political ambitions would be catastrophic, much easier to remove the problem, without it tracing back to him. You know Mehmet Arslan, am I right in thinking that Jack?" Simpson asked.

"I have met him on occasion and found him to be an honourable man, I must say. I have never met the boy personally, the finance was arranged through a broker, but I will be putting that right soon enough, it's time we had a chat, given the circumstances" Riordan said.

"Let me ask you a question Jack, the broker you mentioned, had you used him before?" Simpson asked.

"No I hadn't, we don't know him personally, he was recommended, but I was assured that the money was for the Arslan family, not for the son for his own business, and certainly not behind his father's back, as I said I always found Mehmet an honourable man, so that was good enough for me, Christy spoke to the son on the phone, he confirmed it was a family operation, not his own". Riordan said.

Christy nodded his head in agreement with Riordan's comment.

"I see," Simpson answered.

"Is there something you are not telling me Graham?" asked Riordan.

Simpson pondered the question, taking another long drink from his glass, and placed it down on the table.

"Cards on the table Jack, I know you have a good relationship with Jimmy Walsh, but I have to say, either you are being less than honest with me or you are truly in the dark on this one, and we have always been honest with each other, I know that, so I am assuming it is the latter" Simpson said.

"Of course we have Graham. So tell me? What the fuck does any of this have to do with my Jimmy?" Riordan said, clearly in the dark concerning any involvement that Jimmy may have in these enterprises.

"As I told you, Jack, we have someone inside the Arslan family firm. The man who put Arda Arslan and the Liverpool mob together, and the man who arranged for you to be approached for finance was none other than your own - Jimmy Walsh". Simpson said.

"I don't believe that Graham, how sure are you of this intelligence? Jimmy wouldn't know any of these people, by reputation maybe but not personally. Jimmy is loyal to me - to us - he wouldn't do this to me…". Riordan leaned back in his chair, a look of utter bewilderment on his face and a deep hurt that he couldn't hide showed in his blue eyes.

"Oh no, oh no - not this now, please Lord," Christy muttered to nobody in particular.

Simpson reached inside his jacket pocket and pushed a large envelope across the table to Riordan. Riordan opened the envelope and removed the contents, there were four photographs. Jimmy was standing smiling and shaking hands with a short man of Turkish appearance, another man that Riordan also didn't recognize was in the photographs too. The three seemed to be very happy and content in each other's company, it was clear that Jimmy knew them both from the pictures in front of him.

"That's Arda Arslan shaking Jimmy's hand in the photo. The other man is Tony Fallon, a Liverpool based drug smuggler and armed robber, he is well connected up north, and a very useful ally to have - if you were planning to go to war. I have it on good authority that Jimmy is the common denominator here, he met Fallon while on remand in Brixton prison, they are very close friends Jack, Jimmy introduced Arda to Tony Fallon". Simpson said.

"But what's Jimmy's motivation for this, if he needs to or wants to do a deal, he comes to me for the finance, why would he keep me in the dark this time?" Riordan asked.

Both Christy and Simpson looked uneasy. They could both see what Jack didn't want to see, it was a double power play by Arda Arslan and Jimmy Walsh to get a foothold in their own drugs distribution empire and grow strong together. They saw themselves very much as the future and Jack Riordan and Mehmet Arslan, very much as the past.

Jack Riordan trusted Jimmy Walsh like he was his own son, as his own flesh and blood. He had always listened to Jimmy even when some of his schemes were downright ludicrous, he had always listened, he had always helped him. Riordan knew what he had to do to test Jimmy's loyalty. That plan would be set in motion as soon as he was done here tonight.

"Graham, if what you say is true, and I will find out for sure. I'm going to give you Jimmy Walsh and get rid of Arda Arslan at the same time, but first of all, I'm going to set up that meeting with Arda Arslan, and I'm going to invite Jimmy along - now, drink that whiskey Christy you have been nursing it like it's fucking poison, now let's get to fuck out of here". Riordan said.

"Right you are Jack," Christy said, emptying the glass in one gulp.

Simpson tilted his head in admiration and allowed himself a slight smile in anticipation of the forthcoming arrest of Jimmy Walsh, and of being rid of the Arda Arslan problem. Jack Riordan was a master of manipulation and had always delivered what he promised, Simpson knew very well never to cross this man.

"I will be in touch Graham, I have left your usual package in the usual place," Riordan said as he got up to leave.

The usual package was an envelope stuffed with two thousand pounds in cash in a post office box near Kings Cross station, a monthly arrangement that kept Detective Chief Superintendent Graham Simpson very close to Jack Riordan.

*****

For all intents and purposes, Tony Fallon appeared to be a successful scrap metal merchant and spare car parts dealer. This fronted his illegal drugs business on his native Merseyside. Fallon had been dealing drugs now for six successful years, interrupted only by a spell in Brixton prison in South West London when he had been arrested in London for assaulting a barman in a Pimlico wine bar after a Queens Park Rangers v Liverpool match. The barman's heinous crime was to jokingly tell Fallon that he sounded like Jimmy Tarbuck. Fallon took exception to what he considered to be a malicious slur on his Liverpudlian accent, and proceeded to beat the barman with a metal ice bucket until he was unconscious, he then repeatedly kicked him in the face mercilessly until his two companions pulled him away from the prone and listless body of the young man. Fallon was duly convicted of grievous bodily harm for which he was given a custodial sentence. Fallon had set himself up in business as a drug dealer and importer, through his success as an armed robber, banks, building societies and cash delivery vehicles had all been the victims of his unscheduled withdrawals programme. Mob handed and violent was the tactic Fallon preferred, more cutlass than a rapier, and certainly more brawn than brain. Fallon wasn't one for planning too much, fear, noise and violence being the order of the day. Fallon and his crew had been linked to over half a dozen robberies throughout the United Kingdom over the past five years, over one point five million pounds in cash had been stolen in these *blags*, but neither Fallon or any of his accomplices had ever been charged with any crimes.

It was while in Brixton prison that Fallon had met Jimmy Walsh. Jimmy was on remand for the attempted murder of the two Jamaican Yardies. Fallon and Jimmy Walsh had hit it off almost immediately. After their initial meeting, Jimmy found Fallon very engaging, and amusing. Fallon was always the centre of attention and looking to take the piss or set up a prank at any time, he was popular among the other inmates, always looking out to help those less fortunate than himself with cigarettes and other goodies that were hard to come by.

The first time Fallon encountered Jimmy was in the prison exercise yard. Jimmy had just arrived. Fallon had already been in Brixton for six months. He had been sentenced to two years for the violent attack in the West London wine bar. He was also ordered to pay five thousand pounds in criminal compensation to the unfortunate barman. Jimmy was mooching around, hands sunk deep into his trouser pockets and not in the best of moods.

Fallon noticed Jimmy because of his bright ginger hair, something that had always either made Jimmy stand out from the crowd or got him picked on. But as clever as Fallon always was, he already knew who Jimmy was having checked him out through the reception orderly and learned a thing or two about the famous Jimmy Walsh.

Fallon watched as two men approached Jimmy. The shorter, stockier of the two men decided to try his luck with the new boy.

"Hey you, *Ginger*, he called back as Jimmy passed by, give us a snout"

"Fuck off, you mug," Jimmy shot back.

"Hey you're new here, you want to mind who you're speaking to with that attitude pal," the taller skinnier man said.

"Why who the fuck are you two pricks? Someone important, someone fucking hard are you" Jimmy snarled, marching head up hands balled into fists straight towards the two men.

"No - no - we're from Manchester that's all," the taller man said, backing off.

"Fucking Manchester? So are United and I don't fucking like them either you northern monkey" Jimmy said almost nose to nose with the man now.

Fallon laughed out loud and clapped his hands with glee.

"I love that line lah, so are United and I don't fucking like them either" he repeated still laughing.

Fallon walked towards Jimmy to diffuse what might turn into a bad situation for the two shaken Mancunians.

Jimmy was taken by surprise and turned towards Fallon, who was still laughing. Fallon held his hand out.

"I'm Tony Fallon from Liverpool, and I hate Manchester United too," Fallon said, still laughing.

Jimmy took Fallon's outstretched hand and shook it warily.

"Jimmy Walsh, I just got here today, are these two mugs with you?" Jimmy said.

"Oh I know who you are my friend, I do my homework, these two Mancs are harmless, they think anyone coming in here on the first day is a soft touch". Fallon laughed again.

"Hey *Mancs*, come here" Fallon called after them.

The two Mancunians wandered over sheepishly towards Fallon and Jimmy. Heads down, hands in pockets.

"This is Jimmy Walsh, he's not the kind of man you try and mess with, now take these and remember he's here for two attempted murders, on people who were trying to murder him, so unless you want him to want to make it four. I would apologize and fuck off" Fallon told them as he held out two cigarettes to the men, who were standing with their heads down shuffling their feet like two scolded schoolboys.

"Yeah sorry Tony, we didn't know, we just needed some snout, you know how it is brother," the taller man said.

"Yes I know exactly how it is, and you two are going to come a cropper one day, you'll ask the wrong man the wrong way, and its game over for you two". Fallon said.

"We can look after ourselves Tony" the shorter man argued.

"No, no, no - you can't, that's just it - need I remind you two fucking halfwits how you got in here in the first place?" Fallon laughed.

Jimmy just stood watching, an amused onlooker at what was turning out to be a bit of a pantomime.

Tony Fallon then proceeded to regale Jimmy with the story of the downfall of the gruesome twosome. The two men had no choice but to stand helplessly by, as shamefaced they listened, not for the first time, and no doubt not the last, to their tale of woe.

The incident Fallon was referring to was the event on Clapham Common that led to the incarceration of the two men here in Brixton prison in the first place. The Mancunians had been down on their luck after losing their jobs on a building site. They decided to forego the shackles of gainful employment and embarked on a career of robbing gay men and those engaged in a bit of *"cottaging"* on the Common. Their criteria for this particular new venture were twofold.

Number one was that they assumed gay men to be a soft target, and number two they figured, quite rightly in most cases, was that the robberies would not be reported due to the systemic anti-gay feelings in the Metropolitan Police, and the fear of "outing" of any of the married men practicing their extra-marital activities on the chosen hunting ground of the Mancunian predators.

All had gone to plan for around six weeks. The two men were very happy with their newfound vocation and the income which it brought them. This was far more lucrative and enjoyable than humping bags of cement around a building site for ten hours a day. Their chosen hours of work suited their lifestyles much better too, no early mornings to face. No getting up at the crack of dawn in all kinds of weather, traipsing off to catch the tube to get across to the other side of London. Life was good, they were enjoying being both unemployed with their social benefits from the government paid fortnightly. The government would also generously pay the rent on the small bedsits they had found in privately owned buildings in the Battersea area. This coupled with the income from their self-employed nocturnal criminal enterprises, allowed them the time and freedom to enjoy the fruits of their labours in a far more relaxed manner than they had previously been accustomed to - that was of course until that fateful night of shame and humiliation when they met Liberace - and - Wonder Woman!

Our heroes had been on the Common for around two hours, carefully vetting the assorted prey that wandered the landscape like the seasoned professionals they now believed themselves to be. The pickings seemed few and far between this Thursday night and our heroes wondered why?

What they were not aware of was that not three miles east of the Common, there was a massive Gay Pride costume event going on, and the usual gaggle of assorted, rent boys, cottagers and still in the closet married men, were all there enjoying the parade and making new friends.

Not so for Liberace, a gay man in his late twenties who made his living doing impersonations in the many gay clubs of London as the "love of his life" and namesake. Liberace was late and wanted to get to the parade very badly. Against his better judgement, he had taken a shortcut across Clapham Common to try and pick up a stray taxi, but he knew he was clutching at straws. All the cabs would be around the centre of the parade.

As Liberace made his way quickly down a gravel pathway, his highly shining sequined costume caught the light of the overhead lamp post sending colourful reflective patterns into the night sky like a laser show. Liberace stopped briefly and sighed - damn he thought to himself forlornly, why couldn't there be someone else around to witness what must be quite a spectacular vision - even if he thought so himself, he must look "*absolutely fab-u-lous*".

At this point, Liberace was not aware that he did indeed have a couple of admirers, and they were just about ready to introduce themselves. They fell in behind Liberace and followed at a safe distance.

"Here have a look, hero one said to hero two, what's he come as do you think?"

"What's he come as? Are you kidding me? It's bloody obvious ain't it? "Hero two answered.

Liberace remembered his mission and hurried onward. About twenty seconds later he heard a voice a little way behind him.

"Where do you think you're going Elvis?" Hero two demanded.

Liberace turned with a look of disgust on his face.

"Bloody Elvis you cretinous oaf, he spat the words at our heroes, how very dare you?".

Without warning Liberace suddenly turned and ran, fearing that he was about to be mugged or worse, these two northern ruffians were no good, of that he was sure. Unfortunately for Liberace the three-inch heels on his patent leather boots were not made for sprinting and he slipped on the gravel, his left leg went west and his right leg east, he tripped and went full head over heels, flashing through the night air as the lamplight caught his costume like a fiery Catherine Wheel.

The sight of Liberace spinning arse overhead was too much for our heroes. They fell about laughing as Liberace lay on the gravel a whimper escaped from his mouth, as he feared the worse. Hero one moved in for the kill.

"Hand it over Elvis and don't waste our time, he growled, and peel those rings off while you're at it". He said.

Liberace burst into tears, his rings, no not the rings.

"Please don't take my rings, they belonged to my mother and grandmother, please I beg you, I have cash, take that" Liberace pleaded.

"Don't be telling me your life story Elvis, just give me the rings," said Hero one.

The sound of running footsteps caused our heroes to turn at once to face whatever danger might be approaching. What they saw, would haunt them forever!

A large figure in a Wonder Woman costume was hurtling at some speed towards them, her blue cape billowed behind her as she covered the ground between them like a winged greyhound, a look of evil on her face that would put the wind-up Freddy Kruger.

Wonder Woman was Lola Lombardi, a lesbian female wrestler standing six feet three inches tall and weighing in at one hundred and ninety-five pounds, and as it happened, a very good friend of Liberace. Lola raised her arm and crashed her elbow into the face of the smaller stockier man. He went down like he had been hit by a runaway truck. Without breaking stride and as silent as the grave she sped towards the skinnier of the two men. Hero two fancied himself as a bit of a boxer and took a defiant pugilistic southpaw stance, although this in no way camouflaged the fear burning in his eyes having seen his brother-in-arms immobilised with one swift mighty blow from the brutal Amazonian.

"Bring it on you scrawny rat" Lola growled at him.

Hero two threw a wild haymaker which Lola parried with ease grabbing a handful of his hair as she did, as if in slow motion Lola crouched down, grabbed him by the balls and squeezed, the screams of agony could be heard in Lambeth. Lola hoisted him above her head, spun him around helicopter style and threw hero two face-first into an oak tree ten feet away. He landed dazed and semi-conscious in a pile on the ground.

Liberace squealed with joy as Wonder Woman walked over and helped him to his feet.

"Oh Lola, thank God you are here, I snapped a heel" Liberace gushed.

"Are you ok Libby?" Lola asked, just as other stragglers either going to or coming from the Gay Pride costume party arrived after they had witnessed the commotion and heard the screams from across the common. Three of them were dressed as the Native American, the motorcycle cop and the construction worker from the Village People music video, these were soon joined by Snow White and two of her Dwarves, and judging from the look on the Dwarves faces ...neither of them was *Happy*. To complete the angry ensemble, a bearded drag queen with a poodle, for some inexplicable reason known only to the bearded beauty, had been dyed Canary yellow.

Having quickly assessed what had taken place, and the fact that two men with northern accents had plagued the common and the gay community in general for some time now, the assembled entourage started to kick and batter our defenceless heroes into bloody submission, to make matters worse for the two, if that were at all humanly possible, the motorcycle cop then produced a set of handcuffs, which were attached to an ankle of each man, they were pulled to their feet and frog-marched off the common. Further humiliation was heaped upon the two men as a passing police car stopped. The police officers listened in awe to the story of the attempted mugging and subsequent rescue. They were eventually arrested and detained, only after one of the arresting officers had regained his composure long enough, having rolled around on the grass holding his stomach as if he were suffering from severe cramps, in a fit of laughter.

To finally end their ordeal, the two men were bundled into the back of the police car. The howling, jeering, bloodthirsty mob still baiting them as they were driven away. The two arresting officers still hooting with laughter at the sight of the fallen heroes in the rearview mirror, heads hung shamefully in self-loathing. Thus ended their reign of terror on Clapham Common, and the assorted gentlefolk of that particular manor lived in harmonious peace once more.

As fate would have it, and to make matters even worse, the national press had picked up on the story. At the arranged court hearing one national newspaper had invited their vanquishers to attend in full battle costume, for a photo-shoot. The story ran for three days in the newspaper, including the photographs, first-hand eye witness accounts, a public comments section and a "which superhero would you like to be rescued by?" competition.

Jimmy looked at the two men, tears of laughter rolling down his face.

" I never heard anything like that in my life, oh for fuck's sake, that's priceless," Jimmy said.

"Shackled and beaten up by a gang of poofters and lesbians and midgets, you're lucky you two got away with your arseholes "*Virgo intacta*". Fallon said.

This last remark was too much for Jimmy to bear; he fell against the wall doubled over in mirth.

"Oh no, stop it Tony   please," Jimmy said, still doubled over and laughing himself sick.

This was the beginning of what was to become a long friendship for Jimmy Walsh and Tony Fallon.

Chapter 8

South London October 1983

The meeting had been arranged to begin at eleven o'clock, it was to take place in an Irish themed bar named Bradys'.

Bradys' was a typical London style pub, lots of dark colours in the decor of the curtains and carpets, mainly reds and greens. The deep oak wooden bars were also a feature which reflected in the booths, tables and chairs which were still littered with Saturday's night debris of glasses, bottles, overflowing ashtrays and crisp packets. The usual Irish memorabilia adorned the walls, shalaleighs, Irish proverbs in glass frames and a scattering of Gaelic football teams' colourful shirts.

The landlord of the licensed premises was an Irishman of about forty years of age from Dublin by the name of John Driscoll. Driscoll had been the proprietor at Bradys' for close to fifteen years. He was a tall man standing over six feet in height and weighing a hefty eighteen stones, his well-rounded belly hanging proudly over the belt of his trousers, his round ruddy face and cheeks flushed even redder now due to his endeavours at getting the bar ready to receive his pre-legal opening time guests. Driscoll had a team on early duty buzzing around the bar, glasses being collected, cleared and washed, vacuum cleaner humming in the background, tables being washed down and polished, windows being polished, and the smell of fried sausages, bacon and black pudding coming from the kitchen behind the bar.

Driscoll owed his livelihood to Jack Riordan. Riordan had put up the fifty thousand pounds Driscoll had needed to buy Bradys' from the previous owner, Keiran Brady. The purchase carried out in Driscoll's name, as a director holding the power of attorney for the purchase, on behalf of a shell company, owned by a shell company, owned by a parent company, owned by an offshore trust fund registered to an office in Nicosia, Cyprus, none of these companies of course actually did any business, the trust fund just a front for the cash businesses.

The real owner, as in the case of six other popular watering holes in and around the manor was none other than Jack Riordan. Any cash business is invaluable to any group or individuals dealing with large amounts of illegal cash and the need to legitimise it. Money goes through the pub's books, invoices and receipts are produced to make the books balance, and a vehicle for cleaning the money is established. Public houses are a particularly good way of laundering money especially if you have a loyal hardcore clientele of a few hundred thirsty Irishmen. Bradys' was a great business, it was everything a local Irish community bar should be, a great location, great management, the food was superb and the Guinness even better.

At Christmas, Easter and St. Patrick's Day, parties and family days were fantastic fun occasions where the generous donations that covered all the costs were courtesy of the philanthropic Jack Riordan. Bradys' was possibly the only Irish pub in London, or anywhere else for that matter, that had never had a barroom brawl. There was an unwritten code that determined this was a family environment and everyone was welcome, however, any shenanigans that needed to be settled, the warring parties were free to pick any one of the other five locations in the Riordan portfolio and tear it up to their heart's content, anyone ignoring that rule would be dealt with swiftly and more often than not violently. Word gets around, strangers didn't come here looking for trouble, everyone knew this was Jack Riordan's place, whatever it said above the door and whatever protestations John Driscoll may have made if indeed anybody dared to put it to him, although nobody ever seemed to feel the need to explore the complex origins of the ownership of the aforementioned drinker.

The phone at the bar suddenly rang. Driscoll picked it up.

"Good morning Bradys', he said, right you are, we're ready for him so we are".

Driscoll hung up the phone and clapped his huge hands together. "Right the boss man will be here in five minutes, get that Guinness on the go Sean" he boomed out across the barroom.

Driscoll went to the preferred booth that Jack Riordan always occupied when he visited Bradys'. He placed two bottles of Jameson Irish whiskey on the table, along with six glasses and a full ice bucket. The table was already laid with cutlery, napkins, and condiments. A loud knock at the door stopped him in his tracks.
Driscoll pulled back the curtain and peered out, he could see Jimmy Walsh, Billy Kelly and the other two usual suspects, Paddy and Tommy whoever, were standing outside.

Driscoll went across the bar to the door and opened it a crack.

"Lads I can't be doing an early one today, Mr Riordan has business here this morning, a meeting of some importance" he blurted out.

"Indeed he has, and that's why we are here John, and by the way, very good morning to you too," Jimmy said.

"You fellas have a meeting with the boss here, now, this morning?" Driscoll asked almost in disbelief.

"We do John, so if you would be so kind, to let us in, I don't want to keep Mr Riordan waiting". Jimmy said.

"Of course no problem, come in Jimmy, how are you doing lads?" He asked as he stepped aside ushering the boys into the bar.

"Fine thanks John, how are you yourself?" Billy asked.

"Top-notch Billy boy, top-notch" Driscoll answered.

The boys sat at a table not far from the booth they knew Riordan would occupy on his arrival. Sean the barman brought over a tray on which four pints of Guinness stood.

"On the house boys, compliments of John" Sean said as he rested the tray on the table.

"Cheers Sean, how's your mum these days?" Jimmy asked.

"She's good Jimmy, thanks for asking," Sean said.

"That's good, give her my regards won't you? " Jimmy said.

"I sure will Jimmy, thanks again" Sean replied.

The boys picked up their glasses and held them out to the middle of the table touching them together the clink of glass against glass rang out across the empty bar.

"Sláinte," Jimmy said. The traditional Irish toast which simply means "health".

"Sláinte" the boys replied as one. They lifted the glasses and drank.

Billy was still feeling uneasy about this meeting. He still didn't know what the meeting was about, and Jimmy had pulled out of the arrangement to meet earlier this morning to brief him. Billy liked Riordan but didn't trust him as much as the whole community seemed to. Riordan had a much closer relationship with Jimmy than with any other member of the younger Irish community.

Billy had often wondered why his father never came to Bradys' or frequented any of the other Riordan pubs, he chose to take a drink at home occasionally or even less occasionally go further afield. He had never told Billy why. His father had always nodded respectfully and greeted Riordan with a handshake whenever their paths had crossed at church, but it always seemed there was an unspoken mistrust of the man. Anyway - that's how it appeared to Billy.

"Jimmy, are you going to fill us in? What's the fuck is this all about?" Billy asked, his eyes fixed firmly on Jimmy's face.

"What's up with you Billy, it's just - look I'm sorry I couldn't make it this morning to meet you. Riordan has a job for us that's all, said he wanted to meet us here. He said he would introduce us to a business acquaintance who is meeting with him to discuss whatever it is they want from us." Jimmy said.

"So there is no problem with Riordan? Everything is fine, no problems you haven't told us about Jimmy?". Billy said.

"For fuck's sake Billy he's here, let's just find out what he wants we can talk later". Jimmy said.

Jack Riordan had just walked into the pub. His number two Christy Monaghan beside him. The two men approached the empty booth and slid inside. The sound of glasses being overturned and the cap of a whiskey bottle being spun off onto the table could be heard as Christy attacked a bottle of Jameson.

John Driscoll came over to the booth, greeted and shook hands with each man in turn.

"Something to eat Jack?"

"Not right now John, we have a bit of business to take care of first with the lads here, we will eat later," Riordan said to Driscoll as he turned to the boys' booth.

"How are you lads? Riordan asked, the breakfast of champions I see. John, would you get the boys another round on me please?" Riordan looked straight at Jimmy.

"Jimmy - would you and young Billy kindly join us, please? Tommy and Paddy, I'm sorry, but I'm expecting another to join us, and as you can see it's a bit of a squeeze so it is, I hope you don't mind lads?" Riordan said.

"No not at all Mr Riordan" Tommy blurted out.

"It's fine Mr Riordan," Paddy said. Neither of the two was aware that Jack Riordan even knew their names.

Jimmy and Billy went to the booth to join the two older men. Christy Monaghan poured a generous shot of Jameson into two glasses and topped up his own glass and Riordan's.

"Sláinte," he said and emptied the glass in one gulp.

"Sláinte," came the reply as they all drank.

Riordan eyed Jimmy carefully. "You must be wondering what I need you for Jimmy calling you here in this clandestine manner?" he said.

"You're the boss, Mr Riordan, I'm sure we can help whatever you need". Jimmy answered.

"How's your dad Billy?" Riordan asked, taking Billy by surprise.

"Err - he's fine Mr Riordan, thanks," Billy said.

"That's good Billy, he's a good steady man your dad, I'm sure you are aware of that". Riordan said.

"I am, thank you". Billy replied.

"Good lad Billy, good lad….". Riordan said and let the sentence trail.

"Anyway to business. Some time ago I entrusted a quarter of a million pounds sterling to one slippery bastard to buy some supplies from Holland. He now tells me that the drugs were seized by the old bill on a fucking houseboat on a river in fucking Essex" Riordan was becoming redder in the face as he told the story.

"I want my money back, and I want it back quick, the man in question is coming here in a few minutes to explain to me in person how he intends to pay me back. I want him to understand that I want my money - now - within a week, otherwise I'm going to get nasty, and by me - I, of course, mean you two". Riordan said.

"No problem Mr Riordan, you just tell us what you want to be done, where and when," said Jimmy.

"You can count on us Mr Riordan" Billy piped up.

"Good lads, let's see what he has to say for himself when he gets here then we can make a plan if need be".

The four men continued to drink whiskey and make small talk until John Driscoll came over to the booth about ten minutes later. He leaned into Riordan and whispered something discreetly in his ear.

"Ah that's grand John, let them in, I'm expecting them, Riordan said, It would appear our guest is here lads".

The slippery bastard that Jack Riordan had referred to earlier was a man by the name of Arda Arslan. The same man discussed at the meeting previously with Detective Chief

Superintendent Graham Simpson. Arda Arslan was a second-generation Turkish immigrant whose parents had come to London in the 1960s from Istanbul.

Arda Arslan controlled the Arslan family drug business operations, mainly large hashish imports from Turkey and Pakistan through Holland. The hashish was then shipped by small fast-moving motorboats to the coast of England, mainly along the Kent and Essex coastlines. The Arslan crime family was based in Islington North London and was headed by Arda's father Mehmet. A man in his late sixties now, but still feared and respected throughout the North London Turkish Cypriot communities.

Arda Arslan was a stocky man of about five feet nine in height. His companion, on the other hand, was standing six feet five and weighing in at two hundred and twenty pounds of steely sinew and hard muscle, a scar ran from the crown of his shaved head to the bridge of his nose. This man was Arda Arslan's personal bodyguard and attack dog, Hamza Yılmaz. A former Turkish special forces soldier and close protection specialist.

Riordan sat straight as the two men approached, standing to greet Arda with an outstretched hand.

"Mr Arslan, welcome to South London, I trust the air agrees with you", Riordan smiled as he looked warily up and down at Hamza.

"By the holy, he's a big one your man there, what are you feeding him?". Riordan smiled jokingly. Hamza smiled back, an uncannily genuine and pleasant smile.

"Oh don't worry about Hamza Mr Riordan, he's not fussy he eats whatever I tell him too" Arda replied as the men shook hands.

Everybody laughed at Arda's witty response.

"Will you take a drop of whiskey? I'm sure you must have a terrible thirst after your travels" Christy Monaghan said, extending his hand to Arda, Christy had noticed the sideways glance Arda had given Jimmy when he had first approached the booth, Jimmy had looked away quickly, not very Jimmy Walsh like at all.

"Thank you, Mr Monaghan, I don't mind if I do," said Arda.

Christy poured whiskey into the two remaining glasses and refilled the other four.

"Sláinte,", Christy said he emptied the glass in one gulp again. Riordan, Jimmy and Billy replied in unison as the two Turks looked on. The Turks had no idea what the toast meant, so just muttered "cheers" as a reply.

"So now, this is an unfortunate business, Arda. May I call you Arda?" Riordan asked.

Arda smiled and nodded his assent.

Arda looked calm while considering his reply. He knew of Jack Riordan's reputation as a businessman, and he knew this was about nothing more than the money. He didn't want a war with the Turks, he was a reasonable man. He wanted his product or he wanted his money back.

"Very unfortunate Mr Riordan, very unfortunate indeed. But rest assured your money is safe and as soon as I regroup the deal we had will go through sweet as a nut" Arda said.

"Well now Arda that's good to know so it is, unfortunately for you though I want no part of any further deals, you have drawn unwanted and unnecessary attention to yourself and your family. Do you even know how the police were waiting, with Customs and Excise no less? Riordan asked.

"We had an unlucky week is all Mr Riordan, these things happen in our business, you know that" Arda replied.

"Well, this is the attention I don't want on me or my organisation. I have always made sure that the people I deal with are clean, they are trustworthy and they don't have any leaks in their firms" Riordan continued.

"Are you suggesting that this was a set up by someone inside our family Jack, may I call you Jack?" Arda said as he smiled at Riordan.

"No you may not call me fucking Jack sonny, remember where you are and who you are fucking dealing with here, you think I have 250K to piss away on the likes of you? You get me my money and you get it quick." Riordan snapped at Arda.

Arda's face dropped the smile and his eyes became hard.

"If that's what you want you can have it, there are no grasses in my family or my firm, I will have your money by the end of the month". With that Arda was about to get up and walk away.

"Sit the fuck down and listen to me you little shit, you needed money from me and you got it twenty-four hours later. Out of respect for your father…, Riordan let the sentence trail off for effect, the look of surprise on Arda's face told him all he needed to know, I will give you forty-eight hours to get my money back to me before I tell Mehmet it's his debt, and I will take it one way or the other, do I make myself fucking clear Mr Arslan?" Riordan said.

Arda was visibly shaken by Riordan's words. Not the threat or the fact that Riordan knew his father, but the fact that Arda's father knew nothing about his extracurricular activities. Arda had been raising money and dealing directly with his own suppliers for some time now, this was the biggest deal so far and it had gone wrong, badly wrong. He was 250K in the hole with Riordan and the same to a very nasty firm from Liverpool, whom he intended to pay this very day. He did have enough to cover the full debt but was hoping that Riordan would have been more reasonable and given him more time. He wanted to use the 250K to set up another deal with the Liverpool firm. He was going to buy into that deal when Tony Fallon came for his money tonight. He would give Fallon the full 500K.

"This has nothing to do with my family Mr Riordan, my father knows nothing about this piece of business - and I don't like being threatened, Hamza here will rip you four apart with one word from me," Arda said.

Arda's face was now flushed with embarrassment and fury. On hearing Arda's words, Hamza had stood up towering above the small booth, Jimmy and Billy both stood a fraction of a second later, as Tommy and Paddy moved in behind.

"Lads, lads, enough of this now - sit the fuck back down big fella," Christy Monaghan said to Hamza, at the same time pulling back his jacket to reveal a gun holster holding an Italian made Beretta nine millimetre automatic pistol.

"*Rahatlayın Hamza - relax,*" Arda said, using the English word too, so everyone was aware it was not instruction or a trick.

Hamza took no longer than a second to decide that even for a man with his pure physical strength and skills, the odds were still very much against him.

"You have forty-eight hours; you want to go to war with me? Or you want war with those scouse scum? Yes, I know all about your dealings Mr Arslan, and I also know your family does not. Either way, you don't have the money to cover us both without going to your daddy, and I also know you won't do that. Choose wisely Mr Arslan - now get the fuck out of my pub, and get to fuck out of South London while you still can." Riordan said.

"Fuck you old man, I will pay you when I'm ready," Arda said as he got to his feet again.

"You speak to Mr Riordan like that again I will put you in the ground you fucking no mark Turkish prick" Jimmy snarled at Arda.

Rising from the table Billy also stood facing directly to Hamza, Tommy and Paddy took up their previous positions, this time closer to Hamza, who shuffled his feet to a wider combat stance.

Christy tapped his jacket and Hamza sat down again.

John Driscoll kept his hand firmly on the stock of a shotgun under the bar as he watched the men argue.

Arda looked at Jimmy and sneered.

"I'm looking forward to meeting you again *Ginger* - and believe me, we ain't no fucking Yardie pussies, you won't get the fucking drop on me."

Arda turned and walked away, Hamza followed.

"Forty-eight hours Mr Arslan" Riordan called after them.

Arda and Hamza carried on walking as if nothing had happened, no break in step no hesitation. Riordan beckoned Tommy and Paddy to join them, he smiled at his assembled troops around the table.

"Another round for the boys' John". Riordan called out to Driscoll.

"What's the plan, Mr Riordan?" Jimmy asked.

"Oh quite simple - Jimmy my boy, he's got to go, Riordan said, I want him and his monster dead - today, he has no intention of paying me, and I'm not going to give him time to get organized, Riordan said raising his glass, Sláinte..."

"I liked the way you told that upstart to watch his mouth Jimmy, thank you for that" Riordan said, referring to Jimmy's brief exchange with Arda.

"No problem Mr Riordan, Jimmy said, it was very disrespectful".

Riordan watched Jimmy intently, he searched his face for any sign of him giving away his secret. Billy was very uncomfortable with the order that Jack Riordan had just given them. Riordan had them asked to commit murder, a double murder in fact. They all sat quietly waiting for Riordan to continue the conversation.

"You know; I can't help thinking I've seen those two before somewhere. Have you boys come across them before today anywhere? Are they known across the parish here? Riordan asked.

"Or have you seen them in North London anywhere, up West, who knows, anywhere at all".

"I've heard of the bodyguard Mr Riordan, he's a right handful. They reckon it took five old bill and two dogs to get him in a van once after he mutilated three black geezers outside a club up west, then he bit one of the dogs ears off and threw it at the arresting sergeant, a right nutter they reckon". Billy said."

"They say that the dog had to have therapy and retire... every time it saw a big skinhead after that night it pissed itself and attacked its handler" said Tommy.

They all burst out laughing at Tommy's story. There were two things now that Jack Riordan was certain of, Jimmy Walsh was in cahoots with Arda Arslan, and even his best friend and business partner Billy Kelly didn't know.

"What about you Jimmy? You ever come across those two before, he did seem to take a dislike to you for sure, I thought you might have had a bit of previous, I saw the look he gave you when he came in" Christy asked.

"No nothing like that Mr Monaghan, just sizing me up I suppose in case things kicked off" Jimmy replied.

"Ah yeah for sure, I think had anything kicked off he would have left the big fella to sort it out, and ya man would have had it away on his toes," Christy said. More laughter rang out from the booth.

Jack Riordan looked away in despair on hearing Jimmy's answer. Any last hope he had held that this was all a mix-up, some sort of terrible mistake had gone, Riordan now knew he had to move quickly.

"Ok Jimmy, are you in?" Riordan asked.

Jimmy quickly weighed up the pros and cons of taking out Arda Arslan, on the one hand, he knew that the deal had gone pear-shaped, and he knew it wouldn't take long for Riordan to find out about his involvement. He also knew that Tony Fallon was waiting for Arda to make restitution on the money that was lost by his Liverpool firm, and that payment was due to take place this evening at eight o'clock at the Turks gambling club in Islington. If Jimmy took this job, he just might be able to pull off a real coup, take out Arda and the ferocious Hamza Yilmaz, dead men don't tell tales.

Jimmy had to make sure Tony Fallon got his money first. It was all about the timing. He would call Arda and arrange a meeting. He would also call Tony Fallon with a proposal.

"You know me, Mr Riordan, I'm your man, I'm in I won't let you down," said Jimmy.

"Good lad - I want this over by tonight, I want them gone Jimmy, well and truly gone," Riordan said.

"Understood Mr Riordan" Jimmy answered.

"I had them checked out through a friend of mine north of the river. They own a gambling club in Islington, just down from the Angel, Riordan said, it's called The Casbah Club. Arda is there every Sunday from three o'clock in the afternoon onwards, he likes to gamble and drink until the early hours of the morning, another of his lifestyle choices that bitterly disappoints his father, anyway that's where they will be tonight, the place doesn't get busy until around nine or ten, so the earlier you do it the better" Riordan said.

"Don't worry we will find it, you can rely on us Mr Riordan," Jimmy said.

Billy sat silently watching this surreal conversation between Jimmy and Riordan. He couldn't understand why Jimmy was just agreeing to commit double murder with a few hours' notice, not to mention the moral implications of the actions. The firm had been involved in some pretty heavy-duty armed robberies and there had been beatings doled out during their debt collecting and enforcement jobs, but this was murder. Beatings, drug and cash rip-offs or robbing thieves or drug dealers, didn't get reported, that was low-risk stuff. Murders on the other hand always drew unwanted attention, and the amount of time they were looking at if they were caught was a very high risk indeed, for what Billy could see was for no return.

Billy was not happy with this arrangement and was going to let Jimmy know it.

"I expect I will hear from you later then Jimmy, is there anything you need from me, except my gratitude, loyalty and friendship?" Riordan asked.

Billy looked at Riordan as he noticed the emphasis he had put on the word loyalty, something wasn't right here, something, in fact, was very wrong. Jimmy didn't seem to notice or was playing it very cool if he had.

Riordan and Christy got up to leave bidding farewell and good luck to the lads as they went.

"Are you away Jack? You're not going to eat something?" Driscoll called out.

"Not today John, whatever the lads need, put it on my tab, make sure they have a good feed before they go now, they are going to need it," Riordan said.

"Right you are Jack, consider it done," said Driscoll.

The door closed behind Jack Riordan and Christy Monaghan as they disappeared from sight.

"Fucking double murder Jimmy, are you sure? What the fuck is wrong with you, just like that you say yes, you don't ask for anything - you don't even speak with us, you just agree?" Billy said.

"Listen, Billy, you don't say no to a man like Jack Riordan, they are two worthless Turkish scum, what's the problem?" Jimmy said.

"I don't like it either Jimmy, that's me and Tommy - right Tom?" said Paddy looking for Tommy's support.

Tommy nodded in agreement.

"Then you should have told Riordan when he was here, I can't call him now and tell him we ain't got the balls to do it can I? Jimmy protested, so let's just make the best of it, we need a plan. I know this club it's on Camden Walk opposite Islington Green".

"How do you know the club Jimmy, you never said that to Riordan, you said we will find it, said Billy, have you been there before? What were you doing on that side of the river Jimmy, we never go there, we never have - well not unless Palace is playing there".

"Fucking hell Billy what's all this, it's like the third degree here. I went there once with a mate I met in Brixton nick, it's no big deal for fuck's sake, Jimmy argued, I need to get my head straight over this, I need to know if you three pussies are in or out, I will do it on my own if I have to"

"Yeah - that's the problem right there Jimmy I know you will do it alone, you are getting reckless, snorting that white powder morning, noon and night, you are not thinking straight, and it's making you paranoid," Billy said.

"I'm not paranoid Billy, I'm just asking you three are you in or out? And who said I'm paranoid - was it you Tommy? Did you say I'm paranoid? Jimmy asked menacingly.

"I ain't said a word to anyone about you Jimmy, why would I say something like that? Tommy said.

"Ok - ok I will ask you all again then, are you in or out, we need to get organized' Jimmy said, we've only got a few hours and we need to do this right".

Jimmy looked around the booth at the faces of the other three. Billy nodded - Tommy and Paddy did the same.

"Ok then all in - sweet, Jimmy said, John another round and give us the works on the Irish breakfast times four".

Chapter 9

London 1983

Jack Riordan was still hurt. He could feel his anger towards Jimmy Walsh growing by the second. Jimmy was like a son to him but now all he felt was pure hatred.

"That treacherous little bastard Christy, Riordan roared, everything I did for that little shit, and he sits there and lies straight to my face, siding with those fucking lowlife's, would you credit that?"

Not waiting for Christy to answer Riordan ploughed on.

"Well, we will see how he gets out of this one now tonight, let's go to the Emerald club, I have an important phone call to make and I need some privacy. I hope Jimmy Walsh and his friends like porridge because there will be plenty of that where those fellas will be going for some time" Riordan said.

The Emerald Club was another of the drinking establishments in the Riordan portfolio and was located in the backstreets of Penge, South London. Jack Riordan kept a small office at the back. The office was located on the first floor of the premises that he used occasionally for his more private meetings and discretionary phone conversations, such as that he was about to have with Detective Chief Superintendent Graham Simpson.

Riordan entered through the fire escape entrance at the back of the Emerald Club, an external black metal staircase with a small landing at the top that led directly into the small neat office. Jack went straight to the desk, sat down and lifted the handset from the cradle of the telephone set. He jerked his thumb over his shoulder indicating to Christy to fix drinks from the bottle of Jameson Irish Whiskey on the small drinks tray sitting on top of a small oak bookcase.

Riordan sat patiently as he waited for somebody to answer the phone at the other end of the line as Christy placed a large drink in front of him.

"I'll go and fetch some ice Jack, two ticks now," Christy said.

Riordan nodded as Christy left through the office doorway that led to the small kitchen downstairs.

A voice at the other end of the line answered.

"Ah Graham, good afternoon to you, how was your golf game this morning, not too rusty I trust," Riordan said.

"Good afternoon Jack, it was very pleasant thank you, not my best round but always good to be out there hitting a few after a bit of a prolonged break" Simpson replied.

"Indeed. Well, that's grand Graham - Riordan said pausing slightly, my meeting this morning told me all I needed to know about my own people. I've arranged another this afternoon on your patch, you know the place on Camden Walk owned by your philandering friend I take it?" Riordan asked.

"Indeed I do, this is the real thing Jack, we can take the whole lot down today?

Simpson confirmed he knew the Casbah Club and that he was expecting the whole operation to be over with today. He didn't want this business dragging on, especially with his political contact, who desperately wanted Arda Arslan out of the picture as soon as possible.

"I's dotted T's crossed Graham, you need to give my fella's a bit of time to do the necessary then, they are all yours Graham, with my compliments. If it wasn't for the intel you gave me I would still be none the wiser now". Riordan said.

"All understood Jack I will have a team on standby ready to pick up the pieces, we will be ready and in position by three o'clock, and thanks for this Jack, it won't go unnoticed in the corridors of the house you will have made a powerful political ally. I will make sure credit is given where it is due" Simpson said.

"We've always made a good team Graham, long may it continue, I will be in touch," Riordan said, just as Christy came back through the door with the ice.

"Goodbye, for now, Jack," said.

Christy brought the ice to the desk and dropped three rocks into Riordan drink, then did the same for his own.

They both picked up their glasses and raised them to each other.

"Your very good health Jack, Christy said, Sláinte"

"The same to you Christy, Sláinte," Riordan said.

Chapter 10

North London 1983

Billy felt his stomach turn over again, there was something wrong here and he wasn't sure what it was. Tommy was at the wheel of the white BMW 3 series as they made their way through the light Sunday afternoon traffic towards North London.

"Alright remember boys, in and out, no hanging around and if that big geezer is there take him out, don't mess around with him and don't try to be a hero he will definitely do you some damage - all right, Jimmy said, everyone knows what we are doing, this is for real boys, no fucking about".

"Yeah, we got it Jimmy" Billy answered for everyone.

After they had left Bradys', and before they had set off on their journey to North London, Jimmy had made his excuses to get away from the others for a while. He took the opportunity to say he needed to pick up his gun and a clip of ammunition from home.

Jimmy had called both Arda Arslan and Tony Fallon, taking a calculated risk that neither of the two was as treacherous as he himself was, and wouldn't call the other to verify Jimmy's new plan. Jimmy intended to tell each just enough to make it easy to change the plan quickly if he had to. He made his call to Arda Arslan first.

"Hello," Arda said as he answered the phone on the fifth ring.

"Arda, it's Jimmy we need to meet, Jimmy said, I have just finished up with Riordan. He's not happy but I've managed to get you a couple of more weeks. That will help sort this mess out. I have a plan - so I'm going to ask Tony to come and meet us at the club too, is that alright with you?

"Ok Jimmy, no problem. How did you manage that? He seemed pretty pissed an hour ago, I wanted to talk to you about Tony again, I mentioned to you last week I wanted in on his deal, this will work out now if we can persuade him, Arda said, it will solve all our problems".

"I'm not too sure, to be honest, Irish charm I guess. So what do you mean exactly? Do you have Riordan's money? You have his money but you want to give Riordan's money to Tony Fallon as a buy-in on his deal? Jimmy said acting dumb.

"Yes that's exactly what I want to do, said Arda, do you think he will go for it?"

"Great minds think alike Arda, that's exactly what I was going to suggest if we could lay our hands on some cash, but we need to convince Tony, I don't think he needs any more cash for the deal he has in hand," Jimmy said.

"You think he will knock me back?" Arda asked.

"He might be a scouse scally but Tony's an astute businessman. He will always use other people's money where he can, double the money, double the product, double the profits. Anyway let's see, let me chat with him now and look at that option. I will be at the club around four o'clock Arda,".

"Yeah ok Jimmy see you later then - Jimmy, make it work mate, I need this" Arda said as he hung up the phone.

The next call Jimmy placed was to Tony Fallon.

"Hello Tony Jimmy here" Jimmy spoke into the mouthpiece.

"Ah Tony lah, how are you, bro," Fallon said in his distinctive Liverpudlian accent.

"What happened with your boss, did you meet with him? Did you manage to buy us some time?".

"No I didn't mate he's none too pleased, he scared the shit out of Arda and told him he was going to go after his old man if he didn't get his money today," Jimmy said.

"What - he doesn't have the money - only my fucking money, I'm picking that up today" Fallon protested.

"Calm down Tony, I will tell you what happened, he has your money - and he has Riordan's too - and he wants in on your deal" Jimmy explained.

"No fucking way lah, I don't need more cash to do the other deal with my own suppliers, I wish I had never got involved with these Turks," Fallon said.

"Tony - think about it mate, he's going to give you another 250K today on top of your 250K. He doesn't need to know anything other than you are going to do him a favour and get him out of the shit with Riordan and with his family, they won't need to know". Jimmy said.

Jimmy continued his pitch.

"Look I know you have that other bit of business lined up - so what if we take the cash? - and anything else that might be there in his club? Jimmy said.

"Riordan has told me to get rid of them both".

"Ah - now you're talking lah, I like it, Jimmy, I like it, Fallon said, you do this and Riordan will know you're kosher Jimmy, you sneaky bastard you," Fallon said.

They both laughed at the thought of getting rid of Arda and Jimmy putting one over on Riordan.

"Yeah I thought you might like it son - ok I'm going over there at four o'clock, you are due there this evening, I told Arda you would come with me - that way he can persuade you to give you what's his" Jimmy suggested.

They both laughed again.

"What about that fucking great gorilla he has with him all the time Jimmy, who is going to handle him? Fallon asked.

"Don't worry about the details Tony, let's just get in and get the money out of there, Jimmy said, and as for Hamza. I'm not stupid Tony, I'm going to be well tooled up for him no sweat son. Just be inside that club by four o'clock Tony"

At just before four o'clock that Sunday afternoon, Tommy pulled the BMW into the curb outside the Casbah Club in Islington.

Jimmy jumped out of the car and waited for Billy to join him on the pavement.

"Alright Billy, change of plan ok, Jimmy said, I'm going to go in there and just have a chat with him first. I want to scope the place out and see what's what"

"Ain't that a bit risky Jimmy, let me come in with you, Paddy and Tommy can stay outside with the motor running just in case we get trouble". Billy answered.

"It's ok - Riordan has a guy inside, just watch the door, Billy, I can handle whatever goes down inside with Riordan's man" Jimmy lied, of course, the man inside waiting for Jimmy Walsh was Tony Fallon.

Jimmy pulled a gun from the waistband of his trousers, he released the magazine, checked it and rammed it back inside the butt. Billy looked at Jimmy, he knew there was something Jimmy wasn't telling him.

"Where the fuck did this guy come from Jimmy? When did Riordan tell you this? He never mentioned anything to us when we were in Bradys" Billy protested.

"Look Billy just do as I say ok? I don't want you involved in this, keep out of it as much as you can, you will understand soon enough, but just for now, let me do what I need to do - please?" Jimmy said.

Billy was still not happy with the answer, but he knew whatever the reason was for Jimmy's secrecy, that there would be no changing his mind now.

"Just be by the door Billy that's all I ask, make sure Tommy and Paddy are ready if I need them, do that for me?" Jimmy asked.

With that Jimmy turned up the collar on his jacket, pulled a baseball cap from his pocket, put it on his head and turned towards the doorway, there was nobody at the door. The gambling didn't start until seven in the evening so the security didn't arrive until six o'clock, the only people around were a few afternoon drinkers at the small bar. Jimmy went inside and looked around, Tony Fallon was already there, sitting at the bar head down, looking deep into a pint of lager.

Jimmy moved up alongside Fallon at the bar.

"Give me the same as my mate here please pal, Jimmy asked the barman, and tell the boss we are here please, he's expecting me".

"Oh yeah, and who should I tell him you are then," asked the barman.

"Not your concern son, I'm sure Hamza will see me on the CCTV," Jimmy said.

"Ah ok then, no problem, I guess if you know Hamza is with him …then you must be friends" the barman laughed.

"Oh yes, we're all friends here," Jimmy said.

The barman walked out of hearing range and Jimmy took the opportunity to speak in a hushed voice to Fallon.

"Alright Tony you know what I have to do in there - Riordan is expecting it. I don't want you linked to me, so let's get the cash first, Jimmy said, you tell him you have to get back to Liverpool sharpish to tie up that bit of business. Tell him you're under pressure from your supplier, and you have a car waiting for you. Take the cash and get out - ok? My guys are right outside, one by the door and another two in a white BMW, keep your head down and get out of this manor quickly".

Fallon nodded that he understood Jimmy's instructions. The barman returned with Jimmy's drink. He picked up the phone and pressed the number one.

"Two gentlemen here to see you, boss, the barman said into the phone, obviously speaking with Arda - he wouldn't say, he just said that Hamza would recognize them if he's watching on the cameras...ok boss I will send them up".

Both Jimmy and Fallon looked up at the camera and waved.

The barman replaced the handset. He turned to Jimmy and Fallon.

"Ok you can go up, I'm sure you know the way but just in case, up those stairs and left at the top". The barman said.

"Ok thank you my good man' Fallon said throwing a five-pound note on the bar, keep the change"

Jimmy and Fallon walked to the staircase at the back of the bar. They ascended the steps quickly, just as they turned left at the top and turned towards Arda's office, the door opened and Hamza stepped out.

"Hey Hamza, how are you?" Fallon asked. Jimmy just walked by him and went through the door into Arda's office.

"I'm good Tony, thank you, I see your friend is as polite as ever," said Hamza.

The small office was in a state of disarray, files scattered around the desk, boxes of spirits piled up in the corner of the room, a row of three metal filing cabinets stood drawers open, files piled inside in no apparent order.

"You're early Tony," Arda said as Fallon entered the office.

"Jimmy explained what you wanted, if you don't want in on the deal, just give me my cash and I'm gone mate, Fallon said, I have a bit of a problem in Liverpool with my supplier Arda, I need to get the cash up to him tonight, they moved things up. You know I have to get this deal done, otherwise, it's going to cost me even more money, so like I said - in or out?" Fallon said.

"Keep your hair onTony, I've got the cash here, your two and a quarter and ours, half a million in total," Arda said.

"Ok nice one, I've got to get going, so if you don't mind can we get it done, we will make some real money now," Fallon said with a smile.

Arda bent forward, fiddling with a small safe under his desk, Jimmy and Fallon exchanged glances listening to the dial on the safe turning one way then the other.

"Hamza, get me a bag can you?" Arda said.

Hamza left the room to get the bag. Arda sat back in his chair and looked at Jimmy.

"So the Irishman, what's the score with him, you think he knows right? He's making you nervous Jimmy I can see you're edgy" Arda said.

"When this deal comes off I don't care what he knows" Jimmy lied.

"Are you sure Jimmy, you look a bit worried to me?" Arda asked.

"I told you I would take care of Riordan - and Monaghan - if I have to, at the moment they are not the problem, the problem is we need to get some money coming in before we are forced to do something we don't want to that will draw attention to our plans, and you don't want daddy finding out now do you?" Jimmy answered.

Arda nodded silently as Hamza returned with a canvas hold-all for the cash. Arda stuffed the piles of tightly packed notes into the bag and pushed it across the desk towards Fallon.

"Count it please Tony, I don't want any misunderstandings," Arda said.

"No need Arda I trust you, we're partners after all - right?" said Fallon, the smile still illuminating his face.

Fallon zipped-up the bag up containing the half a million pounds lifted it from the table and hoisted it over his shoulder.

"Right then gentlemen I will see you next week, I have business to the North" Fallon said dramatically as he laughed, saluting the three men as he turned and left, patting Hamza on the back as he went.

Hamza followed Fallon out and down the stairs, the two men went through the bar, shook hands and Fallon left through the open door, turning left after he was on the street outside. His head down Fallon didn't look at the man hanging around outside the door to the club and only threw a cursory glance at the white BMW at the curb.

Hamza turned around and went back to the bar to speak with the barman.

Jimmy and Arda sat opposite each, more than a little friction in the air.

"What's that all about Jimmy, your snide remark about my dad?", Arda demanded.

"Chill out Arda, you're too sensitive, did I get upset when you called me *Ginger*?" Jimmy teased.

The two sat for about thirty seconds in silence, just staring at each other. Each willing the other to speak first, like a silent game of chicken. Jimmy spoke first.

"Anyway you got more to worry about than me making little remarks Arda, you need to work out a plan for Riordan, you only have a couple of days left to live - remember". Jimmy said smiling.

"You said you got us a couple of weeks," Arda said nervously, suspecting a rip-off.

Arda stared hard at Jimmy Walsh, searching his eyes for any deception. Convincing himself there was none he bent down to the safe, was about to close it when Jimmy spoke again.

"Arda," Jimmy said.

Arda looked up. Jimmy was pointing a gun straight at his head.

"Call down to the bar and get your attack dog back up here Arda, do it now - and Arda do not try anything clever, speak English," Jimmy said

Arda lifted the phone and punched an angry finger at the keys.

"Send Hamza up here right away" Arda demanded and hung up.

"So what's this Jimmy?" Asked Arda nervously.

"Just business Arda, I can't risk Riordan finding out about us, and you - my friend - are now a loose end, get your hands where I can see them". Jimmy said.

Jimmy got up from the chair, the gun still levelled at Arda's chest, he moved back across the small office and stood about twenty feet from the door. The sound of Hamza's footsteps on the stairs could be heard clearly in the office.

"One word Arda and I swear I will kill you" Jimmy snarled.

"Fuck you" Arda screamed as Hamza came through the door at a run now, alarmed by the raised voice of his boss. Hamza saw the gun in Jimmy's hand, took a quick glance at Arda and pulled out a commando knife with a ten-inch blade from inside his jacket. He screamed something in Turkish at Jimmy and lunged forward. Jimmy squeezed the trigger twice and the gun roared. Hamza stopped dead in his tracks and slumped to his knees, blood pouring from two wounds to his chest. He fell forward onto his face.

Jimmy turned towards Arda and squeezed the trigger twice more, Arda fell forward onto his desk dead.

Jimmy sprang into action knowing exactly what he had to do, remove the security tapes from the video recorders and check the safe. The tapes he got out quickly pulling the celluloid from the reels one after the other, he emptied the metal waste paper bin that was under the desk and threw the unwound tapes inside, Jimmy then produced a can of lighter fluid and squirted the liquid inside the bin, he then lit a piece of notepaper from the desk and threw it inside. The tapes exploded into flame and started to disintegrate.

The safe was all but empty, maybe two thousand pounds in notes, Jimmy scooped them up and stuffed them in his pocket. He heard a noise behind him and turned. Hamza had managed to clamour to his knees and had turned around to face Jimmy, a grotesque gurgling sound coming from his chest.

Jimmy moved from behind the desk and aimed the gun at his head, he shot Hamza through the forehead. This time there was no coming back, Hamza spun around as particles of bone and brain matter covered the back wall. Jimmy then grabbed Arda by the shoulders and heaved him back in the chair, he shot Arda through the forehead also. Arda's body bucked in the chair and slumped down, his head lolling on his shoulder, his arms across the armrests of the chair, blood trickling from the pound coin-sized hole in the middle of his head. Blood and matted hair covered the headrest of the chair.

Jimmy moved fast again, he pulled up the office window and jumped to the flat roof of the terraced shops ten feet below. At the far end of this flat roof was a staircase to a side-street. Jimmy had moved maybe fifty feet towards it when he was stopped by the sound of a man's voice.

"Armed Police put down your weapon! Armed Police do it now! Get down on the floor, get down now, drop your weapon. Armed Police" the voice shouted.

Jimmy looked around, two armed police officers were positioned behind him, a helicopter circled overhead, anticipating Jimmy's escape and ready to track his movements.

At the top of the staircase, two more uniformed armed police officers appeared, blocking Jimmy's escape route, their guns trained on Jimmy. Jimmy looked up, his eyes looking heavenward he dropped the gun and the plastic carrier bag.

"Fuck my luck," Jimmy said, as he got onto his knees and prostrated himself on the damp flat roof, he could hear the sound of footsteps crunching on the rooftop shingle as they approached him.

Jimmy felt his arms being pulled back, the cold steel of the handcuffs and the bite of the ratchet mechanism on his wrists as it locked tightly in place. Two officers hauled Jimmy to his feet, a man in his fifties, dressed in plain clothes smiled happily at him as he approached, he bent his face towards Jimmy's ear.

"Hello, Jimmy - *Jack Riordan sends his regards*" whispered Detective Chief Superintendent Graham Simpson.

*****

Billy didn't take much notice of the man that came out of the club door with a canvas hold-all slung over his shoulder, the man moved quickly down the street, turned the next corner and was gone.

Jimmy Walsh had never mentioned Tony Fallon to Billy, not even just to say they were friends in Brixton prison. Billy was totally unaware of Fallon's existence, so he had no idea that the man with the bag containing half a million pounds sterling, was Jimmy's accomplice and business partner. Jimmy knew that Billy was wary of strangers and knew that Billy wouldn't have liked Jimmy bringing in an outsider.

Billy walked to the white BMW parked at the curb.

"Just stay alert boys we are going to need to get out of here quickly when Jimmy comes out," Billy said to both Paddy and Tommy. They both nodded silently.

Billy was getting quite edgy now. They had been waiting for nearly ten minutes and wondered whether he should go in or not. Just at that moment, Billy heard gunfire, two shots, another two - Tommy wound the window down.

All three men jumped at the noise.

"Come on Billy he will be here now, get in, keep the door open for him, he's coming now I bet" Tommy shouted.

Armed Police! Down on the floor - Armed Police! Get out of the car - do it now! Get down on the floor, get down now, Armed Police" the voices shouted.

The car was all of a sudden surrounded by armed police officers. Billy dropped to the ground as Tommy and Paddy were hauled unceremoniously from the car and pushed downward in the middle of the road.

Another shot, then another - Billy turned his head to see armed police officers flooding into the Casbah Club. Billy, Tommy and Paddy were all handcuffed and thrown into a police van. Billy was praying Jimmy would surrender, he would be killed for sure if he didn't.

Chapter 11

North London 1983

After their arrests, all four men were taken to Stoke Newington police station. Jimmy was bundled into the back of a police car and driven off at high speed. The other three boys, Billy, Tommy and Paddy were taken in a police van, both vehicles moving rapidly through the traffic, blue lights flashing and the wail of sirens warning other vehicles out of their way, police vans carrying armed police officers followed in close proximity.

The vehicles arrived at the police station. Jimmy was taken directly to a cell; he was ordered to strip to his boxer shorts. His clothes were removed for forensic examination. He was then given a white all in one coverall, that resembled tissue paper and had about the same tensile strength.

"Going to be some time before we can interview you, Walsh, firearms protocol. No doubt some bleeding heart liberal bullshit about your human rights and the fact you might be traumatized from murdering two people - ain't it fucking fair - hey" said the police officer on custody duty.

His three companions just stood and stared at Jimmy, shaking their heads and tutting in disbelief at this rule.

"Yeah well, I don't reckon I'm going anywhere - do you? Jimmy quipped and smiled, "Any chance of a cuppa - oh - and my brief please?" Jimmy added asking for his solicitor.

The police officer just smiled back, he knew Jimmy was a stone-cold killer, but he had made their job easier, two dead drug-dealing scumbags now off the streets, nobody but their nearest and dearest would give a shit about them. The police were certainly not concerned with the victims of this particular crime, but more the chance to take down another little firm that had killed them, and put them away so they are off the streets too.

"Yeah sure, I reckon you deserve it," the police officer said. His colleagues laughed as they walked away from the cell, a plastic bag full of Jimmy's clothes tagged as evidence and heading for the forensic laboratory.

Outside in the area of the reception and booking, Billy, Tommy and Paddy were separated and led to different cells. Their clothes were not needed for any forensic testing, so they were allowed to keep wearing them, their shoes were removed and they were shoved into cells to await for interviews. Each one of them had asked for a solicitor to be present, as they were not going to say anything until they had spoken to a brief. Billy knew that Davie Malone would soon be here and had told both Tommy and Paddy to keep quiet until then, just keep asking for a solicitor if the police try to get you to answer any questions.

Two hours later Davie Malone arrived at the Stoke Newington police station and asked to see Jimmy Walsh. Davie had represented Jimmy on previous occasions and was well aware that this was far and away the most serious crime he had been involved in or accused of. Davie knew this was going to be a battle from the start to keep Jimmy from going to prison for what could be decades, he also knew that this news would not be the kind of thing that Jimmy would want to hear right now.

Davie was told that Jimmy would be facing two charges of murder. His friends would be charged with accessory to murder and various other charges that would be forthcoming as the facts and evidence in the case were gathered. The legal representative for the Crown Prosecution Service also advised Davie Malone at that time of the possibility of a conflict of interest were he to speak to any of the other men involved as it was in the interests of the CPS to offer reduced charges to the other men to secure a conviction in the case of Jimmy Walsh, who indisputably had been the gunman.

Davie Malone also knew that this was news that Jimmy Walsh would not want to hear. Jimmy was not the most level headed of people when forced into a corner or faced with the pressure of any sort Jimmy would react to threats or manipulation with the only weapon he knew, violence, or the threat of violence to others if he could not reach the targets himself.

Davie Malone was taken to Jimmy's cell. Jimmy was ordered to move back from the door and to sit on the floor. He did as he was asked as Davie was permitted entry to the cell. The cell door was closed behind him after he had entered.

"Alright Davie, how are things?" Jimmy asked.

"Alright Jimmy, what the fuck have you got yourself into now?" Davie asked.

"They were going to kill me, what was I supposed to do, he pulled a fucking great knife on me, so I shot him," Jimmy said.

"Ok Jimmy you know the drill, say nothing unless I'm with you, I need to get something sorted out for the others, they have all asked for a solicitor so they can't interview them yet, that's something at least," said Davie.

"What do you mean, you're their solicitor Davie, you're the firm's brief, what do you mean sort something out?" Jimmy asked, confused.

"The police are going to try and use them against you Jimmy, the CPS has told me there will be a conflict of interest if I speak to them now, they intend to offer them deals to secure a conviction against you. They want you, Jimmy, I don't know who you have pissed off but they want you - and they intend to get you" Davie said.

"I know who it was I pissed off, that Detective that arrested me whispered in my ear," Jimmy said.

"Whispered what?" Asked Davie.

"It was Riordan, Riordan fitted me up," Jimmy said.

"You're Riordan's man, why would Jack Riordan want you nicked?" Davie asked he was totally confused by this revelation.

"I was working with the Turks behind Riordan's back, he must have found out," Jimmy said.

"Well, this just got a bit messier Jimmy, if they can link you to this Turkish firm, your self-defence plea is gone, it will look like something totally different. Tell me how you are linked to them, what business you are in, or were in with them, and where Riordan fits in?" Davie said.

"There are only Riordan and a friend of mine that knows about my business with the Turks, they won't be able to link me to them, not even Billy knows," Jimmy said.

"So if Billy doesn't know I assume Tommy and Paddy know nothing either?"

"Yeah that's right"

"Somehow Riordan must have found out. But whoever his source was, they won't be able to come forward because they will know that Riordan bankrolled a drug deal for the Turks, and that will give him a motive for what really happened - he told me to kill them because they were holding back his quarter of a million"

Davie looked stunned, this was a bigger problem than he had anticipated. One thing was true though if Jimmy claims self-defence it wouldn't be in anyone's favour to link themselves to the drug deal.

"The Turks came to meet us at Bradys' today, I had arranged for them to borrow a quarter of a million from Riordan, for a deal that was busted on a houseboat in Essex. A load of Ecstasy pills, the pills were confiscated so now Riordan wanted his money back. They laughed at Riordan and told him that he would get his money back when they were good and ready. After they left, Riordan told me to take them out - he didn't just tell me, Billy, Tommy, Paddy and Christy Monaghan were there too" Jimmy said.

"So we actually have four potential witnesses that could put you - and Jack Riordan away for life Jimmy! The premeditated murder of two men in cold blood is not the easiest of charges to beat, and both judge and jury take a very dim view of it" said Davie.

"Then you need to speak to them Davie don't you, and tell them all to keep their mouths shut?" said Jimmy menacingly.

Davie Malone left Jimmy's cell that night a worried man. Jimmy Walsh was a dangerous man, a man he could not and would not cross. But Jimmy was basically ordering Davie to start intimidating witnesses. Not only does that crime carry a long stretch of time, but also if Davie were found to be involved he would never practice law again and would be stripped of his license.

Davie had to think of a way to get the message to the others without implicating his own involvement. Davie went directly to his office to make some phone calls.

All four of the men were interviewed the next morning. Tommy and Paddy elected to go with the duty solicitor firm that was present at the police station at that time, a small firm named Gibbs & McCall from Islington. Brian Gibbs, one of the partners in the firm was briefed by the CPS as to the current situation. The decision had been taken the previous evening to warn Davie Malone of a possible conflict of interest for his client, and the protection of the rights of the other accused was they to be represented by the same firm of solicitors.

Having consulted with Tommy and Paddy. Gibbs stated, and then instructed, both of them, that they were to say nothing in the interviews until he had established what exactly they were offering in exchange for their testimony against Jimmy Walsh. It was the intention of Brian Gibbs to have all charges dropped or at the very least to be reduced to a minor charge. He warned both men that they faced two charges of conspiracy to murder and that they could face the real possibility of life imprisonment if they were charged and convicted of this offence. This had come as a sobering thought and surprise to both Tommy and Paddy who were only now realizing the true gravity of their situation.

Brian Gibbs sat in the first interview with Tommy. Gibbs was a thin-faced man in his mid-thirties with a hawkish nose. He was competent and experienced in the negotiations of plea bargaining. The interview started with Detective Constable's Malcolm Wright and Roland Fletcher speaking out loud for the benefit of the tape recorder, giving first their names, rank and Stoke Newington CID as their unit and asking both Brian Gibbs and Tommy to do the same, to officially record the attendees at the time, place and date also recorded, and the nature of the interview that was about to take place.

"Tommy, you were at the Casbah Club in Islington yesterday afternoon, is that correct?" Asked D.C. Wright.

"Gentleman, my client will not be answering any questions until we have firmly established for the record what the CPS is offering in return for his testimony against James Walsh, that is why we are here, right?" Gibbs asked.

"Mr Gibbs, we are just trying to establish your client's whereabouts yesterday" Wright continued.

"I think having been arrested outside the Casbah Club and appearing in a supporting role in the police video recordings of the incident has firmly established my clients' whereabouts D.C. Wright, his whereabouts at the time of the incident are not in dispute, what is, however, is just what the CPS are willing to offer for his testimony" Gibbs concluded.

"That's not something I can comment on at this moment in time until we establish his usefulness to the CPS in their pursuit of any case against James Walsh" D.C. Fletcher interjected.

"I see, then I think we have nothing further to discuss until the CPS stops their fishing expeditions and puts something solid on the table for my clients. I include Mr Patrick Meehan also in that statement. I would like to suspend this interview until such time as you can give my clients a written guarantee of immunity from prosecution in exchange for their testimony, that will include, driving and accompanying James Walsh to the Casbah Club, waiting outside to drive him away from the crime scene, watching him enter the premises and witnessing gunfire coming from the club, whilst James Walsh was inside" Gibbs said.

Tommy was impressed, the detectives looked at each other, then at Gibbs, nodded their agreement. D.C. Wright again spoke loudly to record the fact the interview had been suspended at the request of Brian Gibbs to meet with the CPS to discuss a plea bargain for his clients.

Three hours had passed until Brian Gibbs had returned and arranged to see both his clients together, as the CPS had agreed to grant immunity from prosecution for both men for their joint testimony, this was not a one will one won't deal.

The CPS wanted two competent witnesses with the exact same statement of events to bolster their already strong case against Jimmy Walsh. The CPS had wanted to build a watertight case as they had already been informed, unofficially, that James Walsh would be pleading not guilty as he was acting in self-defence. Knowing that he had already beaten a double attempted murder charge previously they were not willing to take any chances this time and agreed to Gibbs wishes with that one proviso.

Gibbs put the deal to Tommy and Paddy in a small sparsely furnished interview room.

"The CPS has agreed to give you both immunity from prosecution for both of your testimonies. That means as a collective, not individually, my advice is that you take it, no actually my advice is that you grab it because as I told you looking at the evidence against both you and James Walsh the CPS have a very good chance of making this case without you. You will not get a better deal, you should take it now, make your statements go home and decide what you are going to do with the rest of your lives, you both need to get out of this life,". Gibbs said.

"It's not that simple Mr Gibbs, Jimmy is a mate, we can't just roll over and grass on him," Paddy said.

"Yes Paddy, it is that simple, you have a son right? If you want to see him grow up I suggest you start acting like a father and an adult, this isn't a fucking game sonny, you could go away for twenty-five years, did I not make that clear?" Gibbs said.

"He's right Paddy, we have to take this, I don't want to be banged up for years on end, it's not like a stint on remand or a detention centre this is proper behind the door, we will be in there with murderers, rapists, all fucking sorts," Tommy said.

Paddy stood up and walked to the door, he was clearly torn between his loyalty to Jimmy and to his family. He understood what Mr Gibbs and Tommy were saying to him, any loyalty he was feeling should first and foremost be with his family.

"Ok Mr Gibbs - make the deal," Paddy said.

Gibbs smiled. "It's the right decision Paddy," he said.

Tommy and Paddy both made statements within the hour. They were now to appear as witnesses against their friend Jimmy Walsh, they were both released from custody without any charges and immunity from prosecution guarantee less than twenty-seven hours after their arrest.

Billy had arranged a solicitor through the yellow pages earlier that morning. He had made it clear to the police that he would not answer any questions until he had spoken to his newly appointed legal advisor. Billy had called a company based in Lewisham named Howell Davis & Little.

The solicitor that arrived two hours later was a young lady by the name of Belinda Phillips. Belinda was a very stern looking woman, twenty-nine years old and single, she met Billy for the first time in his cell at Stoke Newington police station.

Belinda entered the cell all business, shoulder-length brown hair pulled back in a tight ponytail and horn-rim glasses, her dark eyes darting around the room like reptiles, a sturdy handshake and then the briefest of introductions.

"Good afternoon Mr Kelly I'm Belinda Phillips from Howell Davis & Little in Lewisham. I understand you are at present facing two conspiracy to murder charges relating to an incident yesterday afternoon in Islington, is that correct?" Belinda said in a very Sloane Ranger type voice.

"Well nobody has actually mentioned any charges to me at the moment, but the incident you refer to is correct," Billy said.

"Well let me be very clear Mr Kelly, you are in a world of trouble and if you are not actually being charged with the murders you can expect to be charged with conspiracy or at the very least aiding and abetting after the fact, all of which carry lengthy prison terms up to and including life imprisonment," Belinda said bluntly.

"Fucking hell - you're a happy soul you ain't you? - I need you don't I... Billy said, knowing he was in a right fix.

"Let's be clear, I'm not here to make you happy Mr Kelly. I'm here to represent you, counsel you, protect you and to make the best fucking deal we can to get you out of this shit, do you understand me? I'm not here to entertain you or make you feel better about yourself, so shall we get to work?" Belinda said.

"Yeah, sounds good, Billy said, can you do one thing for me first though please?" Billy asked,

"And what might that be Mr Kelly?"

"Can you check on Tommy and Paddy; see how they are holding up? I'm a bit worried about them, we're all best mates you see, I just want to know they are ok" Billy said with a friendly smile.

"I assume you are referring to Callaghan and Meehan, the other two arrested with you?" Belinda asked.

"Yeah that's right" Billy replied.

"They were released about an hour ago without any charges and immunity to prosecution guarantee for their testimonies against James Walsh, Mr Kelly. Did they not ask how you were before they left? I would assume they are now either having a cold beer or having their dicks sucked - I'm sure you would much prefer to be involved one of those activities right now too, to what presently occupies you?" Belinda smiled.

"What -? Those slippery no good wankers, those no-good fucking lousy toe-rags have gone, no charges…." Billy was dumbfounded.

"Mr Kelly...as I said to you before, I'm not here to make you feel better, we need a strategy or you will be going away with your friend James Walsh for a very long time. The CPS have what they need, two corroborative statements from your, so-called *bessie* mates already. So if all you have is what they know already then I do not see a lived happily ever after for you, in this particular fairytale" Belinda said.

Billy looked like he was going to be sick, Tommy and Paddy had turned on Jimmy. They had turned on him to save their own skins. The more Billy thought about it, the more he understood it. Paddy has a family if what this Belinda is saying is true Billy could be facing a long, long stretch behind bars. He had no choice, he didn't kill anyone, he hadn't even been there when they were shot, he was outside, he'd never even been inside the Casbah Club.

"Mr Kelly - I need you to help me, help you! Unless you have anything other than what the CPS already have, you will be charged with conspiracy to murder, can you help them further in their enquiries?" Belinda asked.

"You want me to turn on Jimmy too, is that what you are asking me to do?" Billy asked.

"I'm asking you to save your own skin Mr Kelly, nothing more nothing less," Belinda said.

"I won't do it, I won't turn on Jimmy, he's my friend I can't do it," Billy said.

"Look around you Mr Kelly, this will be your life for the next God knows how many years, is this what you want"? Belinda asked, her voice devoid now of all emotion.

Billy looked at her, defiance in his eyes.

"I'm not going to grass on Jimmy, I don't care what they do," Billy said.

"Very well Mr Kelly, as you can see I do not get emotionally involved in my work, if you change your mind please call me, if you feel I'm not the right legal representative for you, please feel free to change to another firm of solicitors. But before you do, just understand and consider this, your friends do not give a fuck about you, and for all you know James Walsh could be making his own deal right now to put you right in the frame, so to speak, so - it's your choice, my advice will not change - Billy. I do not want to see you go to prison for something you did not do, or a crime you did not commit, so please consider my advice and call me. And my apologies, it was most unprofessional of me to address you by your given name Mr Kelly…" Belinda said.

"Billy is fine - Belinda, Billy said, I need time to think about it, you understand right"

"As I said, I understand but your options are limited and the window of opportunity could be closing as we speak, so please think quickly…and clearly," Belinda said.

"Give me half an hour, I just need to get my nut straight," Billy said.

Belinda agreed to the recess and left the cell. Billy was running through everything in his mind, he would not incriminate Jimmy, but his statement would basically be the same as Tommy and Paddy's unless they had lied and really tried to stitch Jimmy up.

If what Belinda said was true then he might not even be offered a deal like she said, if he has nothing to offer other than what they already had, why would they even bother giving him a way out of this mess. Then it came to him all at once, he didn't have to give them Jimmy - he had something far more valuable to give them.

Billy called the custody Sergeant and told him he needed to see his solicitor, and that he was ready to make a statement. Belinda returned to the cell happy and a little surprised to hear the news.

"So you have come to your senses Billy, I'm glad to hear it," Belinda said.

"I have, but I'm not going to grass on Jimmy, I don't have anything other than what the other two will have already told them about Jimmy. I will not say I saw a gun, I will not say I knew what he intended to do. But I have something they will want, and I need you to get me a deal Belinda, and to be honest, it might just hurt Jimmy more, but that's a chance I have to take," Billy said straight-faced.

Billy explained in detail the information that he had to offer. Belinda, after hearing his story, knew this was something that she could very well bargain within her negotiations with the CPS. All there was to do now was to take Billy's offer to the CPS and hope they were in a negotiating mood.

Two hours later Belinda returned, with an offer from the CPS. It wasn't as good as the offer Tommy and Paddy had received, but given the circumstances, it was as good as Billy was likely to get.

"Ok Billy, this is as good as it gets I'm afraid. Given your story, you cannot expect to walk away without serving time, you are openly admitting to conspiracy to murder. They are willing to greatly reduce the sentence for your testimony, but the only guarantee is no more than five years" Belinda said.

"Well if I don't take it I'm going to have to stand trial and I will be found guilty, and I'm going to get a lot more Belinda. I'm a realist, I'll take it, let's get it done" Billy said.

Belinda left the cell again and returned five minutes later. Billy was handcuffed and led to the interview room. Billy and Belinda had taken their places at the table opposite the two detectives. The time was now close to one o'clock on Tuesday morning nearly thirty-three hours after the shootings had taken place.

"If you are happy to proceed Ms. Phillips, I will introduce ourselves for the benefit of the tape, and I would ask that you do the same for yourself and your client," D.C. Wright said.

"Please do Detective Constable, we are ready and happy to proceed" Belinda replied.

With the formalities completed D.C. Wright proceeded to question Billy.

"Mr Kelly, do you acknowledge that you were arrested on Sunday, October 14 outside the Casbah Club in Islington North London?" he asked.

"I do," said Billy.

"And you were outside the Casbah Club with Thomas Callaghan and Patrick Meehan, is that correct?" D.C. Wright continued.

"It is," Billy replied.

"What were you doing outside the Casbah Club," D.C. Wright asked.

"We were waiting for our mate," Billy said.

"The mate being James Walsh, is that correct Mr Kelly?"

"Yes it is," Billy said.

"And did you know why James Walsh went into the Casbah Club?" D.C. Wright continued.

Billy looked at Belinda who nodded at him by way of an affirmative response to answer the question.

"Yes I do, he went inside to negotiate the return of some money that was owed," Billy said.

"And what money was that Mr Kelly, was it money that belonged to James Walsh?"

"No it didn't belong to Jimmy it belonged to someone who asked Jimmy to get it back from the Turks on his behalf," Billy said.

"And who might that be Mr Kelly? "

"It belonged to Jack Riordan," Billy said.

Just at that moment, the door opened. Billy, Belinda and the two detectives looked towards the door, standing there was Detective Chief Superintendent Graham Simpson.

"For the benefit of the tape, Detective Chief Superintendent Graham Simpson has entered the room, and will remain for the rest of the interview," D.C. Wright said.

"So Mr Kelly to clarify, the money you claim was the topic of discussion at this meeting between James Walsh and the dead men, belonged to a Mr Jack Riordan, is that correct" D.C. Wright asked.

"Yes that is correct" Billy confirmed.

"Can you explain how you know this Mr Kelly, how were you privy to this information?"

"Because I was at the meeting in Bradys' on Sunday morning with The Turks, Riordan, Christy Monaghan and Jimmy," Billy said.

"Are you telling us that before the fatal shooting on Sunday afternoon there was a meeting in Bradys' - that's a pub I assume? - D.C. Wright waited for confirmation.

"Yes it's a pub on our manor in South London," Billy said.

"And at that meeting, Riordan asked James Walsh to retrieve his money for him, is that correct?" D.C. Wright asked.

"Yes, that was one of the things that he asked for" Billy confirmed.

Simpson was sitting very uneasily in his chair, he fidgeted with his notepad and scribbled something on the pad and pushed it towards D.C. Wright.

"I would like you to tell us exactly what was discussed at this meeting on Sunday morning, prior to your visit to the Casbah Club on Sunday afternoon," D.C. Wright said.

Billy looked again to Belinda.

"At this juncture, I would like to state for the record that the information my client will now reveal is subject to an agreement with the Crown Prosecution Service for a significant reduction in any sentence he may receive for charges arising out of these enquiries," Belinda said.

"That is our understanding also Ms. Phillips" D.C. Wright agreed.

"Thank you, please continue Billy," Belinda urged.

"The meeting was at Bradys' on Sunday morning, Jack Riordan had called it. He invited Jimmy Walsh. Jimmy then, in turn, asked me along with Tommy Callaghan and Paddy Meehan. The four of us were already in Bradys' when Jack Riordan and Christy Monaghan turned up. We just made small talk, Riordan then told us he was waiting for somebody else to join us…"

D.C. Wright interrupted Billy.

"Did Riordan say who this someone was? Did he refer to the person by name?" he asked.

"Not at that time, his actual words were that he had lent a quarter of a million pounds to *"one slippery bastard"* some time back. The guy had told Riordan that the deal had gone tits up, the pills they had purchased from Holland had been seized on a houseboat on a river in Essex" Billy explained.

"Ok go on," D.C. Wright asked.

"Anyway a little while later, Arda Arslan and his minder turn up, the big guy Hamza something. So we have a drink, you know, the usual pleasantries, welcome to Indian country and all that, Belinda looked at Billy a little confused, that's you know what anyone not from south of the river calls it when they come over there" Billy said.

"Yes we are aware of the term Mr Kelly," D.C. Wright said.

"So it gets a little heated when it becomes obvious that this Arda geezer thinks he can take liberties with Riordan, you know when Riordan asked for his money, he sort of laughed and then said, you will get it when I'm good and ready, Billy said, Riordan somehow knew that Arda had taken money from a Liverpool firm too, and didn't have enough to cover both ends of the debt without going to his father for help, he also knew that the old man Arslan knew nothing about the deal".

"So then what happened next," D.C. Wright asked.

"Well they left, the Turks I mean, and that's when it all got a bit strange. I mean Riordan had given them forty-eight hours to come up with his money, then all of a sudden he wanted them gone" Billy said.

"Are you telling us that Jack Riordan ordered a hit on Arda Arslan?" D.C. Wright asked.

"Not just Arda, he said he wanted him and his monster dead, meaning Hamza, and he wanted it done today," Billy said.

"And did James Walsh accept this proposal?" D.C. Wright asked.

"No comment," said Billy.

"What did Jack Riordan offer James Walsh to do this job ?" D.C. Wright pushed his questions.

"No comment," said Billy.

Billy looked at Belinda.

"My client has no further comment to make pertaining to these unfortunate incidents, having fulfilled the conditions of the agreement with the Crown Prosecution Service as agreed," Belinda said.

Detective Chief Superintendent Simpson rose from his chair and hurriedly left the room. D.C. Wright spoke aloud to record his departure and the termination of the interview. Belinda and Billy were led back to the cell. Belinda explained that Billy would now be charged and remanded in custody to appear before a magistrate in the morning, this was a formality hearing to plead and hear bail applications. She further explained that an application for bail on this charge would not be permitted, however she would put in the application as a matter of course. Belinda also explained to Billy that his testimony against Riordan really would make him a marked man and that she requested solitary confinement in the first instance, as an arrest warrant would be issued for Riordan the following morning.

Billy was remanded in custody overnight. The next day he appeared in the Magistrates Court. He remanded in custody again and sent to Swaleside prison in Kent to await trial for conspiracy to murder Arda Arslan and Hamza Yilmaz.

*****

Chief Superintendent Graham Simpson waited patiently for the phone to be picked up
and answered, it was two thirty-five on the morning after the shooting of Arda Arslan and Hamza Yilmaz.

"Hello" Jack Riordan rubbed at his eyes and tried to see the time on the digital bedside clock, his voice still croaky, his throat dry after being awakened from his peaceful slumber.

"We have a problem, we need to meet now, the usual place for the early morning chats, and hurry it's urgent," Chief Superintendent Graham Simpson said.

"Ok I'm on my way, I won't be alone" Riordan answered.

Riordan jumped out of bed, walked briskly to the bathroom and splashed water on his face. He brushed his teeth quickly and dressed in a tracksuit and trainers. He knew there must be a major problem that had occurred with the shootings in north London early yesterday afternoon. Jimmy Walsh and his cronies had all been arrested and banged up in jail, that was the plan, the Turks were gone, also part of the plan. Maybe Jimmy had offered up Riordan as the man who ordered the hit, as a bargaining chip.

Riordan kissed his still-sleeping wife on the forehead and headed down the stairs, he picked up the phone near the front door and dialled a number, and spoke to Christy Monaghan.

"I'm going to meet our friend, there seems to be a problem, he just called me now, maybe someone is saying too much, get that young one who works in the office out of bed and arrange flights for tomorrow morning Christy," Riordan said.

"I'm on my way, the usual place I take it," Christy asked.

"It is; I'll have the tea ready ya big lump ya" replied Riordan.

There is an all-night cafe not far from Battersea bridge. This particular cafe was always busy around this time of the morning with the night workers and early morning stragglers from the various entertainment centres' local to this part of London. The customers here would normally just be stopping by to pick up tea, coffee or sandwiches as they made their way on their varied journeys to carry out their nightly duties. There was also a small back room to the cafe that Jack Riordan used for such nocturnal activities, away from prying eyes.

Riordan arrived and waved at the owner, he then proceeded to walk to the back of the cafe. The owner, a small man in his fifties, waved back. He then took a key from under the counter and went to meet Riordan at the rear, where he opened a door and let Riordan into the back room. The room was sparsely furnished with a table in the middle of the room and four chairs, all that was needed for clandestine early hours of the morning meeting, that was not going to draw attention from any nosy passerby in the main area of the cafe.

"Mr Riordan, I'll bring tea and sandwiches, how many are you expecting?" the small man asked.

"Just a pot of tea, and grab a bottle of Jamie too, that will be fine Ronald, there will be three of us, thank you," Riordan said.

Ronald returned with a tray, crockery piled on it with a large teapot and a plate of assorted biscuits. No sign of the whiskey.

Riordan was pacing the room, growing more anxious by the minute. His mind was racing and going into overdrive.

"Will you be needing anything else, Mr Riordan?" Ronald asked.

"Nothing thank you, Ronald, Riordan answered shaking his head, I will bring my own fucking whiskey next time, the doddery *old feck* that you are" Riordan was muttering under his breath.

Simpson arrived a couple of minutes later, Riordan was pouring tea into cups just as Christy walked into the room to join them. The men greeted each other. Riordan finished pouring the tea into mugs and looked expectantly at Detective Chief Superintendent Graham Simpson.

"Well, Graham, what's the problem?" Riordan asked.

"The problem Jack is that there will be a warrant issued for your arrest tomorrow morning for conspiracy to commit murder," Simpson said.

"Oh for fuck's sake," said Christy.

"Is there nothing to be done, Graham? Who can we get to, to make this go away?" Riordan asked.

"This isn't going away Jack, it's a matter of record, you have been put in the frame for ordering the murders of both Arda Arslan and Hamza Yilmaz. What the fuck were you thinking of Jack, giving that order in front of four fucking witnesses?" Simpson said, clearly more than a little upset.

"Oh let's not start pointing fingers now Chief Superintendent, you gave the exact same order in front of us two, you marked his card - not me - so you did, you wanted him gone to keep your political friends happy and we provided that service - a service for which I am yet to be fucking paid I might remind you, Riordan snapped back, did you by any chance bring the money with you?

"Ok, Jack - *touché* - Simpson said, you need to get out of the country and soon, tomorrow by midday there will be a nationwide alert for you Jack, you have to get out of England for the next few months at least, go to Spain and get a plan together, you have a place there I believe?

"Yes I do, I'll make arrangements. And what about my money and safe passage Graham, we kept our part of the bargain. I want my money, and I want out of here - because if I don't get my money, or if I'm arrested by chance at the airport, you can tell that fucking politician if I go down for this there will be no bastard left standing, and that includes you Chief Superintendent, do you think I don't have insurance" Riordan growled at Simpson.

Christy Monaghan pulled an envelope from his pocket, this time the envelope contained photos of Simpson and a well-known political and public figure. Simpson turned a shade paler than his already ashen complexion and shook his head.

"Do you think you are the only one with intelligence and leverage Graham?" Riordan asked.

At eight-thirty that same morning Jack Riordan, his wife and three daughters breezed through immigration and boarded an Iberian Airways flight at Gatwick Airport, bound for Alicante for a prolonged spot of sun, sand and sangria.

*****

Simone Dawson could not remember ever being so happy. Her boyfriend of three months Billy Kelly would be coming tonight to spend a long weekend with her at her flat. Simone had been busy all week arranging viewings for properties in the area, as last week Billy had asked Simone to look for a place for them to buy together and to start their lives together for real.

This dinner had to be special, this was the night Simone was going to tell Billy that she was expecting their child. There was a bottle of champagne on ice in the fridge, tonight was going to be perfect, it just had to be, she could feel it in her bones, she was the luckiest girl in the world...and she was so in love. Billy was the kindest, gentlest man she had ever met, they were going to be so happy - all three of them.

Simone had lined up two viewings tomorrow morning from ten o'clock to look at two bungalows with sea views, two other houses on Saturday on a more exclusive inland part of the town, and another on Sunday morning to look at a large detached property on the outskirts of town.

The whole of that afternoon Simone had spent busying herself in the small kitchen in the flat above her hair and beauty salon. She had cooked a Cottage Pie and was going to serve it with fresh vegetables this evening, as she knew this was a particularly favorite dish of Billy's.

Billy was due to arrive around eight o'clock that evening. The journey from London usually took anywhere between ninety minutes to two and a half hours, depending on the traffic coming out of London on the M2 or M20 motorways.

The documents containing the details of the properties were laid out in viewing order on the table to be discussed over dinner. It was now six-thirty in the evening and Simone couldn't hide her excitement. She sat down to try and relax at the breakfast bar, stood again to pour a glass of wine and moved to the small lounge area where she settled on the sofa. The wine was a crisp Chardonnay that Simone enjoyed as her thoughts turned yet again to the future. She couldn't help but see Billy and herself in any other circumstances than that of sheer bliss, in the three months they had been together they had not had one crossword between them, and had enjoyed every single minute of each other's company.

By seven forty-five Simone could hardly contain her excitement. Pacing to and fro the small flat like a caged tigress. Simone put a large saucepan of water on the cooker and lit the gas ring below it with the electric ignition device. She had prepared broccoli and carrots earlier and removed them from the fridge, she didn't want to cook them too soon, so she left the vegetables on the breakfast bar, and reduced the gas under the boiling water to a simmer. She took the already cooked Cottage Pie from the fridge and lit the oven to a low flame, waiting exactly an impatient two minutes for the oven to warm before sliding the tray into the oven to slowly reheat.

It was now eight-thirty and there was a hollow feeling in the pit of Simone's stomach. She had turned the oven and gas ring off and removed the Cottage Pie, placing it on the breakfast bar next to the vegetables. Simone then poured another glass of wine. By nine-thirty the bottle of wine was all but gone and impatience and frustration had been replaced by real anxiety and worry, had something happened to Billy, had he been in an accident, was he lying in a hospital somewhere, or had something delayed him, maybe heavy traffic, Simone tried to relax.

As the hands on the wall clock moved to eleven o'clock worry had turned to irritation and anger. The second bottle of wine was now only half full. Simone walked a little unsteadily to the kitchen, picking up the Cottage Pie she threw it into the wall above the cooker, the vegetables were swept aside to the floor in a fit of pure frustration.

Why had she been so stupid yet again, falling for all the sweet talk of this charming man? She really had thought that Billy was different, but it's the same old story with these men, they get fed up and need variety and excitement in their lives, what would a big city London boy want with a girl from a small seaside town, she must have been crazy to believe that he really wanted to leave London to live on the coast.

By midnight, Simone, now mentally exhausted and very drunk by her own admission. She had a few minutes earlier, in deep conversation with her reflection in the bathroom mirror conceded she was drunk and decided she should go to her bedroom, she lay down on her bed, pulling the quilt tight to her chest, she laid the palm of her hand on her tummy. Simone cried silently thinking about her unborn child, and the future they would now face alone.

The last thoughts Simone had that night before she fell asleep were that she now had to tell her parents she was pregnant; this was not nearly as painful as the thought that Billy had abandoned her for no reason.

The following morning Simone woke with a massive hangover. Her head pounded, her temples throbbed and her mouth was dry, as she walked through the lounge to the kitchen the sight and smell of the Cottage Pie adorning the kitchen wall and the cooker made her heave, she turned and ran back to the bedroom throwing up just as she reached the sanctuary of the bathroom. Her head bowed in the toilet bowl she wretched again, thinking this was the last time she would endanger her unborn child in this way, no man was worth the life of her baby. The mixture of alcohol and morning sickness kept her occupied for the next ten minutes.

Chapter 12

The Old Bailey 1984

The day had arrived, some nine months after Jimmy's arrest. The police van, flanked by two motorcycle outriders and followed by a Specialist Firearms Command unit (SCO 19) in another unmarked van, pulled through the portcullis type gated entrance at London's Old Bailey central courthouse.

Jimmy looked pensive. His short-cropped ginger hair matted to his scalp with sweat, as he climbed from the back of the prison van.

"It's like a fucking oven in there mate," Jimmy snarled at the prison officer, as he undid the ankle shackles on Jimmy's feet.

"Oh I do apologise, Mr Walsh, the transportation is not to your liking? I will see if the stretch limo is available for our return journey" the prison officer replied sarcastically.

His colleagues laughed, Jimmy spat on the floor at the prison officers' feet, covering the highly polished toe caps of his black boots in saliva.

"You sarky cunt, when I get out of here I will be looking you up you fucking mug". Jimmy snarled again.

The prison officer smiled.

"I won't hold my breath Walsh, that's not going to be anytime soon now...is it?" The prison officers' colleagues laughed again. Jimmy stared coldly at the man, then unexpectedly launched himself forward screaming like a banshee at the prison officer as he did.

"You fucking scumbag screw I will fucking do you". Jimmy screamed.

The prison officer stepped back from the attack, as his colleagues restrained Jimmy and pulled him away towards the entrance to the underground holding cells. Jimmy laughed at the look of shock and fear on the prison officers face, his laughing continued as he was led through the door and out of sight.

Jimmy was booked in and taken to a cell, pushed inside and left to wait until he was to be called for the trail to begin. The small shutter opened in the thick metal door. A white polystyrene cup appeared on the flap.

"Cup of tea here Walsh, the voice from behind the door said, your brief will be down in five minutes".

"Stick the fucking tea you nonce, you probably gobbed in it" Jimmy replied.

"Suit yourself, no skin off my nose, drink it or don't drink it, it's your choice" the voice outside the cell answered.

Jimmy ignored the last remark, as the tea disappeared again, a loud slurping sound followed by a satisfied "*Ahhh lovely*" a short chuckle and the sounds of footsteps moving away.

"Fucking wanker" Jimmy muttered with a smile. He was used to the tricks and the somewhat sadistic behaviour of the prison officers. It was all part of the game, psychological warfare on the prisoners, a game of strength to see who can get the upper hand, the screws needed to understand which of the prisoners they could bait, and which they knew to be wary of. They weren't quite sure about Jimmy Walsh - they would be soon enough.

Jimmy lay back on the bench that served as a bed. The wooden slatted platform only rose six inches above the concrete floor level, this, of course, to serve as a precaution to injury, and for the safety of the occupant in the cell to avoid falling from a higher version of a bunk bed.

Jimmy closed his eyes. His thoughts turned to his childhood, his mother, whom he loved, his father whom he loathed, and his closest friends all of whom he had sworn to kill.

Billy Kelly, Paddy Meehan and Tommy Callaghan. They had grown up together, same schools, the same church where they all served as altar boys, the same football teams and boxing clubs and the same firm. Jimmy's firm, where he had looked after all of them as if they were his brothers. He still couldn't come to terms with the betrayal, they had all turned on him, they had all had pointed the finger at him. He was here at the Old Bailey, not for the first time it had to be said, but the reason he was here, and the only reason he was here, was because his so-called brethren had grassed him up to the old bill and that was something Jimmy couldn't live with.

Jimmy was looking forward to seeing them give evidence against him, his eyes would bore into their very souls, he would never take his eyes from them from their traitorous faces, they would feel his wrath, the anger that welled up inside him day after day and the overwhelming feelings of hatred and vengeance would not be quelled until he had taken their lives, one by one, as they were about to take his from him.

Jimmy, eyes still shut tight against the world, let his mind drift off into the deepest realms of his subconscious, the depths of long-forgotten events, of triumphs and disappointments, of happiness, misery and despair. He recalled a time at a birthday party when they were just kids, all four of them together, Billy, Tommy, Paddy and Jimmy. It was Billy's thirteenth birthday, Jimmy could recall the table laden with a lovely spread of food and drinks, the birthday cake, the girls in party dresses, mainly Billy's cousins and a couple of his mum's friends' daughters. He remembered the presents and the music, but most of all he remembered the house. The house was full of love and how Billy's doting parents made the whole event and day about Billy. Jimmy loved Billy's parents, they were kind and generous towards him, they made him feel special whenever he visited or he saw them at church, he, in turn, was polite and courteous, and as much as he loved his own mother, he secretly wished they were his parents. Jimmy would have changed places with Billy in a heartbeat.

Jimmy remembered crying that night as he lay in bed. Although he had enjoyed the party, the melancholy feelings that swept over him as he remembered Billy's dad making a small speech were something so alien to him that he covered his face with his blanket in shame and confusion. Billy's father had told everybody present how proud he was of his son, and how the day that Billy was born both he and Billy's mum knew he was a gift from God Almighty, they prayed and gave thanks for this most precious of gifts, and Billy had repaid them every day since.

He laughed as he told of a conversation the night before when Billy had thanked his parents for the party in advance, but begged them it was to be the last one, as he was getting too old for this sort of thing now, he was tomorrow to be a teenager after all. He kissed and hugged Billy and unashamedly, and nearly shed a tear as the gathered attendees gave him a round of applause. How Jimmy wished he had a father like this man. He could never remember his father saying a word to him of pride, love or anything positive, the only words he could recall were to scold and shame him. Jimmy watched as Billy opened his presents and thanked everyone in turn for their generous gifts. Jimmy had never received such gifts before on any of his birthdays, expensive clothes and shoes from his parents, an Atari from his aunt and uncle and other assorted books, gift tokens and cash.

It was now Jimmy's turn to give his gift to Billy, he wanted to turn and slink off before anyone could see him. The small box containing the gift now felt so insignificant among the other offerings. The box contained a small penknife. Jimmy had only stolen it the night before from the local hardware store two streets away, he had wanted to steal a Swiss Army knife, but he just couldn't get his hand around and into the glass case far enough, so had to settle for the penknife with an authentic bone handle and three-inch blade, he wondered who's bone it was? And what part of the body it came from? He knew that Billy liked the Swiss Army knife and wished with all his being that he had succeeded in getting it, but it was too late now, he just hoped that Billy would like this one too.

Jimmy stepped forward towards Billy who was standing on a small wooden decking in the garden. Billy was smiling at his best friend as he approached him, head down, eyes peering upwards, this was the way Jimmy had always dropped his stare in times of embarrassment. The small box was five inches long and covered with an imitation brown leather casing, it had originally housed a small silver bracelet that Jimmy's mum still wore, she had stuffed the box with white tissue paper and laid the small knife inside.

Jimmy held out the box to Billy at arm's length. Billy waited for Jimmy to look at him, as he knew he would. Jimmy looked up at Billy's smiling face.

"Happy birthday Billy," Jimmy said.

Billy took the box from Jimmy and opened it. His eyes lit up when he saw the small knife inside.

"Oh mate, cheers Jimmy," Billy said as he stepped forward and hugged his friend, how did you know I liked this knife? I never told anyone, I was going to buy it tomorrow".

"Lucky guess I reckon Billy, I'm glad you like it," Jimmy said, his face beaming a big smile. The two friends stood and looked at each other.

"We will be mates forever Jimmy," Billy said.

"Yeah, mates forever Billy" Jimmy replied.

When Jimmy finally fell asleep that night, it came as mercy. His mind wondering what it must be like to be a part of a family such as the Kellys'. Thoughts that he didn't want to have, thoughts that tormented him because the more he felt them, the less respect he felt for his own dad. But, try as he might, he couldn't shake them from his mind. What must be like for Mrs Kelly to have such a stable man like Billy's dad, a good honest, hard-working loyal and loving husband and father? Billy knew his mum deserved such a man, but that was not part of God's great plan for either Jimmy or his long-suffering mum.

Jimmy, some years later during a psychotherapy session, while being held as a violent, high-risk prisoner at Parkhurst prison on the Isle of Wight, was asked about his formative years. More specifically, when he stopped feeling like a child. He thought for a few moments before answering. It was, in fact, that night when he was alone in bed after Billy's thirteenth birthday party with tears streaming down his face hiding under his blanket, that was the exact time he could pinpoint...that was when his childhood had ended.

When pressed further as to why he believed and felt that was the time, Jimmy just responded with a sadness in his eyes.

"I never went to another birthday party…" he replied quietly.

On another occasion, Jimmy was asked to think about the first time he had felt empowered and in control of his own life and his own destiny. Jimmy recalled the first and only violent confrontation he had ever had with his father. He remembered the incident with such vivid clarity and regaled the story with such a lack of emotion that it was clear that this had been a watershed moment in the young life of Jimmy Walsh and in a strange way the only time he had ever hurt his mother by taking something away from her that he knew she had loved.

At the age of fifteen, Jimmy had put an end to his father's reign of domestic terror with a beating he had fantasised long and hard about and had longed to deliver. One afternoon Jimmy had arrived home from school to find his mother sitting sobbing in the kitchen, her head hung low, rosary beads clutched to her chest in her pale thin hands praying to the Virgin Mary in a voice so faint he could hardly hear her. Jimmy's mother seemed unaware of his presence and continued to beseech Mother Mary to help her find peace in this life and to protect her husband from the devils and demons that tormented his soul. Jimmy turned his mother's face towards him and recoiled in horror upon seeing her busted lip, swollen, split and bruised. Her right eye was black and almost closed.

Jimmy screamed in anger, tears running down his face. This seemed to shake his mother out of her trancelike adoration.

"Jimmy its ok son, don't fret so, it's only a couple of bruises so it is, it's not his fault you know that it's the drink, he can't help himself, you know that son", Jimmy's mother pleaded.

"I'm going to fucking kill him, I'm going to fucking kill that bastard I swear to God I'm going to kill him" Jimmy screamed at the top of his voice, he ran from the house, his mother followed behind him.

"Jimmy, Jimmy come back here son - please come back".

Jimmy was gone through the front door and onto the street he ran down the road, his mother's vain cries dying in the distance.

After ten minutes Jimmy had located his father in a local pub. He was holding court at the bar with about half a dozen or so other drunks, as Jimmy referred to them mentally. Jimmy's stomach turned over at the thought of what this man had done to his mother earlier that day. Jimmy knew he had to do what he had planned to do now before this man killed his mother, every time the beatings were getting worse, more frequent and more intense, a slap became a punch became a beating became a - murder, "well not my mother you fucking drunken bastard" Jimmy said aloud to himself.

Jimmy waited almost two hours outside the pub as his father became more and more intoxicated. At just after nine o'clock that evening he had, at last, decided it was time to move on from this particular watering hole and bid farewell to his cronies. Jimmy watched as his father stumbled through the doorway onto the street. He steadied himself against the wall arms outstretched for balance, legs apart and planted firmly on the ground he kept himself upright. Fishing a cigarette packet from the breast pocket of his jacket, he retrieved one and lit it with a match at the third attempt, while swaying around as if he was caught in an invisible vortex, he proceeded to stagger in the general direction of the family home.

Jimmy followed closely, about fifty feet behind, his father totally unaware of his son's presence, or at least that was what Jimmy had thought!

Jimmy dodged into an alleyway, his eyes darting all around the ground for a weapon of some description. He knew his father would put up a fight and didn't fancy his chances of overcoming the much bigger, stronger man alone with nothing more than his fists. Lying about twenty feet away, among the windblown crisp packets, newspapers and a covering of broken glass, Jimmy saw a long piece of scaffold pipe about fifteen inches in length and three inches in diameter, a bit cumbersome, but it would do. He picked it up and concealed the bulky tube in the back of his jeans. Jimmy hurriedly came back out of the alleyway to continue his pursuit of his father. As he emerged from the alleyway he bumped smack bang into his father who was standing waiting for him just out of view. Jimmy took a step back into the alley and continued to back off.

"Your fucking old one sent you no doubt you little shite you, I expect you will be running back to tell her where I am and what I'm doing you little grass that you are" his father growled at him.

"You think I didn't notice you following me, you will have to get up very early to catch Niall Walsh unawares boy" his father continued.

"Fuck you - you drunken pig, you've beaten my mother for the last time you bastard" Jimmy was screaming in a high pitched voice at the bigger man.

Niall Walsh lunged forward and threw a clenched fist hard into Jimmy's stomach, the powerful blow knocked the wind out of him and sent him reeling back to the ground. Jimmy yelped in pain as the scaffold tube jarred into his back. Niall laughed and moved menacingly towards Jimmy, who was backing off in a crawl, his hands scraping the ground and broken glass as he went. Niall bent forward and grabbed a handful of Jimmy's hair.

"And what will you do about anything you little runt? Are you a hard man all of a sudden? Well get up now, let's see how hard you are then boy?" his father mocked him still laughing and twisting Jimmy's hair in his hand. Jimmy struggled to his knees, leaned on the wall for support and pulled himself upright. Jimmy knew he had to get off the wall to stand any chance of winning this battle. He pulled away hard feeling his hair rip from his scalp, he spun around and backed off two steps into the open alleyway.

"You're nothing but a drunken bully, you always have been you fucking loser" Jimmy taunted his father. With that Niall launched himself forward at Jimmy who sidestepped the lunge as his father collided with the wall, the pipe appeared in Jimmy's hand as if by magic, his father turned back towards him and felt the cold metal connect with his face, the blow breaking his nose cleanly across the bridge. His father screamed in pain and shock, blood pumping out of both nostrils and a wide gash at the point of contact. Jimmy swung again, the pipe connected with the side of his skull opening a two-inch cut. Niall slumped forward and fell to his knees, Jimmy aimed a kick to his stomach that made him fall forwards onto the filthy floor of the alley.

"Get up you drunken pig, Jimmy snarled, get up and fight".

"You little bastard I will fucking kill you" Niall screamed in anger and tried to get up from the ground, the pipe connected again, this time with his jaw, smashing bone and teeth in one heavy swipe. His prone father lay still breathing deeply. Blood covering the ground where he lay. He moaned in agony, Jimmy stood over him also breathing hard.

"You come home again old man, there's more of that waiting for you, in fact, every time I see you I will do you if you understand me then grunt like the fucking pig you are". Niall moved slightly and felt Jimmy's boot connect with his ribs. Niall grunted loudly in pain, as the breath left his body.

"I guess we understand each other then" Jimmy sneered, tossing the pipe over his shoulder and walking towards the street. As Jimmy entered the open space of the road he noticed two of Niall's drunken buddies staggering along the opposite side of the road.

"Oi" Jimmy shouted at them to get their attention.

"Your pal is in a bad way down there, he's bleeding all over the place, must have fallen over".

The two drunks decided to go and look, more out of curiosity than anything else. Jimmy walked back to the alleyway and listened as they made the gruesome discovery.

"Ah by fuck its Niall so it is, quick call an ambulance, Niall, Niall are you ok?" one of the two men asked. Jimmy laughed and walked away at a brisk pace, he could hear the song *Crocodile Rock* by *Elton John* playing in an Italian cafe across the street, for some unknown reason it made him smile warmly.

Jimmy felt a new power in his body as if he had been reborn, a weight lifted from his shoulders, a veil from his eyes, he was sure he could see things more clearly now, a newfound sense of invincibility that until he stood up to his father a few short minutes ago he had never experienced. In that one violent action, Jimmy had seen the future, he was never going to be a victim again, he was going to take control of his life and violence was to be the trademark of Jimmy Walsh.

After a slow ten-minute stroll Jimmy had reached home, his mother pulled him close and hugged him when she saw him standing in front of her when she opened the door.

"It's ok mum, he won't be back again" Jimmy whispered as he kissed the crown of his mother's bowed head. Neither Jimmy or his mother ever saw or heard from Niall Walsh again.

*****

Jimmy shook himself out of his state of daydreams. He stood up and paced the cell back and forth. Unintelligible conversation and footsteps in the outside corridors echoed through the building, the footsteps growing louder as they approached.

"Stand back from the door Walsh" the voice from the corridor ordered. The same voice from the earlier tea saga. The flap dropped down and two men entered the cell as the door opened. The taller of the two men was Davie Malone, dressed in a smart dark blue tailored double-breasted suit, plain white shirt and blue tie.

Davie Malone had known Jimmy Walsh since they were at junior school. Davie had been two years older than Jimmy but was aware of his violent reputation even then. Davie had subsequently lost touch with Jimmy when he passed his eleven plus exam in junior school and went on to attend the local Grammar School, he then attended Southwark University where he studied law.

Davie Malone hadn't seen Jimmy for some years when he, as the duty solicitor at the local police station, Jimmy was brought in for questioning about a violent incident involving two men who had broken into Jimmy's home to harm him or worse.

The two men seemed to get along fine, and Jimmy agreed to let Davie's firm represent him. Davie thought this was a real coup, he was sure that Jimmy's name on the signing form was going to guarantee a lot of future business for his law firm.

Davie had sat with Jimmy through all his interviews, while Jimmy sat looking at the detectives with disdain and boredom, not even affording them the courtesy of a no comment answer. This went on for forty-eight hours.

Jimmy was then charged and remanded on two counts of attempted murder. He was sent that evening to Brixton prison to await trial.

"Alright Jimmy, this is your barrister Mr Bamford, he will be representing you throughout the trial," Davie said.

Mr Bamford was dressed in the full regalia of Queens Councilor, wig, gown - the *full Monty*.

"Alright, Davie good to see you, good morning Mr Bamford, pleased to meet you," Jimmy said, holding out his hand to both men in turn.

" Good morning Mr Walsh, I'm pleased to make your acquaintance. Mr Malone has fully briefed me on your case over the past two weeks. I have seen the statements of the three witnesses they have lined up, and I have to say it makes compelling reading" Bamford said.

"They have you at the scene, two dead bodies at your feet, so to speak, gun in hand when you are arrested, your fingerprints on the magazine of the gun, gunpowder residue on your gloves, three eyewitnesses - and you wish to enter a not guilty plea I understand?" Bamford drew breath awaiting Jimmy's response.

"Yeah - is that a problem?" Jimmy said, a quizzical look on his face.

"Problems - plural Mr Walsh, I understand that you want to go with the self-defence plea, however, I cannot make a case that you took appropriate and proportionate steps to defend yourself from one man with a knife when two men were shot dead, two bullets to the chest apiece, and another from close range to the head - apiece," Bamford said with exasperation.

"Listen Rumpole, that fucking Turk was going to cut me - I heard he had already killed one geezer if I hadn't shot him then I would have been his second, he would have carved me up like a kebab, surely to fuck - I'm allowed to defend myself? I'm not saying I didn't shoot the slags, I'm saying I had very good reasons to shoot them - apiece or not apiece - I thought his mate was going to pick up the knife and come at me, it was a preemptive strike - if you will". Jimmy said almost regally.

"Quite - "Bamford replied, looking at Davie for some kind of support.

"Look, Jimmy, Mr Bamford is one of the best in the business, he reckons if you cough on the first charge he can you down to ten years for manslaughter and the other will be dropped if you plead not guilty and they find you guilty Jimmy - which they will - you are going to get twenty at least, you could get thirty, think about it please - you could be out in seven mate," Davie said.

"Out in seven you prick, fuck you, Davie I'm not pleading guilty, you got that Mr Bamford if you are as good as he says you are, you will find a way to sway it - ok?" Jimmy said.

They could both see the anger in Jimmy's eyes, that much was evident from his outburst, and Davie knew that no amount of talking was going to change Jimmy's mind now.

"As you wish Mr Walsh, I have my instructions, I will do my very best...but I have to warn you, this is the most difficult self-defence case I have seen in my long and illustrious career, you need to prepare for the worst, but you as the client have spoken, my advice to you is on the record," Bamford said.

"Ok then Mr Bamford thank you, I have every faith in you and the British criminal justice system, I will be eating fish and chips in Margate again before you know it" Jimmy laughed, making a reference to his celebration after being acquitted previously on attempted murder charges.

"Quite -" replied Bamford looking puzzled, banging on the door to be let out.

The door opened and the two men left. Jimmy was alone with his thoughts again, waiting for the trial to begin.

A half an hour later Jimmy was led from the cell and up into courtroom number one of the Old Bailey. He was seated in the dock flanked by a prison officer on either side of him. The opening arguments were to be heard. The prosecution made a very strong case. The Crown claimed that the accused had met earlier in the day with both the dead men. They had argued over missing drug money that the accused claims his boss was owed, death threats had been made. Later that evening in a gambling club in Islington North London, the accused had shot dead both men in cold blood. Both were already dead from shots to the chest before another close-range shot, execution-style, was fired into the heads of both Arda Arslan and Hamza Yilmaz.

The jury of eight men and four women sat silently as they attentively listened to the opening statement from the prosecution counsel. His Honour Judge Keeble sat on his bench wisely overlooking the proceedings like a human owl, ready and willing to pounce at any opportunity to arbitrate, offer his opinions and overrule or sustain any objections with the wisdom of a latter-day Solomon. His pince-nez glasses perched on the end of a bulbous ruddy nose, no doubt reddened by the more than occasional expensive scotch or port consumed in his chambers.

The charges relating to the murders of Arda Arslan and Hamza Yilmaz on Sunday, October 14 1983, had been read to Jimmy, and when asked by the usher how he would plead? He had replied with just two words "not guilty".

Mr Bamford had begun his opening statement for the defence of Jimmy Walsh in a manner of a man who was not ready to accept defeat. It appeared to Jimmy that his sole purpose and mission was to lay down a strategy of self-defence by concentrating on the dead bodyguard Hamza Yilmaz, the man who was actually wielding the knife while staying away from the nearly indefensible self-defence plea of the unarmed boss Arda Arslan. Jimmy sat uncomfortably in his seat and listened intently.

"Ladies and gentlemen of the jury, you have heard from my learned friend Mr Alcott for the Crown, that James Walsh is a cold-blooded killer. I put it to you that this is not the case. Mr Walsh is, in fact, the victim of this unfortunate circumstance, and found himself that fateful evening in North London, in a kill or be killed situation. His actions merely that of a man defending himself from a much bigger and stronger man, a man with a violent criminal record and a penchant for violence surpassed only by his appetite for the consumption of class A drugs. This was no innocent passerby that was gunned down in the crossfire of a gang war, this was a seasoned and hardened criminal, part of a violent gang of drug traffickers hurtling towards Mr Walsh with a brandishing a commando knife with a ten-inch blade. He was intent on killing Mr Walsh in that attack, and may well have succeeded had he not been stopped by Mr Walsh with his lawful actions and quick thinking in shooting him dead. This was self-defence plain and simple, self-defence is not a crime, the law clearly states that there are four elements for a self-defence plea to be recognized by law and justifiable in its execution - no pun intended" Bamford had recognized his faux pas in using the word execution, smiled weakly and had moved quickly to rectify it. Bamford continued on unabated.

"The four elements I mention are as follows. One - an unprovoked attack, which Mr Walsh, by the prosecution's own admission, was certainly the victim." Bamford, for dramatic effect, held up his index finger of his right hand.

"Two" the middle finger flipped upward to join the index.

"That the unprovoked attack threatens imminent injury or death. And again ladies and gentlemen of the jury, by the prosecution's own admission Mr Hamza Yilmaz the man carrying the large knife intended with the possibility of murderous intent to bring imminent harm or death to Mr James Walsh". Bamford smiled broadly at the jury, he was beginning to believe he was getting some sympathetic looks for his client and moved quickly to capitalize on his beliefs.

"Three".

 The ring finger joins the other two, the three-fingered salute made Bamford appear to be a centre forward celebrating the third goal of a hat trick.

"An objectively reasonable degree of force used in response to such an imminent threat is lawful   and please ladies and gentlemen of the jury this is where you must be clear in the law and not be swayed by personal feelings or by the fact that Mr Hamza Yilmaz was killed in this incident - the action taken by Mr Walsh was lawful, he was defending himself against a man intent on killing him - which brings me to element number four ". The pinky finger rises to join the other three.

"Four - an objectively reasonable fear of injury or death. Put yourself in Mr Walsh's terrifying position and ask yourself this question, if you were being attacked by a man who again - by the prosecution's own admission earned his living as an enforcer and bodyguard for a drug trafficking gang."

"Objection my lord" interjected the barrister for the prosecution, a man in his forties with a pale thin face and pencil line moustache, giving him the look of a 1920's silent movie villain.

"My learned friend continues to testify during opening arguments m'lud, the sadly departed Mr Yilmaz is not on trial here, neither m'lud is his career choice, I respectfully ask that my learned friend be reminded of those facts".

"Yes indeed Mr Alcott, I agree entirely, Mr Bamford you will adhere to the facts only please" the judge decreed.

"Quite - as your lordship pleases," Bamford said.

"Mr Walsh was in fear of his life and took this unfortunate but necessary step out of panic and fear for his well-being, this was the only course of action open to him, he knew his life was in danger - he defended himself - lawfully. Ladies and gentlemen of the jury I ask that you return a verdict of not guilty by way of self-defence on all charges against my client Mr James Walsh. Thank you."

Bamford sat down and looked in Jimmy's direction, Jimmy nodded approvingly at Bamford, who visibly breathed a sigh of relief.

"Mr Bamford?", the judge leaned over, his pince-nez balancing on the bulbous snout with an enquiring stare, you mentioned all charges but referred only to those pertaining to the case of the murder of the deceased Mr Yilmaz".

"Quite - my lord" Bamford said, standing and taking his seat again in one swift motion.

"I see - as you wish," the judge said knowingly.

"My lord" Bamford responded, again with the up and down motion.

Mr Alcott the barrister for the prosecution stood and waited for the judge to instruct him to proceed.

"You may call your first witness Mr Alcott," the judge said.

"Thank you, my lord, the crown calls Mr Thomas Callaghan". Alcott said.

Tommy ambled into court head down, doing everything in his power to avoid any eye contact at all with Jimmy Walsh. Tommy was dressed in a navy blue suit and pale blue shirt that was unbuttoned at the collar.

The usher approached Tommy in the witness box.

"What is your religion?" the usher asked.

"Roman Catholic" Tommy answered.

"Take the book in your right hand and read from the card," the usher said.

"I swear by Almighty God that the evidence I shall give shall be the truth, the whole truth, and nothing but the truth," Tommy said.

Mr Alcott stared at Tommy and opened his questioning.

"You are Thomas Peter Callaghan of London?" Alcott said.

"Yes" replied Tommy

"You know the defendant James Walsh?" Alcott continued.

"Yes," Tommy replied, eyes fixed firmly on the floor.

"And do you see Mr Walsh in court today?"

"Yes, that's Jimmy over there," Tommy said, looking up for the first time, seeing Jimmy glaring at him from the dock, Tommy felt a sense of unease coursing through his body as he saw the look of hatred etched on Jimmy's face.

"Let the record show that Mr Callaghan has indicated the defendant.

"Now Mr Callaghan can you remember your whereabouts on the afternoon of Sunday, October 14 1983?" Alcott asked.

"Yes I can," Tommy said.

"Please can you tell the jury in your own words where you were?" Alcott continued.

"Well from around eleven o'clock that morning I was in Bradys' pub with my friends, we had a few drinks, then we left and went to North London," Tommy said.

"And which friends are you referring to Mr Callaghan?"

"Well, there was Paddy Meehan, Billy Kelly and Jimmy Walsh,". Tommy answered.

"Ok, so Bradys' pub is in South London, is that correct?" Alcott said.

"Yes it is, it's our local I guess," Tommy answered.

And who's idea was it to go to North London?".

"It was Jimmy's," Tommy answered.

"You mean Jimmy Walsh the defendant?" Alcott asked.

"Yes," Tommy answered.

"And why did Jimmy Walsh want to go to North London that afternoon?"Alcott pressed on with his questions.

Before Tommy had a chance to answer Bamford was on his feet.

"Objection my lord, the witness cannot possibly know what Mr Walsh was thinking and it calls for speculation," Bamford said.

"I agree with Mr Bamford, said the judge, Mr Alcott, please can you keep your questions to the facts, the witness is not to the best of my knowledge a mind reader ?".

"As his lordship pleases, I will rephrase the question," Alcott conceded.

"Mr Callaghan, did Mr Walsh say why he wanted to go to North London that afternoon?"

"Yes he did, he wanted to go to the Casbah Club in Islington," Tommy said.

"And that is where all four of you went that afternoon, is that so Mr Callaghan?" Alcott asked.

"Yes, it is," Tommy answered.

"And how did you travel to the Casbah Club in Islington?".

"We took my car, I was driving, Paddy was beside me in the passenger seat and Billy and Jimmy were in the back," Tommy said.

"And when you arrived at the Casbah Club, what happened?" Alcott went on.

"Well Billy and Jimmy got out, and they were talking, Billy didn't want to be there and was arguing with Jimmy asking him to not go inside, Jimmy said that it was ok, that we just had to wait here that there was somebody to back him up inside already, Billy wanted to go inside with Jimmy but Jimmy wasn't having it, so we just waited outside in case there was trouble, while Jimmy was inside,"

"Did you know who it was that was waiting inside the club to back the defendant up?" Asked Alcott.

"No I didn't," said Tommy.

"And why did the defendant need back up Mr Callaghan, did he say?" Alcott asked.

"Earlier he had said that the big geezer would be there, and not to mess about with him," Tommy said.

"The big geezer - to whom was Mr Walsh referring, did you know?"

"He meant Hamza Yilmaz, Arda Arslans' bodyguard" Tommy said.

"So, as far as you knew Mr Walsh was going to see Arda Arslan and was well aware that Hamza Yilmaz was going to be there, but did not seem in any way concerned about the fact" Alcott said.

"Nothing scares' Jimmy, that's who he was, nobody scared him, ever," Tommy said.

"I see, so it didn't matter what the defendant faced that afternoon in the Casbah Club he was not going to be scared, is that correct to the best of your knowledge Mr Callaghan?" Alcott said.

"Like I said nothing ever scared Jimmy," Tommy answered.

"So you waited outside the club, then what happened after that?" Alcott asked.

"We waited for about ten minutes, we were getting edgy and I asked Billy to get in the car, Billy just said stay alert and wait, then we heard the gunshots, next thing we were all face down on the ground surrounded by armed police, as I was being handcuffed I heard another two shots, but the interval was different, it was like a couple of seconds between them, not likc thc other shots, which were like double taps," Tommy said.

"Double taps Mr Callaghan…?" The judge asked, eyes peering over the pince-nez at Tommy.

"Yes your honour, two shots fired in quick succession, these last shots were a couple of seconds apart, unlike a double-tap" Tommy answered.

"I see, thank you for the clarification," the judge said.

"And what were you to make of that, the change in the speed of the gunfire Mr Callaghan?" Alcott asked.

"My lord, the witness, by his own admission was outside face down on the pavement in police custody, he was not in any position to comment, let alone testify to any reason for the alleged change in the speed of any gunfire, it again calls for speculation" Bamford interjected.

"Mr Alcott, your last warning, please do not lead the witness with this line of questioning or ask him to speculate again" the judge scolded.

"I apologize unreservedly my lord, and if it pleases the court I have no further questions for this witness," Alcott said.

The judge looked at Bamford.

"Your cross-examination Mr Bamford," he said.

Bamford rose to his feet, looking at the sheaf of papers in front of him.

"Mr Callaghan, you were good friends with the defendant, is that true?" Bamford asked.

"Yes, we were," Tommy said.

"In fact, your very living was dependent on Mr Walsh, would you agree?". Bamford continued.

"Yes," said Tommy.

"Mr Callaghan, why are you testifying against your former friend here today?". Bamford said.

"Objection my lord" Alcott said.

"Please rephrase your question Mr Bamford, I am aware of the point you are trying to make, but it needs to be a little more subtlety put," the judge said.

"As your lordship pleases, Mr Callaghan, you were there that day, having driven the defendant to the scene, you were also there to drive him away, is that correct" Bamford asked.

"Yes," Tommy said.

"And what criminal charges are you facing Mr Callaghan?" Bamford continued.

"None," said Tommy.

"I'm sorry Mr Callaghan I or I'm sure the jury, didn't quite hear you, could you speak up please?" Bamford said.

"I'm not facing any criminal charges," Tommy said.

"I see so no conspiracy to the two murder charges before and after the fact, no aiding and abetting a criminal before and after the fact, you must be very lucky Mr Callaghan, Bamford said, or is it you have been given immunity from prosecution for your testimony against Mr James Walsh?"

Tommy hesitated, his head bowed down. Tommy lifted his head up and looked straight at Bamford.

"Yes that's right I have been given immunity from prosecution for my testimony against Jimmy Walsh," Tommy said.

"I have no further questions for this witness my lord," Bamford said.

"Very well, the judge said, Mr Callaghan, you are free to go, we will adjourn for lunch".

"All rise," said the usher as the judge rose from his bench.

The court quickly emptied out, as public and journalists alike rushed to find the nearest pub, to imbibe a well-deserved lunchtime pint with their ploughman's lunch.

Jimmy was led back down the stairs to the holding area, where he was locked inside a cell again and served a passable lunch of chicken and vegetables. It must have come from the canteen on the premises as it was warm and hygienically packed.

He lay down on the low wooden bench to sleep for a while just to kill the time. That fucking little prick Tommy he thought, proud as punch telling the world that he was a grass, no criminal charges for my testimony against Jimmy Walsh, he had said - fucking outrageous!

Jimmy must have drifted off and was startled awake by the voice of the prison officer.

"Get away from the door Walsh, the officer said, hands on the flap"

Jimmy got up and walked to the cell door, put his hands on the flap to be cuffed and walked back from the door. The door opened and Jimmy was led up the stairs again for the afternoon session of the trial.

"You may call your next witness Mr Alcott," the judge said.

"Thank you, my lord, the crown calls Mr Patrick Meehan," Alcott said.

Paddy claimed the three steps up into the witness box one hand on the rail. Unlike Tommy, Paddy quite openly stared back at Jimmy Walsh, acutely aware of the hushed threats that had already been made by Jimmy. Paddy was wearing a black pinstripe suit with a white shirt and plain dark grey tie.

The usher approached Paddy in the witness box.

"What is your religion?" the usher asked.

"Roman Catholic" Paddy answered.

"Take the book in your right hand and read from the card," the usher said.

"I swear by Almighty God that the evidence I shall give shall be the truth, the whole truth, and nothing but the truth," Paddy said.

Mr Alcott looked directly at Paddy and opened his questioning. His strategy was to ask the same questions to the first two witnesses as they had been together the whole time during the journey to the Casbah Club and throughout the entire incident.

"You are Patrick Phillip Meehan of London?" Alcott said.

There was a press blackout on reporting full addresses given the seriousness of the offences and the safety of the witnesses and their families.

"I am" replied Tommy.

"Do you know the defendant James Walsh?" Alcott continued.

"Yes, I do" Paddy replied, eyes fixed firmly on the floor.

"And do you see Mr Walsh in court today?"

"Yes, he's the one over there in the dock" Paddy said, still looking straight at Jimmy. Jimmy glared back at Paddy who kept eye contact and didn't drop his stare.

"Let the record show that Mr Meehan has indicated the defendant.

"Mr Meehan, can you recall your whereabouts on the afternoon of Sunday, October 14 1983?" Alcott asked.

"Yes, I can remember," Paddy said.

"Please can you tell the jury in your own words where you were?" Alcott continued.

"I had been to Bradys' pub. We had been drinking after that we went to North London" Paddy said.

"And by "we" you are referring to whom Mr Meehan?"

"Tommy Callaghan, Billy Kelly and Jimmy Walsh" Tommy answered.

"As we have already established Bradys' pub is in South London, is that correct Mr Meehan?" Alcott said.

"Yes, it is" Paddy answered.

"And who's idea was it to go to North London?".

"Jimmy Walsh". Paddy answered.

"You are referring to the defendant?" Alcott asked.

"Yes, I am" Paddy answered.

"James Walsh actually said that he wanted to go to North London that afternoon" Alcott pressed on with his questions.

"Yes he did," Paddy answered.

"Mr Meehan, did Mr Walsh say where he wanted to go to in North London?" Alcott asked.

"Yes, he wanted to go to the Casbah Club, it's a gambling club in Islington, near The Angel," Paddy said.

"And that is where all four of you went that afternoon, is that so Mr Meehan?" Alcott asked.

"Yes, it is" Paddy answered.

"And how did you travel to the Casbah Club in Islington?".

"We went in Tommy's car. Tommy drove us there, Paddy said, I was in the passenger seat and Billy and Jimmy were in the back".

"And when you arrived at the Casbah Club, what happened?" Alcott went on.

"Well Billy and Jimmy got out, and they were still arguing. Billy had already told Jimmy we shouldn't be there and that it wasn't a good idea" Paddy said.

"And did Mr Walsh at any time go inside the club?" Alcott asked.

"Yes he did," Paddy said.

"And who accompanied Mr Walsh inside?" Alcott said.

"Nobody, he said he had someone inside waiting for him, he just wanted us to wait for him," Paddy said.

"And by him, you mean the defendant, Mr Walsh? Alcott said.

"Yes, Jimmy Walsh" Paddy answered.

"And do you know who it was that was waiting inside the club for the defendant?" Alcott asked.

"No we didn't, none of us knew," said Paddy.

"Please just keep your answers to what you actually know, you cannot speculate as to what any other individual might or might not have known Mr Meehan," Alcott said.

"And was it usual for Mr Walsh to meet other individuals outside of the four of your group, in such circumstances?" Alcott said.

"No it was the first time anything like that had happened," Paddy said.

"So you waited outside the club, then what happened after that?" Alcott asked.

"We were waiting outside for about ten minutes, maybe a bit more, then we heard gunshots, as soon as that happened there were armed police everywhere, we were handcuffed and on the ground within seconds," Paddy said.

"Did you hear anything else of significance after your arrest, Mr Meehan?" Alcott asked.

"Yes - there were another two gunshots from inside the club," Paddy said.

"These two gunshots were they shall we say, fired in quick succession," Alcott said.

"They were a few seconds apart," said Paddy.

"Thank you, Mr Meehan, I have no further questions for this witness my lord," Alcott said.

"Your witness to cross-examine Mr Bamford," the judge said.

"I'm obliged my lord," Bamford answered.

Bamford rose to his feet, looking up at Paddy.

"Mr Meehan, you were good friends with the defendant, is that true?" Bamford asked.

"Yes," Paddy said.

"In fact, your very living was dependent on Mr Walsh, would you agree?". Bamford continued.

"I wouldn't go that far," said Paddy.

"You wouldn't go that far Mr Meehan, really, what was your primary source of income? Were you not employed by Mr Walsh and Mr Kelly as a security manager, dealing with the supply of - bouncers, door supervisors and events security staff to pubs and clubs across London?" Bamford said.

"Yes I was, I still am in fact," Paddy said.

"Yes my point exactly, you still are Mr Meehan, with Mr Walsh out of the way you have free rein over the business to do as you please, isn't that so Mr Meehan, it serves your purpose to see Mr Walsh out of the picture so to speak, isn't that so Mr Meehan, I put it to you Mr Meehan that you are in this for what you can gain for yourself, and no other purpose, your motives are totally self-serving," Bamford said accusingly.

"No, that's not how it is," Paddy answered.

"Really - what criminal charges are you facing arising out of the incident at the Casbah Club, that October afternoon Mr Meehan?" Bamford asked.

"I am not facing any charges," Paddy said.

"I'm sorry Mr Meehan I'm not sure the jury heard you, could you speak up please?" Bamford said.

"I'm not facing any criminal charges," Paddy said.

"I see, so no conspiracy to the two murder charges before and after the fact, no aiding and abetting a criminal before and after the fact, you must be very fortuitous Mr Meehan, Bamford said, or is it you have been given immunity from prosecution for your testimony against Mr James Walsh?

"Yes that's right I have been given immunity from prosecution for my testimony against Jimmy Walsh".

"A nice little ready-made business and immunity from prosecution, my aren't you the lucky one Mr Meehan, I have no further questions for this witness my lord," Bamford said.

"Very well, the judge said, Mr Meehan, you are free to go, we will adjourn until tomorrow morning at ten".

"All rise," said the usher as the judge rose from his bench.

Jimmy was led from the dock as the courtroom emptied to end the first day of the trial. He was quickly booked out of the custody suite in the Old Bailey and loaded into a prison van.

The vehicle pulled out through the gates of the Old Bailey and into the balmy London streets, the evening temperature unseasonably warm for June. The group of photographers snapping away with their cameras held aloft as they chased the prison van until it made its escape towards Giltspur Street. Jimmy would be back in his cell tonight in Brixton prison reflecting on the day's events and looking forward to seeing Billy Kelly for the first time since the incident nearly eight months previously.

*****

The following morning Jimmy found himself back in the custody suite being led up the stairs to the dock for day two of his trial accused of the murders of Arda Arslan and Hamza Yilmaz.

"All rise" called the usher as His Honour Judge Keeble made his way in and took his place on the bench.

The press box, as it had been yesterday was full to capacity as was the public gallery.

"Good morning Mr Alcott, please call your next witness please," the judge said.

"Good morning my lord, and thank you, the Crown calls William Kelly".

The court was hushed as Billy was brought up into the witness box, flanked by two prison officers. Billy turned and looked directly at Jimmy and nodded. Jimmy, his face that of a seasoned poker professional gave nothing away, he just looked straight ahead.

Billy was wearing a light grey suit and a black shirt that was unbuttoned at the collar.

The usher approached Billy in the witness box.

"What is your religion?" the usher asked.

"Roman Catholic" Billy answered.

"Take the book in your right hand and read from the card," the usher said.

"I swear by Almighty God that the evidence I shall give shall be the truth, the whole truth, and nothing but the truth" Billy read the same oath as Tommy and Paddy before him.

"You are William Joseph Kelly of London?" Alcott said.

"I am," Billy replied.

"You know the defendant James Walsh?" Alcott continued.

"Yes I know him very well" Billy replied, looking at Jimmy again.

"And do you see Mr Walsh in court today?"

"Yes I do, that's Jimmy up there," Billy said, still looking at Jimmy.

"Let the record show that Mr Kelly has indicated the defendant".

"How well do you know Mr Walsh?" Alcott asked.

"I've known Jimmy since we started school together aged five, Billy said, we were - are best friends" Billy said with a tinge of nostalgia in his voice.

"Mr Kelly, can you remember your whereabouts on the afternoon of Sunday, October 14 1983?" Alcott asked.

"Yes I can," Billy said.

"Please can you tell the jury in your own words where you were?" Alcott continued.

"I was in Bradys' pub with friends, then we left and went to North London," Billy said.

"And which friends are you referring to Mr Kelly?" Alcott said.

"Jimmy Walsh, Paddy Meehan, and Tommy Callaghan". Billy answered.

"Ok, so Bradys' pub is in South London as we have already established in previous testimony, is that the pub you are referring to Mr Kelly?" Alcott said.

"Yes, it is," Billy answered.

"And who suggested that you all take a trip to North London?".

"It was Jimmy's idea" Billy answered.

"You mean James Walsh the defendant?" Alcott asked.

"Yes," Billy answered.

"And what did James Walsh want to do in North London that afternoon Mr Kelly, was he specific as to what he had planned when he suggested going there?" Alcott asked.

"Yes he was, very specific," Billy said.

Alcott allowed himself a smile. This was his *Coup de Gras,* the one question that when the jury heard the answer they would convict Jimmy Walsh of a cold-blooded, double premeditated murder, of that Alcott was certain.

"Pray tell the jury what Mr Walsh told you the reason for the visit was to be? Alcott asked, finding it hard to contain the almost orgasmic expectation he felt as he waited for the answer.

Jimmy stared at Billy in the witness box. Billy looked back knowing that this testimony was going to put his friend behind bars for a long time to come. Billy couldn't look Jimmy in the eye as he stammered his reply. Jimmy dropped his stare and held his breath as he waited for Billy's answer.

"We were going there to carry out a request to get rid of Arda Arslan and Hamza Yilmaz," said Billy in a voice just about audible.

"A request to get rid of? Can you be more specific Mr Kelly? Alcott probed.

"We were to kill them, both of them," Billy said.

"By we you mean yourself, the defendant, Thomas Callaghan and Patrick Meehan, your firm, or in fact Mr Walsh's firm, is that correct Mr Kelly?" Alcott said.

Bamford hung his head, this was a big blow to the self-defence plea.

Jimmy jumped to his feet in the dock.

"You're a liar Billy" he screamed.

The gavel slammed down on the judges' desk.

"Order, order, he shouted, Mr Walsh you will not interrupt these proceedings, one more outburst I will have you removed from this courtroom", the judge warned Jimmy.

Alcott looked pleadingly at the Judge.

"You may continue Mr Alcott," the judge said.

"I'm obliged to my lord. Mr Kelly you were given an order by whom to kill Mr Arslan and Mr Yilmaz?"

Billy looked directly at Jimmy this time.

"The order was given by Jack Riordan," Billy said.

"And you were there when this order was given Mr Kelly," asked Alcott.

"Yes, I was" replied Billy.

"Where and when was this order given?" Alcott continued.

"About four hours before it was carried out when we were in Bradys' pub," said Billy.

"And how did you travel to the Casbah Club in Islington that afternoon?". Alcott went on.

"We went in Tommy's car," said Billy.

"And when you arrived at the Casbah Club, what happened?" Alcott went on.

"Jimmy and I got out and we were talking, well arguing actually. I didn't want to be there and was arguing with Jimmy asking him to not do it" Billy said.

"Did you know that Mr Walsh had an accomplice waiting inside the club?" Asked Alcott.

"Not until he told me right before he went in I didn't," said Billy.

"So you waited outside the club, then what happened after that?" Alcott asked.

"Yes we waited for about ten minutes, then we heard the four gunshots, next thing we were arrested by armed police. Then a little while later I heard another two shots" Billy said.

"Same as before, two rapid gunshots?" Alcott asked.

"No not like the other shots, they were separate shots this time," Billy said.

"Thank you, Mr Kelly, Alcott said triumphantly, I have nothing further for this witness my lord"

"Cross-examination Mr Bamford," the judge said.

Bamford stood up and smiled at Billy.

"Mr Kelly, you said you are best friends with the defendant, is that true?" Bamford asked.

"Yes we were," Billy said.

"You were in fact business partners with Mr Walsh?". Bamford continued.

"Yes, I was, well we still are business partners the company is still trading," Billy said.

"Indeed it is Mr Kelly, I put to you that you will be in a much stronger position with the business if my client were out of the way, is that true?" Bamford asked.

"No that's not what is going on here," Billy said.

"So please tell us what is going on Mr Kelly, what exactly does your testimony today get you?" Bamford asked.

"The charges against me have been reduced, and my testimony will be taken into consideration during sentencing," Billy said.

"I see so you have pled guilty to the charges to avoid a trial and you have "*offered up*" Mr Walsh, I believe the parlance is, for a reduced sentence, isn't that about the size of it Mr Kelly?" said Bamford.

"No I have told the truth about who gave the order," Billy said.

"So are the jury to believe your story of this order being given by a Jack Riordan, both Mr Callaghan and Mr Meehan were in Bradys' pub when this alleged order was given, neither of them seemed to have heard it," Bamford said.

"Tommy and Paddy were too far away to hear," Billy said.

"Yes, very convenient Mr Kelly," Bamford retorted.

Both Tommy Callaghan and Paddy Meehan had heard everything that Jack Riordan had said with relation to killing the two victims, but neither was willing to testify to it for fear of reprisals.

"I put it to you, Mr Kelly, that this so-called "order to murder" the victims is a figment of your imagination, you've concocted the whole story to better your own cause, where is this man Jack Riordan? I believe the police looked high and low for him, extensive enquiries at home and abroad with no luck, is he just another imaginary figure of a man looking to shift the blame elsewhere? Bamford said I have nothing further for this witness, my lord".

Alcott rose again, to redirect a question to Billy.

"Just to be clear Mr Kelly, who gave the order to murder Mr Arda Arslan and Mr Hamza Yilmaz?" Asked Alcott.

"Jack Riordan" answered Billy.

"Thank you, Mr Kelly, that is the case for the prosecution my lord" said Bamford.

There was again a loud murmuring in the courtroom, as Billy mentioned the name of Riordan. Jimmy looked directly at Billy and shook his head.

"You fucking grass" he mouthed the words silently.

The court was again brought to order by His Honour Judge Keeble, who then having settled everyone down promptly adjourned for the day and instructed the trial to commence into the third day and to reassemble tomorrow at ten.

Jimmy went through the usual procedure of being booked out of the custody suite, loaded into the van and driven back to Brixton prison, the pack of journalists and photographers outside the court building trying to get photos of anything they could. The van pulled away from the Old Bailey again, the pack of photographs still chasing the vehicle, jumping up to the windows, cameras in outstretched arms trying in vain to capture the elusive and exclusive shot of Jimmy Walsh.

The courtroom was packed the following morning; the atmosphere was electric with the anticipation of what was to come. Jimmy Walsh would be taking the stand to give evidence. The revelation in the evidence yesterday in Billy Kelly's testimony to the involvement of Jack Riordan had put Jimmy Walsh's self-defence case in total jeopardy. If what Billy Kelly had said was true, it would indicate that Jimmy Walsh, on the instruction of Jack Riordan had gone that afternoon to the Casbah Club to carry out an assassination, and had gone equipped to commit murder. This would indeed be damaging testimony against Jimmy Walsh.

Jimmy was brought from the cells up to the courtroom as normal, he was then directed to and entered the witness box, again flanked by two prison officers.

The usher approached Jimmy in the witness box.

"What is your religion?" the usher asked.

"Roman Catholic" Jimmy answered.

"Take the book in your right hand and read from the card," the usher said.

"I swear by Almighty God that the evidence I shall give shall be the truth, the whole truth, and nothing but the truth" Jimmy read in a clear, confident voice.

Bamford stood and looked at Jimmy and smiled.

"Mr Walsh, you have been charged that on Sunday, October 14 1983, you did unlawfully kill Mr Arda Arslan and Mr Hamza Yilmaz, you have in due course pled not guilty to these charges, can you please in your own words, tell the jury what happened that afternoon at the Casbah Club in Islington North London," Bamford said.

"I was frightened for my life. I was attacked with a large knife and I acted in self-defence," Jimmy answered.

"Yes indeed Mr Walsh, however, I need you to go back to earlier in the day and tell the court how you happened to be in the Casbah Club, what business you had there if any, and what were the circumstances that led up to you having to defend yourself in the manner you chose," Bamford said.

"Oh I see, ok, I was in Bradys' pub with my friends, we had had a couple of drinks and I decided that I would go to the Casbah Club to pick up some money that Arda Arslan owed me, so I asked the boys if they wanted to come with me that afternoon, so I went home and met them later, and we went over there," Jimmy said.

"So you went there to collect money that you were owed, what was this money owed to you for Mr Walsh?" Bamford asked.

"I had won four thousand pounds at the poker table a few nights earlier, I didn't want to take all the money with me, so I asked if I could leave it in the club safe and I would collect it later," Jimmy said.

"Was this something that was usual for a gambling club to do Mr Walsh, act as a banker for their members?" Bamford went on.

"Yes of course, they work on the principle that if you come back to the club to get your money, there's every chance you will gamble again and they will win it back, so they are happy to do it," Jimmy said.

"So you have the arrangement to pick up your money and you and your friends arrive at the club, what happened next Mr Walsh?" Bamford said.

"Well when we got there, the boys had changed their minds. They didn't want to come in, so I said ok but I need to get my money, just give me a few minutes and I will get it and come back and we can go somewhere else". Jimmy said.

"And your friends agreed to this and waited outside for you, is that correct?".

"Yes that's correct" Jimmy answered.

"Tell the court what happened when you got inside the club Mr Walsh, was it a nice atmosphere, was there a warm welcome awaiting you as you expected there?" asked Bamford.

Alcott jumped to his feet.

"I must protest at my learned friend leading the witness with this line of questioning my lord," he said.

"Ask a direct question please Mr Bamford, I'm in agreement with Mr Alcott on this point" Judge Keeble decreed.

"My apologies my lord, I will rephrase of course," Bamford said.

"Mr Walsh, were you welcomed warmly at the Casbah Club that afternoon, was Mr Arslan happy to see you?" Bamford said.

"No it was a bit strange, I went to the bar and ordered a drink, and I asked the barman to tell the boss I was there," Jimmy said.

"And by the boss you mean Mr Arslan, is that correct?" Bamford said.

"Yes that's right, I meant I wanted to see Arda, so he called his boss on the phone and told me I should go up to the office," Jimmy said.

"And when you got upstairs to the office, who was there?" Bamford continued.

"Arda Arslan and Hamza Yilmaz his minder" Jimmy said.

"Minder, Mr Walsh? The judge asked, the now-familiar quizzical look on his face.

"Yes sir, his bodyguard, we call a bodyguard a minder" Jimmy clarified.

"I see - a minder -" the judge let the thought evaporate.

"So you are in the office, the two men you mentioned are there also, did anything else happen before you enquired about your money?" Bamford asked.

"Yes Hamza Yilmaz, spun me around, pushed me up against the door and searched me," Jimmy said.

"Really, you were searched by the bodyguard of Mr Arslan before you were allowed to speak with him? Bamford asked.

"Yes that's right, he searched me" Jimmy answered.

"And did the search reveal anything, any weapons or anything at all of interest?" Bamford asked Jimmy.

"No nothing, I wasn't carrying any weapons or anything else that could hurt anyone at all" Jimmy said.

"So what happened next Mr Walsh?"

"Hamza nodded to Arda to indicate I was clean I guess, and I went inside the office, I sat down at the desk and then asked if I could have my money" Jimmy said.

"And did you get your money, Mr Walsh?"

"No, I didn't, they were going to cheat me, Arda asked me what money? He said they didn't owe me any money and if I knew what was good for me I would get out while I could still walk" Jimmy said.

"Oh, so you were not only going to be cheated but now you were being threatened also, Mr Walsh?"

"Yes I was, and I knew they were serious, that Hamza was a well-known nutter on the manor," Jimmy said.

"Nutter - manor - Mr Walsh? The judge asked.

"A nutcase prone to violence sir, Jimmy said, and the manor is the neighbourhood"

"Could you please try and answer in the Queen's English Mr Walsh I would be much obliged" the judge pleaded.

"Yes sir, I'm sorry sir," Jimmy said, playing the polite and remorseful wrongly accused.

"So Mr Walsh, you have been threatened, what did you do next, did you argue your case further?" Bamford asked.

"Yes, I said you owe me two large, and I want it, I know you have it and I need that bit of poke" Jimmy said.

"Mr Walsh, he owed you two large what exactly? And what on earth is a poke?" The judge asked loudly his brow now furrowed in confusion.

"Oh sorry sir, I meant he owed me two thousand pounds, and poke is - money" Jimmy explained, thinking he was speaking very clearly, he couldn't understand why the judge was having any problems understanding him?

"Then please say so Mr Walsh, any more this I may have to call for an interpreter" the judge added seriously.

There were chuckles from the public gallery and the jury, the judge not aware that he had said anything that was in the least bit amusing banged his gavel to bring order to the courtroom.

Bamford, a slight smile on his face continued his questioning of Jimmy.

"So then, Mr Walsh, you had asked for your money and in no uncertain terms you were refused and threatened with what you assumed to be violence if you didn't leave the premises immediately, is that fair to say?" Bamford continued on.

"Yes very fair, I asked for the money and they didn't want to give it to me, so then Arda opens the safe and shows me he has the money, he throws a load of notes on the desk, I went to pick it up and he pulled out a gun, that's when I pushed the desk at him and it knocked the gun out of his hand onto the desk," Jimmy said.

"I'm sure you must have been terrified Mr Walsh, when the gun landed on the desk, what happened next?" Bamford asked.

"Yes I was really scared, so I grabbed the gun and backed off into the office a bit further, I told them I just wanted my money and I was going to leave, I didn't want any trouble, just let me take my money and let me leave," Jimmy said.

"So you now have the gun Mr Walsh, you've backed off and asked again for your money, what was the response?" Bamford asked.

"Well, all of a sudden Hamza lets out this terrible scream and pulls out a massive great knife and runs at me, I was petrified, I didn't know what to do, so I just pulled the trigger and shot him," Jimmy said very hurriedly.

"Take your time Mr Walsh, your answers are very important at this critical juncture of your testimony, please think clearly when you answer my next question," Bamford said mysteriously.

"Mr Yilmaz is now incapacitated on the floor, you still have the gun, how is it that Mr Arslan gets shot also?" Bamford asked.

"Well he stood up and it looked to me like he was going to try and get the knife from Hamza's hand, so I was still so scared I shot him too," Jimmy said, letting his chin fall down to his chest in a gesture of remorse.

"You shot both men out of fear for your own life Mr Walsh, is that correct?" Bamford asked.

"Yes I did, and I regret it very much, every single day. I just wish they had just given me my money and none of this would have been necessary, but they were going to cheat me and I'm sure they would have killed me if I hadn't defended myself as I did, I just got lucky when he dropped the gun" Jimmy said.

"Indeed Mr Walsh you were very lucky. Now tell the court what happened after you had shot the men in self-defence…" Bamford was cut short by the judge.

"Mr Bamford, please, you know better than to make comments such as that, it is for the jury to decide if the gentlemen in question were the victims of murder or if indeed Mr Walsh shot them in self-defence, Judge Keeble said, turning to the jury he added, the jury will disregard Mr Basford's last comments"

"As your Honour pleases, my apologies my lord" Bamford said, knowing that the admonishment was a small price to pay for getting the thought of self-defence into the minds of the jurors.

"Could you please continue Mr Walsh, you had shot the two men, now what happened?" Bamford asked.

"Well it's all a bit of a blur, Jimmy said, I needed my money and it was on the desk you see, so I scooped up a load of notes, you know I thought that's about two thousand, stuffed it in a plastic bag and jumped out the window, I was really scared, I wasn't thinking straight you see"

"I see, said Bamford, and when you had jumped from the window what's the next thing you remember?"

"Well I was surrounded by armed police screaming at me, so I lay down on the roof and they arrested me," Jimmy said.

"I see later that evening you were taken to Stoke Newington police station and charged with the murders of both men, is that correct Mr Walsh"? Bamford asked.

"Well yes and no sir, I was taken to the police station but not charged until the next day," Jimmy said.

"I stand corrected - I would like you to take your mind back to earlier in the day to when you were in the public house in South London, Bradys', we have heard testimony that this incident was premeditated and arranged by Mr Jack Riordan, allegedly over a sum of money owed to him by Mr Arda Arslan, is there any truth to that testimony by Mr William Kelly, Mr Walsh?" Bamford asked.

"No truth whatsoever, I don't know anybody of that name," Jimmy said.

"Quite so, one last question, Mr Walsh, why did you shoot Mr Arda Arslan and Mr Hamza Yilmaz at the Casbah Club in Islington last October?" Bamford asked.

"I was honestly and truthfully in fear of my life, Jimmy said looking directly at the jury, I knew they would kill me if I didn't defend myself with the force allowed to me by law"

This last comment almost drew a snigger from Mr Alcott the prosecutor, who turned it into a discreet cough at the last second, tapping his chest for effect, to avoid a chastisement from the judge, who was glaring in his direction.

"Thank you, Mr Walsh, I have no further questions my lord" Bamford said.

"Cross-examination Mr Alcott," judge Keeble said.

"Thank you, my lord, Alcott said, Mr Walsh, your testimony is that you shot both these men in a mere act of self-defence, is that correct?"

"Yes, it is" Jimmy answered.

"That you didn't at the behest of Jack Riordan kill these men in a premeditated attack over a dispute involving money, and that in fact you Mr Walsh, do not even know a man by the name of Jack Riordan, is that what you are asking this court and this jury to believe?" Alcott asked Jimmy.

"Yes because it's the truth" Jimmy protested.

"Is it indeed Mr Walsh, Alcott said, Mr Walsh, I put it to you that you have woven a web of lies to deceive this court, you have fabricated this tale for the sole purpose of trying to justify your actions on that afternoon in the Casbah Club, the testimony of the William Kelly, identifies not only your relationship with Jack Riordan but that an accomplice was waiting for you inside the club on that afternoon".

"I went in alone and there was nobody else waiting for me inside the club," Jimmy said.

"Mr Walsh, I will remind you that you are under oath," Alcott said.

"I am aware of that sir," Jimmy said.

"Ok Mr Walsh, I want you to consider your answers very carefully to these following questions. Let's look at the agreed facts. You have admitted to shooting both men dead, you have admitted taking money from the premises, and making your escape through the office window, where you were arrested almost immediately by armed police, none of these facts is in dispute is that correct Mr Walsh?" Alcott asked.

"Yes that's correct" Jimmy answered.

"That's good Mr Walsh, so now let's fill in the gaps shall we?" Alcott said.

"I don't know what you mean," Jimmy said.

"Well, let me be clear Mr Walsh, you have left out large parts of the real story, before, during and after the event. When you were arrested you were in possession of the gun Mr Walsh, another undisputed fact, the gun you used to kill both men, a gun you allege was taken from the safe, or from under the desk by Mr Arslan, the gun was not, in fact, yours and you only had the gun after kicking the desk and the gun dropped from Mr Arslan hand, and you very luckily picked it up" Alcott said.

"Yes that's correct," said Jimmy.

"Mr Walsh, why did you burn the security tapes from the club in the waste paper bin?".

This question caught Jimmy a little by surprise.

"I didn't want to be seen on the tapes," Jimmy said.

"I put it to you That you didn't want your accomplice to be seen on the tapes, and you were covering for both yourself and your friend, whoever that might have been," Alcott said.

"That's not true," Jimmy said.

"Ok - so you had the gun in your possession from the time you allege Mr Arslan dropped it on the desk, until your arrest, this must be correct because you were arrested with the gun. How many times did you fire the gun, Mr Walsh?" Alcott asked.

"I don't remember," Jimmy said.

"Then let me remind you, Mr Walsh, from all the testimonies, there were six shots in total, two double taps close together, then some little time after, another two shots were fired, a single shot followed by a single shot. Now my learned friend skillfully skirted around this point. But I put it to you that the two double taps were shots to the chest of both men. The following shots were a shot to the head of each victim from close range - execution-style. Isn't that what happened Mr Walsh?" Alcott asked.

"No I fired all the shots together, they must have been mistaken," Jimmy said.

"Everyone's recollection is exactly the same, but your testimony s that they are all wrong, is that what you are asking this jury to believe?" Alcott asked Jimmy.

"Maybe they were told to say that to fit me up, Jimmy said, I was the only one in the room with those two and I know what happened they were going to kill me if I hadn't done something to stop them after all the old bill are taking care of all of them aren't they, they are all being rewarded in some way or another for their concocted evidence?" Jimmy said.

Bamford smiled, Jimmy's response was perfectly timed just as he had been briefed.

Alcott was nothing if not a worthy opponent, he looked at Jimmy then directly to Bamford, a smirk on his face.

"Just one last question, Mr Walsh. Jack Riordan, the man you never met and don't know - why did he visit you in Brixton prison while you were on remand?" Alcott asked.

This was a gamble from Alcott, he had solid evidence that Jack Riordan had in fact visited Jimmy in Brixton prison whilst on remand, but for a previous offence, and as such it would not be admissible as evidence in this case. The gamble was that the judge would think that Alcott was referring to this case and that Bamford wouldn't object, because of the confusion. He was running the real risk of a mistrial.

Jimmy was stunned, he knew that Riordan had visited him in prison before but that was not this time. It was while he was on remand for the attempted murders of the Yardies, it was the last time he was in trouble, he hesitated a moment too long, he looked at Bamford for help it wasn't forthcoming.

Alcott smiled as Jimmy stumbled for an answer, he turned to look at the judge.

"Err - he - didn't - it was not …" Jimmy stuttered.

Alcott rifled through the bundle of papers in front of him as if trying to locate a particular document.

"I will withdraw the question, my lord, I don't seem to have the correct document here, my apologies my lord, no further questions," Alcott said, turning to his associate in a show of fake reprimand.

"Very well Mr Alcott, Judge Keeble said suspiciously, the jury will disregard the last question".

Some of the jurors were looking at Alcott with a look of admiration and on their faces, some of them had clearly understood the trap that Alcott had skillfully laid, others would have to wait until it was explained to them. Jimmy Walsh however, had stepped right into it!

Jimmy was led back to the dock, feeling like a boxer who, having been ahead on points going into round twelve, had just walked head-on into a sweet left hook. His mind was clouded, he had to pull himself together, this wasn't over yet.

Judge Keeble adjourned for the day and directed the jury not to discuss the case with each other. Closing arguments would commence at ten o'clock tomorrow morning.

*****

The following morning Mr Alcott was first to address the jury.

"Ladies and gentlemen of the jury, you have heard evidence from all parties in this case, and there are conflicting stories on both sides of the defence and the prosecution. However, this is not a complex case, this is merely a case of whether the defendant killed both men in self-defence as he claims, there is no dispute that he actually did kill them, by his own admission he shot both men, he shot them three times each, and this is where the claim of self-defence does not hold water".

"James Walsh, fired two shots into the chest of each man, almost certainly killing them instantly as we had heard in testimony from the pathologist in this case. Each man then had a bullet fired into his head at close range. The shots to the head of each man was an act of execution, there is no other reason for this action, it was the action of a cold-blooded killer. James Walsh concocted a story to cover his tracks. He went there to the Casbah Club that Sunday afternoon last October to kill both men. He went there on the order given by a man named Jack Riordan. This testimony was given under oath by Mr William Kelly, the defendants best friend and business partner. He went there to recover money from a debt owed to Mr Riordan and he intended to collect it. James Walsh lied about his accomplice, he had an accomplice inside the club, he burned the security tapes so as the accomplice was not identified from the tapes and has refused point-blank to name the man".

"James Walsh argued with William Kelly outside the club about what he was about to do. William Kelly asked him to reconsider, and that is why he did not go into the club with him. He did, in fact, offer to accompany James Walsh inside the Casbah Club, but was told by James Walsh that there was no need. That there was someone already inside the club to back him up. Back him up for what you may ask? James Walsh was not frisked by Hamza Yilmaz as he claims, there was not one piece of forensic evidence in the police reports to suggest that Hamza Yilmaz had manhandled James Walsh during a body search that had supposedly taken place before he entered the office. James Walsh brought the gun with him. He went armed and with the sole intention of killing both Arda Arslan and Hamza Yilmaz on the orders of Jack Riordan".

"Ladies and gentlemen of the jury, you must weigh this evidence as you see it, and come to the only conclusion that you possibly can, and that is that James Walsh is guilty of both charges of murder and must be made to take responsibility for his actions. He is not the victim here being swindled out of his money and threatened by these men as he would have you believe, he is, in fact, a cold-blooded killer, and justice must be served. The only possible verdict, you can return is guilty, given the overwhelming evidence against the defendant in this case. Thank you".

Alcott nodded to the jury and took his seat. The judge looked up at Bamford.

"Mr Bamford if you please," he said.

Bamford stood, knowing that the carefully, and cleverly planned trap that Alcott had led Jimmy into had damaged their defence, but he had a duty to give his deliberations as professionally as he could and not let that setback affect his closing statement.

"Ladies and gentlemen of the jury, you have heard from my learned friend Mr Alcott, as he states yet again that James Walsh is a cold-blooded killer. I will reiterate that this is simply not the case and James Walsh was, in fact, acting lawfully as a man forced into this position by two men that were intent on stealing money from him, and to steal that money from him they were prepared to injure or kill James Walsh. They were in fact about to kill him. The knife recovered at the scene had one set of fingerprints on it, those of Hamza Yilmaz, James Walsh did not put them there. This is proof positive that Hamza Yilmaz had indeed drawn that knife from where it was concealed and intended to kill James Walsh. James Walsh might very well not be standing trial here today accused of these murders had he not reacted in the way he did, he reacted out of sheer terror and to defend himself lawfully. Both Arda Arslan and Hamza Yilmaz would be alive today had Arda Arslan not produced a gun from his safe".

"I will again point out that his actions were within the full parameters of the law covering self-defence and all four elements were present, not least of all the imminent threat of harm or death. James Walsh was a frightened man".

"As I stressed to you in my opening statements, and I will reiterate again, Ladies and gentlemen of the jury, these men were not innocent passersby. They were hardened criminals, who would have killed Mr Walsh if he had not defended himself when he saw the opportunity to do so. James Walsh did not bring that gun to that club, it was the property of Arda Arslan, and had he not produced the gun, there is a very strong possibility that he would still be alive today".

"James Walsh was attacked with a commando knife with a ten-inch blade. He was not the aggressor; James Walsh was defending himself. Make no mistake ladies and gentlemen of the jury Hamza Yilmaz was intent on killing James Walsh in that attack. It was his job to protect his boss Arda Arslan, and he attacked with murderous intent".

"Unprovoked attack, imminent injury or death, reasonable force and reasonable fear. All four elements of the lawful defence are present here. James Walsh was in mortal fear of his attacker, the presence of a commando knife sporting a ten-inch blade are reason enough to presume that either imminent injury or death is real, the force in shooting both men were reasonable and the fear was real".

"James Walsh is a decent citizen and businessman. I implore you ladies and gentlemen of the jury to return the only fair and just verdict that you can today, and that is one of not guilty by virtue of self-defence. Ladies and gentlemen of the jury I say again, the only just verdicts that you can return are not guilty on both charges. Thank you".

Judge Keeble turned to the jury to direct them on the points of law.

"Members of the jury. This has been a hard case to listen too in parts and I'm sure you all agree with me that the level of violence on the part of the defendant was shocking. Having said that, I am obliged to remind you of the law on the point of self-defence, as the defence has been at pains to point out very eloquently and very often, self-defence is permissible by law, and if you believe the account of the defendant that he was only in that office to collect what was rightfully his and was attacked, then you must return a verdict of not guilty".

"If on the other hand, Judge Keeble continued, you believe that the defendant was not in harm's way, that he, in fact, had brought the gun with him to kill those two men in cold blood as the prosecution claims then it is your solemn duty to find the defendant guilty on both murder charges. It is ladies and gentlemen as clear cut as that, you know he was there, you know he shot the men, and you know he was arrested fleeing the scene with the murder weapon in his possession. You also need to take into account the witness testimony and forensic evidence also, but again this evidence only goes to show you what you already know, mainly from the defendant's own admission. The lack of forensic evidence on the defendant points to no search having been made of his person as he claims, it is highly unlikely that a search can be made by one person to another person without some exchange of possibly skin tissue or fibre transference, unlikely but not impossible".

"Ladies and gentlemen of the jury you may now retire to consider your verdict and weigh the evidence and testimony that you have seen and heard in this courtroom, you are to disregard any newspapers or television coverage you may have seen and concentrate on the evidence alone. Please retire now, elect a foreman and for your spokesperson and give the trial verdict your full attention, there is no time limit on this procedure at this moment, so please consider carefully and with due diligence. Thank you, ladies and gentlemen, of the jury".

Judge Keeble finished his summing up and dismissed the jury.

"All rise" called the usher as the trial of Jimmy Walsh ended and the tension of the wait for the verdict began.

*****

That night as he lay restlessly in his prison bunk, Jimmy started to think of the different scenarios he was facing in his life right now. A guilty verdict tomorrow could see him jailed for thirty years or more, it could mean he was *lifed* off with no chance of parole. This was the stark reality of how things might just turn out in the life of Jimmy Walsh. He had to stay positive and think he could beat this thing, he had beaten it before, he had been acquitted on two attempted murder charges, in exactly the same courtroom. In fairness, the circumstances were very different, and in that case, there were not two bodies riddled with bullet holes as exhibit one and two, but you never know with juries. It just takes one dissenting voice and I'm free, he thought. One thing was for sure, one way or the other, guilty or not guilty, people were going to pay with their lives for this treachery, of that Jimmy also swore to God during his prayers with his mother.

He still couldn't believe that Billy had turned on him, Tommy and Paddy, yes, but Billy never. Billy had always been there for him; he had always been there for Billy that's just how it was. Mates forever, tears filled Jimmy's eyes, as he shook his head violently to clear this nonsense from his mind, this was no time for stupidity or sentimentality. They had all turned against him. He closed his eyes and thought about the trial, the evidence that had been heard over the three days, the one thing Jimmy firmly believed that was in his favour was that he was the only one who actually did know what happened in that office, he was the only one alive to know. Dead men don't make good witnesses or tell tales.

The one niggling feeling that still bothered Jimmy was the way he had fallen for the last trick question from Alcott. On reflection, Jimmy wished he had jumped right in and said something along the lines of.

"Oh yes, I remember now, I was on remand for two attempted murders at the time, Jack Riordan came to see me, you're not meant to bring my previous up are you?".

That would have forced the judge to order a mistrial. Well, what's done is done, no point in fretting over it now.

Jimmy slept fitfully that night, tossing and turning in his bunk, the lights coming on at six o'clock the following morning came more as a relief than the usual annoyance. Jimmy was ready, come what may - he was ready.

Jimmy waited in the holding cells underneath the Old Bailey. His mother was allowed to see him briefly, she prayed while Jimmy knelt beside her and listened. He watched her tears, they fell from his mother's eyes in a steady stream, the sight of his mother's anguish hurt Jimmy beyond belief. He felt the same pain, although the pain he felt wasn't a sense of feeling sorrow for his own predicament or any sense of injustice, it wasn't even the shame, it was, in essence, a sort of remorse at the circumstances and how he had allowed this whole episode in his life to hurt his mum. He knew whatever sentence he was given if found guilty, it would be much harder, and a far longer sentence for his mum to bear than it would be for himself.

Billy Kelly was being held in a different part of the building and would be brought for sentencing when the verdict was in, and the jury had returned. As Billy had testified during his testimony he had turned Queen's evidence on his former best friend to escape a conspiracy to murder charge for the lesser charge of accessory after the fact. Billy knew his father was in the building, and his solicitor had told him he would be able to see him when the sentencing was over.

Billy had wanted to see Jimmy Walsh, he needed to explain why he had given the evidence that he had against him. Billy had told Jimmy not to do as he was instructed by Riordan. Billy had no part of what had happened inside the club and was not going away for life because of Jack Riordan. Billy's evidence was indeed the strongest testimony against Jimmy. Riordan had given the order. Jimmy knew that, but Billy understood also that if Jimmy had conceded that Riordan had ordered the hit in Bradys', then he would have sealed his own fate, it would have been tantamount to a confession to a double murder. Billy listened as the usual order was shouted out before he was taken up to the courtroom.

"Stand back from the door Kelly" as the prison officer unlocked the door after checking through the flap that Billy had complied with the order. Billy had stepped away as instructed. He was led up to the courtroom.

Jimmy heard the words he was waiting for. His stomach in knots, the palms of his hands started to sweat.

"Stand away from the door Walsh" Jimmy stepped back. The prison officers entered and escorted Jimmy Walsh back upstairs to the dock to hear the jury's verdict. A jury that had deliberated on this decision for less than four hours.

The courtroom looked even more packed than it had been the previous three days. Press people jostled for position, the public gallery was jammed packed, save for the front row. Sat there in relative comfort were some people who had not been at the previous day's hearings. Both Jimmy and Billy recognized the family of Arda Arslan as they sat glaring in their direction. The eyes of Mehmet Arslan burned with hatred for the men in the dock, only one had pulled the trigger, but four had been there to commit this foul act of cowardice. Mehmet Arslan was not a compassionate man, he did not forgive, and he would surely not forget.

Jimmy stared straight back at Mehmet Arslan, a look of indifference on his face, not even the tiniest hint of remorse in his green eyes. Mehmet Arslan thought it impossible to hate this man any more than he already did - however, he was wrong, the arrogance on the face of this man and the half sneer that was now breaking across his face made Mehmet Arslan snap, he stood up pointing at Jimmy.

"You murdering bastard, he screamed I will fucking kill you". The police moved in quickly to quell any further outbursts before the judge arrived and the proceedings started. Mehmet Arslan was warned that even in these difficult circumstances he must remain calm, and let justice take its course.

Jimmy sneered even more at the outburst.

"Fucking peasant, you ain't killing nobody son" he muttered. Billy looked at Jimmy for a split second before incurring his wrath, as he caught Billy's eye.

"As for you, you fucking no good grass, what are you looking at? Whatever way this goes today Billy, no matter what happens we are going to meet again, I swear to God we are going to meet again" Jimmy said.

The usher came through the door of the courtroom. The jury filed into the jury gallery and took their seats. The tension was palpable.

"All rise" the usher ordered as the His Honour Judge Keeble took his seat.

"Good morning ladies and gentlemen he started, I must remind you that this is a court of law and as such, certain protocols and procedures must be adhered to and followed. I understand that emotions are running very high at the moment, but there must be order in the courtroom whilst the verdicts are delivered and any sentencing be it necessary, are passed, do I make myself clear?" Judge Keeble asked.

A hush descended over the courtroom as the usher approached the foreman of the jury.

"On the charge of murdering Hamza Yilmaz, have you reached a verdict on which you all agree?" the usher asked.

The jury foreman, a small man in his early forties replied looking straight ahead towards the Judge.

"Yes," he answered.

"And what is your verdict?" asked the usher.

The courtroom was in total silence as the assembled legal representatives, press, public and most of all Jimmy Walsh held their collective breaths.

"Not guilty" came the foreman's answer.

The public gallery was in an uproar, women screaming, and men shouting threats at Jimmy in Turkish Jimmy himself had shouted in victory as the verdict was read, punching the air in celebration.

"Order-order, the judge banged his gavel down hard four times on the desk in front of him.

"Order-order" he repeated as the hostility towards Jimmy died down.

The judge reiterated his warning that he would clear the public gallery if there were any further outbursts. Peace and tranquility settled over the courtroom again, save for the odd sob still coming from a lady now being led outside so the proceedings could continue.

The usher looked again at the foreman and asked about the second charge.

"On the charge of murdering Arda Arslan, have you reached a verdict on which you all agree?" the usher asked.

"Yes," he answered.

"And what is your verdict?" asked the usher.

As Jimmy watched and waited the foreman paused for just a split second, but the whole scenario seemed to be being played out in slow motion. The foreman licked his lips, cleared his throat and spoke...

"Guilty" came the reply.

This time pandemonium broke out in the courtroom as Jimmy jumped to his feet screaming at the jury and launching himself towards Billy.

"You fucking dirty bastards, I will kill every fucking one of you, Jimmy screamed, I will have your fucking children murdered as they sleep you dirty bastards, I swear to God you will all die, you fucking grass Kelly I will kill you all, you treacherous lousy bastard".

The prison officers grappled Jimmy to the floor, just as his fist collided flush with Billy's jaw, the punch having had most of the power taken out of it by the rugby tackle that hit Jimmy hard as he was taken down, two police officers had joined the fray and Jimmy was handcuffed and rammed back into his seat. Billy had been knocked down in the scuffle more by the collective force of the men taking Jimmy out, than by the punch, but in all honesty, Jimmy had landed a good solid right-hander.

The Arslan family members were cheering and clapping hysterically at the verdict, police officers were moving among them as they tried to restore order once again.

"You will die soon enough Walsh you fucking Irish pig" one man shouted at Jimmy.

"Fuck you, Abdul, you kebab eating faggot" Jimmy screamed back, not having a clue who the man was, let alone if his name was indeed Abdul.

His Honour Judge Keeble was still banging his gavel and screaming for order. Hearing Jimmy's latest outburst he ordered him to be removed from the dock and taken down to the cells until this outrage had been brought under control. Billy remained in the dock, however, he had been handcuffed now, and was also surrounded by police officers, two of whom were sporting holstered side-arms.

A semblance of order had been again restored as Judge Keeble addressed the court once more.

"Ladies and gentlemen of the jury, I thank you for your verdicts, you have returned them in these most difficult of circumstances, and you have based them solely upon the evidence of which we have heard throughout this trial," he said.

Turning to the legal teams, he spoke to Bamford, Jimmy's defence counsel.

"Mr Bamford, your client has been found guilty of the murder of Mr Arda Arslan, and I fully intend to sentence him today. We will adjourn for lunch now, and after that break, I will take the unusual step of first sentencing Mr Kelly for his part in this crime, without the presence of Mr Walsh in the courtroom, Mr Kelly will be sentenced and only when he is safely removed from the courtroom will I allow Mr Walsh to be returned. I must warn you, Mr Bamford I will not tolerate any further disruptions or outbursts of either physical or verbal abuse to any other persons here present, I hope I make myself clear. You, in turn, should make my feelings clear to Mr Walsh that I have not as yet decided if I will add time to his sentence further to his sentence for the animalistic and outrageous behaviour such as we have witnessed here today".

"My lord I beg the court's forgiveness on behalf of my client, and I will personally guarantee to my honour that there will be no repeat of any such unacceptable behaviour throughout the remainder of the proceedings, as His Honour pleases". Bamford responded.

"All rise," the usher said.

The courtroom cleared as the journalists rushed to make their calls to their press offices to get the verdict into the evening papers and the early editions of tomorrow's front pages, the added bonus of having the time to get the copy ready and just adding the sentences and the judges closing remarks.

In the cells, beneath the Old Bailey Jimmy sat knowing his fate had been sealed, it had been so, so close. He could taste freedom with the first verdict going his way, however, the self-defence plea did not work in the case of the unarmed Arda Arslan and he was sure that his fumbled answer to the Jack Riordan question at the end of his prosecution cross-examination had also made him look like he lying to the court - which of course he had been!

Jimmy felt he knew what it must have been like all those decades ago when criminals were sentenced to hang at the Old Bailey and had to take what was known as Dead Man's Walk to the gallows. The narrow alleyway that took on an optical illusion of the ceiling coming down on top of them and the walls closing in to crush them, by the time they reached the gallows there was no room to even turn around. This was what had greeted those convicted men as they approached the end of what would be their final moments on this earth.

That afternoon Billy was stood in the dock for sentence, Michael Kelly sat beside Father Danny Gallagher, the junior parish priest, in the public gallery as they waited for Billy to be brought up from the cells beneath.

As Billy appeared he looked at his dad and felt his heart sink, this was never a part of the plan, it was never meant to be this way he thought. Michael Kelly looked older now, he looked weaker and more vulnerable, the strain on his face was unmistakable, Billy would make this right after all this was over Billy would make it right, he swore to himself.

"All rise" the usher called and the assembled throng of public and press alike obliged. His Honour Judge Keeble addressed the jury.

"Ladies and gentlemen of the jury, having pleaded guilty to a lesser charge for a reduced sentence for his testimony for the Crown, I will now sentence Mr William Kelly. William Kelly, please stand".

Billy stood facing the judge.

"William Kelly you have pled guilty to the charge of aiding and abetting a criminal in commission of his crimes, in this case namely James Walsh in the act of murder. I am well within my rights to hold you collectively guilty of this crime as a principal offender as if you had indeed pulled that trigger yourself and taken the lives of those two men. However, given that your evidence, in this case, was paramount in securing a guilty verdict against James Walsh, I am willing to substantially credit you with a reduced sentence. You will understand that this is in no way a commendation of your actions, but a means to end to get a public menace and a man who is a clear danger to the public of our streets. Taking into account your testimony for the Crown I sentence you to a term of four years imprisonment, this sentence will be backdated to October 15th 1983 the first full day you were remanded in custody. Take him down". The judge said.

Billy looked for his father. Michael Kelly sat slumped forward, with his head in his hands. Father Danny leant over Michael Kelly speaking to him as he just sat forward not moving, as Billy was led away again to the now familiar short journey back to the holding cells.

Billy had never seen his father cry before. Not even at his mum's funeral. His father never cried, but he cried today because he knew he would never see his only son again. He cried openly, he cried like a father would cry if he had lost a son in a tragic accident. He cried because he knew he would rather Billy lived and he never saw or heard from him again than if he had died at the hands of that psychopath Crazy Jimmy Walsh. It was at that moment when Billy had looked into the tear-filled eyes of his father that he knew what the consequences of his actions were, the life he had chosen had now come back to haunt his waking hours as well as the nightmares he endured remembering some of the actions of himself and the firm. He would now be ostracised from his father, the only man he had never wanted to fail, the only man he had ever felt a need to prove himself to, not because of any pressure his father had ever placed upon him but because he genuinely cared what this great man thought of him.

Billy's father had looked him square in the eye and said the words he would never forget.

"Don't come back here Billy - ever - do not come back. No matter what you might hear or read, do not come back here - Jimmy is insane, he will kill you, keep moving, never stop moving Billy".

He hugged Billy close and kissed him on his cheek as he turned away, his head bowed, he looked fragile, lost, a broken man - Billy stood tall in the cell and said just one single word...

"Dad".

As his father turned away - he hesitated, stopped a second, half turned - but never looked back.

Billy felt ashamed of what he had done to his father. The way he had made him feel, the way that Billy without any consideration for what might happen to his father's own life, had embarked on a pathway that had led them to this point, deep in the bowels of London's major criminal court The Old Bailey. To this point that his father was crying for his only child knowing that his life with Billy was over, he would never see his son again.

*****

Jimmy stood in the dock, his head slightly bowed. Bamford had spoken to him earlier through the hatch in the cell door, wanting to keep a safe distance from Jimmy at that particular moment in time. Bamford had admonished him for his behaviour in the courtroom, telling him straight that he may well have earned himself a further five years on top of any sentence he may have got in the first place. Bamford pleaded with Jimmy to apologise to the court at the first opportunity he got. Jimmy told Bamford to go and fuck himself - End of conversation.

His Honour Judge Keeble opened his sentencing of Jimmy Walsh with a question to him.

"Mr Walsh, do you have anything you wish to say to the court, with regards to your disgraceful outburst this morning?".

"No, I don't have anything to say" Jimmy replied.

"James Walsh, you have been found guilty of the murder of Mr Arda Arslan on October 14 1983. I have no doubt in my mind that you are guilty of this crime. You concocted a tissue of lies to cover your intentions on that Sunday afternoon when your sole purpose was to carry out the instructions of a Mr Jack Riordan, a fugitive from justice. I again have no doubt that you conspired with him and perhaps others to kill Mr Arslan in cold blood. You are without doubt one of the most callous and arrogant men I have ever had the misfortune of meeting. Your total lack of respect for the law and this court, and the fact that you went armed to commit this crime, speaks volumes of your ability to plan and execute the most heinous of crimes.

I can only say to you Mr Walsh that I am in no way perturbed by passing upon you a lengthy custodial sentence for your cold-blooded and cowardly actions. You will go to prison for a term of twenty-two years. Take him down".

The judge finished his sentencing as Jimmy jumped to his feet again and screamed directly at him.

"You fucking pedophile cunt, you will burn in hell for this".

The officers again tackled Jimmy to the ground in the dock dragging him through the doors screaming and cursing anyone within earshot. Jimmy kicked, punched and tried to bite anything within touching distance. He was eventually restrained and bundled still handcuffed into a cell.

Sometime later when Jimmy had regained his composure enough to think of the day's events he contemplated just what a jail term of twenty-two years of his life meant. He was alone in this cell, he was going to be alone in cells a lot in the future, he was going to face being in prison until he was in his forties, his life as he knew it was over. Jimmy sat and let his head fall forward onto his shackled hands.

*****

Later that same night, as Billy Kelly started his four-year sentence for his passive role in the murder of Arda Arslan and as he was being transported from London to the Isle of Sheppey, Tommy Callaghan and Paddy Meehan left London. Neither of them had any idea if or indeed when they might ever return. But for now, they both realized that they needed to leave and leave as quickly and as silently as possible.

Chapter 13

Tenerife 1984

Tommy Callaghan had made the right decision; Tenerife was the bollocks. Tommy had been here for three months now since he gave evidence at the trial of Jimmy Walsh in London. He had met a beautiful local girl, rented a nice villa with a pool and was enjoying the better things in life.

Tommy had made himself a big part of the local ex-pat community here. Always happy to help, lend a hand or donate prizes to events like the quiz nights or karaoke at the local bar that he frequented nearly every afternoon from lunchtime until nine or ten at night. In short, Tommy was a man in hiding that was not hiding at all.

Jimmy Walsh had always thought of Tommy Callaghan as the weak link in the firm, he was flash, he was reckless and he talked too much. Tommy had always been popular with the ladies ever since he was a schoolboy with a promising football career ahead of him. Charlton Athletic had taken him on schoolboy terms and he had played regularly in the South Eastern Counties league until at the age of seventeen when he suffered his first anterior cruciate ligament injury. The anterior cruciate ligament in Tommy's right knee had completely torn, the injury came at a time when Tommy had been tipped for a starting place in the first team within six months.

Eighteen months later Tommy was back playing after a prolonged programme of treatment, complicated by Tommy's insistence on not following his medical advisors' directions, and he had further complicated the injury while hobbling around on crutches and playing street football - in the snow. Tommy had inevitably slipped and fallen which further damaged the knee and prolonged his absence from the game. His comeback match was not the success he or anyone else had hoped it would be.

Tommy had been selected to play out on the left-hand side of midfield in a position he neither wanted nor enjoyed. He kept drifting inside taking the ball from the central midfield players, much to the annoyance of his new coach and he was subsequently given the hook ten minutes before half time. The next game he found himself warming the bench, he was given only a five-minute cameo towards the end of the game, and let the coach know his feelings. Things from there started to go downhill rapidly for Tommy Callaghan and his dreams of a professional football career. He was farmed out to nearby local non-league side Welling United, where having starred in his first game and had scored twice, his ACL again popped in the next game, and that was the end of that.

Tommy, when he had had a drink would tell all and sundry of how he was robbed of his big shot at stardom, how good he was, how badly he was treated, and how if the God's, the stars and the planets had not all ganged up and aligned against him he would have become a household name, and possibly, just possibly a future England international star.

The truth was that Tommy had actually found his level at Welling United and he could have been a very, very good lower leagues footballer, unfortunately for Tommy, he never recovered fully, either physically or mentally from the second injury and never played competitively again. By this time Tommy had become further embroiled in the business of his good friends Jimmy Walsh, Billy Kelly and his closest pal Paddy Meehan.

Tommy sat on the edge of the swimming pool, watching his beautiful twenty-two-year-old Spanish girlfriend swim lengths of the pool at the beautiful rented villa that Tommy had leased. Tommy admired her lithe body as she climbed from the pool, her long dark hair dripping water over her tanned pert breasts, her erect nipples visible through the flimsy white bikini top as the water ran down her lean torso and long well-toned legs. Tommy had about enough money to last about another six months of living this lifestyle if he didn't quickly find a serious income to supplement it on this beautiful island, otherwise, it would all be over. This was not information he wanted to share with his current partner, chances were if she knew how desperate his finances were getting, she would quickly become his former partner.

Juanita Perez had met Tommy in the local town centre where she worked in an upmarket spa and health club. Juanita was employed as a beauty consultant and fitness instructor. Tommy had always kept himself fairly fit, even after his turbulent and short-lived footballing days he worked out diligently, staying fit had become not only a good habit but his go-to activity in times of stress or boredom. Tommy had been wandering around the town looking for a gym to use on the day he had met Juanita.

He had found an old school style gym that was fairly good, but Tommy wasn't happy that there were no facilities such as a sauna or steam room. He had just been ambling by looking for a place to have breakfast when he saw this vision of beauty standing talking and laughing with the receptionist through the window of the health club. Tommy quickly checked his appearance in the reflection of the glass frontage of the health club window and dived in through the door as if his very life depended on him becoming a member at that very moment.

The smiling receptionist looked up and greeted Tommy.

"*Buenos Dias Senor,*" she said pleasantly. Tommy, very proud of how he had mastered the command of the Spanish language in his three short months replied with a beaming smile.

"*Buenos Dias Chicas*, he said, I no can speaki-o the Spanish very goodi-o" Tommy jokingly said.

To which both girls laughed genuinely at Tommy's self-deprecating attempt to let them know he needed this conversation to take place in English.

"No problem sir, are you looking for a membership, would you like to see our packages?" the receptionist asked.

"I only have one question miss, Tommy said, turning to Juanita, do you work here?" he asked.

Juanita laughed fairly nervously looking at the strange Englishman.

"As a matter of fact I do" she answered.

Tommy smiled.

"In that case, I shall need a membership - please, whatever includes everything," Tommy said.

The receptionist prepared the paperwork and Tommy signed, having slight palpation of the heart when he saw the monthly cost written on the bottom line, which was about four times the cost of the old school gym - however that did not include the sultry Juanita Perez.

Juanita climbed from the pool and strode like a catwalk model towards Tommy, who had moved and was now sitting at the poolside table sipping a large Bacardi and coke, ice and a slice of lime finished the cocktail. Juanita stopped just ten feet from him with a look of shock on her face.

"What's up, Tommy said, don't you want one? It's not that early" shaking his glass at her, the ice cubes rattled metallically in the glass. Juanita just kept staring ahead, rooted to the spot.

Tommy stood up seeing the look of horror on the face of Juanita, wondering what could have startled her this way.

"What's wrong …" he started to say, as he felt an arm encircle his throat and the cold serrated edge of a steel blade pressed against his jugular vein.

The man pointed with the knife at Juanita. He indicated for her to walk backwards, he moved forward a few steps as Juanita slowly retreated. Tommy opened his mouth to speak, the knife was at his throat again and a gloved finger moved up to Tommy's lips, an instruction to him to remain silent. Juanita kept walking until she got to the edge of the pool. The man indicated again that she was to go to the middle of the pool edge. He followed her again, indicated for her to stop in the centre of the deep end of the pool and pointed the knife upwards. Juanita looked confused. The man pointed the knife at the diving board and then at Juanita, she then understood that he wanted her to climb up the ladder, she climbed quickly, knowing she possibly had an escape route into the water. She reached the top and the man indicated that she should stop. Juanita did as she was instructed again.

The man then pushed Tommy forward and quickly marched him to the shallow end of the pool. They moved forward directly opposite Juanita still standing on the diving board at the deep end. Tommy's toes were over the edge of the pool. The man moved the knife blade to Tommy's throat and with a swift arcing motion, he cut Tommy's throat from left to right, severing the windpipe. A jet of blood spurted into the pale blue water tuning it purple on contact. Juanita screamed in fear and shock, her screams piercing the calm mid-afternoon siesta like a siren's cry. The man pulled Tommy's body towards him and jerked his head backwards, he inserted his index finger and thumb into the open gash in Tommy's throat, blood still pumping from the wound, and pulled Tommy's tongue out through the hole, the elongated tongue just lolled against Tommy's chest. Juanita screamed even more and staggered backwards on the diving board, her knees like jelly she collapsed onto the surface of the diving board, and vomited.

The man looked up momentarily to glance at Juanita, his knee then came up into the small of Tommy's back as he pushed the lifeless body into the pool. The splash sent purple droplets of water flying like a shower of rubies through the air to land poolside in a raindrop like pitter-patter.

Juanita had retreated to the back of the diving board, her uncontrollable sobs made her gasp for breath. The man looked up at her, his black clothing and balaclava making the scene almost more surreal than it already was. He put his finger to his lips in a shushing motion, then pulled the blade across his throat to indicate the fate of Juanita if she spoke of this to anyone, in another bizarre moment of this brutal attack the man fished in his pocket and pulled out a small camera. Juanita watched as he spent perhaps twenty seconds taking photographs of the dead body lying face down in the pool. Juanita was powerless to do anything as the racking of her sobs tore through her body.

The man then produced a can of black aerosol spray paint. He walked to the edge of the pool and sprayed the word *GRASS* on the ground, and the initials *JW* next to it.

The man then blew a kiss to Juanita in a gesture of a fond farewell, he nodded his head towards her and turned and left the villa garden. The whole incident was over in less than ninety seconds. Juanita heard the revving of a motorcycle engine, that then faded into the distance, she sat frozen to the spot in fear and shock, eventually, she clambered down the ladder of the diving board shaking like an autumn leaf on a tree.

Juanita was found wandering along the road close to the villa. She was still sobbing sometime later and taken to a nearby police station. It was maybe an hour before she could speak of the terrible incident that had occurred at the rented home of Tommy Callaghan. The police and ambulance service arrived at the villa some three hours after Tommy had been murdered.

Despite the rumours of the involvement of Jimmy Walsh, and the indications of a revenge attack on an informant. Nobody had ever been arrested for the murder of Tommy Callaghan. Just three days later Paddy Meehan was murdered in Aberdeen, Scotland.

*****

Paddy Meehan had moved to Scotland, the Granite City of Aberdeen to be exact, two weeks after the trial of Jimmy Walsh had ended at the Old Bailey.

Having given evidence against Jimmy Walsh, Paddy Meehan was advised by the police to leave London for the foreseeable future and to take his family with him. They were not offering any help in any way to relocate him. This was, after all, advice and not an instruction.

Paddy decided to move his wife and young son with him. Jimmy Walsh was also Godfather to Paddy Meehan's son Liam Meehan. Paddy had a brother living in Aberdeen and it seemed as good a place as any to hide out for a while. Paddy knew that Jimmy would be looking for him to avenge the treachery that he had undoubtedly bestowed upon him. Paddy had, in all honesty, felt very bad about the sentence that Jimmy had received, but not so bad that he was willing to trade fifteen to twenty years of his and his family's lives for the guilt he felt.

Paddy had found work at a local canning factory, a job that had Paddy going crazy with boredom. His job was watching cans on a conveyor belt filled with different fish products like pilchards, sardines and tuna. The most exciting time of the day for Paddy was being able to change the can sizes in the feeder from small to large. This was very different from the life he was used to leading in London, the tedium and boredom of a humdrum existence in the arse end of nowhere was a far cry from the excitement of his previous employment as a member of Jimmy's Walsh's firm, where every day was different. There was no need to clock in and out, there were no supervisors or foremen, and there was certainly no ball aching routine to speak of, indeed every day had been full of vibrancy and the promise of new adventures and dangerous dealings. Not so now.

The job in the canning factory had lasted just three weeks, after which Paddy had been fired for allegedly trying to drown his twenty-three-year-old dickhead of a supervisor in a vat of tomato sauce. The incident had happened when the Andrew Ridgeley, lookalike, had pushed Paddy once too often, and far too far. On this occasion, he decided to demonstrate his power in front of the other employees on the assembly line of hell by targeting Paddy for a lecture on both hygienic standards and timekeeping. Paddy had indeed that very morning clocked in three minutes after the cutoff of point of five minutes grace time, so was indeed defenceless against the accusations of being a no-good malingerer, with filthy habits. A malingerer no less who should be wearing his hairnet at all times to avoid errant strands of his greasy and dandruff riddled mane contaminating both the cans of fishy treats and the tomato sauce in the nearby vats.

It was one insult too many. Paddy grabbed the spotty little prick by the throat and marched him back towards the stainless steel vats, where an assembled throng of perfectly groomed, hair net wearing, and no doubt early to work employees stood stirring the simmering cauldrons like the witches from Shakespeare's Macbeth. They held their collective breaths as Paddy spun his tormentor around, arm twisted up his back and dispensed him face-first into the scarlet glop, his protestations ineligible as his head was held under the no doubt tasteless, tepid liquid for about three seconds. His screams bubbling to the surface.

Paddy relinquished his grip on the supervisor, threw him to the floor and turned to walk away. Laughter and cries of approval filled the air, punctuated only by the howls of embarrassment and threats of revenge the supervisor was going to carry out on the *"cockney bastard"*.

Paddy turned back towards the supervisor who in turn fled in his panic, his white Wellington boots and overalls now covered in red tomato sauce. The sauce also dripped from his hair, giving him the appearance of a macabre and mutilated victim of a horror movie. Paddy, being a man of few words, had remained silent throughout this episode, allowing himself only a triumphant and theatrical bow from the waist and genial smile to the now adoring crowd, gathered to cheer and clap their new heroes exit.

Paddy had arrived home that morning to his wife Clare and given her the bad news. Clare and Paddy had been married for three years now, they were childhood sweethearts and had attended the same secondary school.

Clare did her best to keep a straight face as Paddy told her the story of his run-in with the supervisor, but nearly cried with laughter when he finished telling her the whole tale. Clare knew that Tommy had hated the job at the canning factory, the tedium, the smell of the fish and the management, she was only surprised that he had lasted this long.

After about twenty minutes Clare told Paddy she had to go into the nearby town to pick up a few things and wanted to take Liam to the park when they came back. Paddy agreed to meet them in the park in an hour or so. Paddy wanted to call his brother and speak with him to try and sort out a job with the building contractor that employed Paddy's brother as a carpenter. Clare left the house and Paddy made his phone call.

As Clare reversed the small family Fiat Uno out of the driveway she didn't notice the car pass her as she drove away. The dark green colour ford escort pulled into the curb and waited until Clare disappeared from sight in the rearview mirror. The occupant of the car was a man of around thirty-five years of age, he sat motionless in the car for about five minutes before reaching behind for a small bag. He removed a pistol and silencer from the bag, he screwed the silencer into the barrel of the gun, pulled a balaclava over his head and exited the car in a calm manner. He made his way up the short path to Paddy's front door. From inside his jacket, he produced a clipboard.

Paddy had just finished his conversation with his brother, and was feeling in a much better mood as his brother had told him he would put in a word for him with his boss, he couldn't make any promises, but he would try to get him sorted. That was all Paddy could ask after all. He thanked his brother, made arrangements to meet him for a drink the coming weekend and said his goodbyes.

Paddy walked to the kitchen, he was feeling hungry. He opened the fridge and removed sliced ham, sliced cheese and a salad bowl filled with lettuce, tomatoes and sliced cucumbers. Paddy had just finished assembling his lunchtime sandwich when he was alerted by the chime of the doorbell. Paddy wasn't expecting anybody but wasn't duly alarmed as he looked out through the curtain of the bay window in the lounge. This being a style of house with an arched recessed porch, Paddy couldn't see anyone at the door, the bell chimed again, and Paddy walked carefully towards the front door. He could see the bowed back of the head of a man standing facing the road through the opaque glass in the door. As Paddy approached the front door the man turned and placed something against the window - Paddy froze - he then almost at once breathed a huge sigh of relief, it was a clipboard, he smiled inwardly to himself, jumpy he thought. He went to the door and opened it, releasing the door from the jamb.

With the door, just inches open the man threw the full weight of his body into the door knocking Paddy to the ground. The man stepped inside and pushed the door closed again. He pointed the gun at Paddy and beckoned him to his feet. Paddy got up cautiously as directed, and backed away. The man followed him into the kitchen. Paddy, still in retreat opened his mouth to speak, the man put a gloved finger to his lips motioning Paddy to be quiet, he then motioned again for Paddy to turn around. Paddy did as he was instructed. It felt like his heart was about to burst it was beating so fast. He could feel his mouth sandpaper dry; his throat was on fire.

The man raised the gun and fired, it spat a silent bullet into the back of Paddy's skull.

He fell forward with a sickening thud to the kitchen floor. Blood started to seep across the checkerboard pattern tiles. The man stood over the prone body and fired a second shot, the bullet entered the temple of Paddy's motionless head, his eyes wide open as if in shock.

The man then walked casually around the breakfast bar, pulled open a drawer, smiled when he saw what he was looking for and removed a small box containing plastic sealable sandwich bags. The man then picked up the ham salad sandwich that was to have been Paddy's lunch, and carefully placed it in the bag.

The man then took from his pocket a small camera, walking around the body to cover different camera angles of the corpse he snapped a number of photographs of Paddy lying dead on his kitchen floor.

In a final gesture, the man put away the camera and removed from the opposite pocket an aerosol can of black spray paint. He walked to the patio doors and sprayed the word *GRASS* on the glass and the initials *JW* beside it.

He then left the house the same way that he had come, swiftly, silently and unseen.
He walked the two minutes to the back of the house, removing the balaclava when he was inside the car, placing the sandwich on the passenger seat, he smiled and drove off.

Thirty minutes later Clare Meehan arrived home to find her husband dead in the kitchen of their home, her screams alerted a couple passing by on the opposite side of the street, they immediately called the police and ambulance service.

Paddy was, of course, announced dead at the scene by the police doctor, and to this day, despite the rumours of Jimmy Walsh's involvement, nobody had ever been charged with the murder of Paddy Meehan.

Chapter 14

South London 1984

Breda Brennan had been born and raised in the Drumcondra area of Dublin. She was one of six children. Her mother and father worked hard for their money and provided a good upbringing for their family in a stable home environment. Breda's father worked at the local brewery as a drayman delivering barrels of beer to the local pubs and assorted clubs in the Northside of Dublin and up and down the main Drumcondra Road. Her mother worked in the local newsagents and corner shop, mainly part-time, but always working full days on Friday and Saturday.

Breda had always dreamed of one day being married and moving to London like her two aunts before her. Her aunt Rose was forever telling Breda in her letters, of the wonders of London and how it was a beautiful, lively and vibrant city, the work was plentiful and Rose was sure her sister would allow Breda to join her aunt there soon enough.

Breda was just seventeen when she met Niall Walsh, a handsome young man two years her elder. Niall had just finished a three-year apprenticeship as a carpenter, and like Breda, he shared her dream of moving across the water to London.

Breda's father did not take to Niall Walsh, he found him a shiftless, lazy young man who was too fond of the company of his friends and the pub where they hung out. Breda's father's prostrations did nothing but fuel her infatuation with Niall and have the exact opposite effect that he was hoping for.

Around eighteen months after they had met Breda announced that Niall had asked for her to move to England with him, further adding that if it didn't work out then she could come back to Ireland. Breda's father roared with laughter at that suggestion.

"What the fuck does he think this is, sale or return? he scoffed, you won't be going anywhere with that jumped up little swine, unless you are married to him". Mr Brennan spurted out, he immediately realised what he had said and instantly regretted it. Breda, of course, had taken this as her father's approval to be married and six months later she and Niall were wed.

A month after the wedding they were on their way to England where they went to stay with Breda's Aunt Rose in Forest Hill, South London.

Six months later Breda was expecting their first and only child, so they decided to move and rented a small flat in the Elephant & Castle. James Patrick Walsh was born in July of 1958, the only child of Breda and Niall Walsh.

Breda Walsh woke early that morning as always, and of course, her first thoughts turned to her only son Jimmy.

She offered her early morning prayers to the Lord Jesus Christ and asked him to watch over and protect Jimmy from any harm and danger that anybody may want to do to him. Breda as always would attend the nine o'clock mass at the parish church and light a candle for Jimmy also, a ritual she performed every weekday morning.

On her way down the stairs, she heard the usual rattle of the letterbox as the postman delivered the first post of the day. Breda picked up the mail, the usual bills from the electric and gas companies, two pieces of junk mail from insurance and double glazing outfits, she skipped through the envelopes to the last one on the bottom of the small pile.

An A2 size envelope bearing a first-class stamp and a postmark from Devon. Breda was a little confused, she certainly didn't know anybody in Devon, but the handwriting on the envelope clearly indicated that this letter was for her.

Breda walked to the kitchen and laid the envelopes down on the table, she filled the electric kettle with water from the tap. She flicked the power on the switch of the kettle as she removed a teapot from the cupboard. Along with this, she selected a tin tea caddy with pictures of Geishas serving tea to a circle of people seated on the floor and spooned tea into the teapot.

The kettle clicked off at the point of boiling and Breda moved to the table to fill the teapot with boiling water. She placed a china teacup and saucer, adorned with the popular fox hunt pattern of the seventies on the table and stirred the tea in the pot. Adding milk first to the teacup, Breda lifted the pot and poured the tea, her morning tea making ritual complete, she raised the cup to her lips and took the first glorious sip. A satisfied smile lit up her face as Breda reached for the envelope, her curiosity now intense to find out who in Devon would be writing to her.

Taking a butter knife to the flap of the envelope, Breda slit the paper seamlessly along the crease and shook the envelope to free the contents. The envelope did not contain a letter at all, what fell to the kitchen table caused Breda Walsh to scream out and recoil in horror at what she saw, her foot catching the leg of the table rattling the crockery upon it.

The assorted photographs fell on the tabletop surface. They were photographs of Paddy Meehan lying dead on his kitchen floor, his open eyes staring into space, his face a grotesque, twisted mask of death, and Tommy Callaghan face down in a swimming pool, the water in the pool had been turned purple, the scene reminiscent of the victim of a shark attack that Breda had once seen on a wildlife nature programme.

The common denominator in the photographs of the two victims, apart from they were both very dead, was the single word *GRASS* sprayed on the patio door glass, and also on the ground near the edge of the swimming pool along with the letters *JW*, her son's initials.

Jimmy Walsh was still in Brixton prison six months after his sentencing at the Old Bailey for the murder of Arda Arslan. This was a constant relief to Jimmy's mother on visiting days. Brixton prison was less than half an hour from her home.

Breda was still feeling very frightened and upset since the arrival of the package she had received yesterday containing the photographs.

Jimmy sat waiting patiently for his visitor in the visiting room of Brixton prison, the motley crew of prisoners assembled therein also sat with a childlike expectation on their faces, looking anxiously at the door, rising from their chairs and beaming broadly on recognizing the face of a loved one or relative. Hugs, kisses and warm welcomes were the order of the day.

Jimmy rose from his chair as he saw his mum come through the door, she wasn't her usual smiling self. Jimmy could tell there was something bothering her. Breda Walsh threw her arms around her son, hugging him close as she kissed his cheek.

"How are you son?, Breda asked him, are they feeding you enough, are you getting enough to eat, who should I talk to here…?" she said.

"I'm fine mum, no need to speak to anyone, I'm ok don't worry, Jimmy said, you look worried mum, has something happened, has someone upset you?"

"I got an envelope in the post, Jimmy, it has photographs in it, horrible photographs," Breda said.

"What do you mean photographs mum, what kind of photos, is some nonce sending you porno photos, Jimmy asked, just tell me who mum I will get this pervert sorted," said Jimmy his blood at boiling point.

"No Jimmy it's nothing like that son, Breda said making the sign of the cross as she said it, pornography indeed, it was terrible photos of Tommy Callaghan and Paddy Meehan when they were killed son, it scared me, Jimmy - the photos must have been taken straight after they were killed, somebody had sprayed the word grass on the wall and on the floor in capital letters - and your initials were sprayed there too," Breda said.

This was information that Jimmy was already aware of. When both men were murdered earlier in the year, Jimmy had of course been interviewed by the police, but even the police couldn't hope to fit him up for these murders without arresting an actual murderer that claimed Jimmy Walsh had ordered the hits, as Jimmy had been safely tucked up in Brixton prison for three months at that time, as everybody was well aware.

"Don't worry mum, I had nothing to do with Tommy and Paddy being killed like that, somebody is just trying to scare you" Jimmy said.

Jimmy's mind was jumping ahead now, who could have sent those photos to his mum, nobody but the police - or the killer - could have had them. The photos had not even been released to the press. The fact that the rumours had started about Jimmy having Tommy and Paddy taken out had enhanced Jimmy's already fearsome reputation.

He had to turn this to his advantage. There was an opportunity here, it was low risk for Jimmy, because the fact was, as much as he wanted the world to think that he had his two friends murdered for grassing on him - he hadn't, that was the truth of the matter.

"Look, mum, don't worry I'm going to get my friend to come and see you, he will take those photos from you. His name is Tony Fallon, ok?" Jimmy said

"Who's this Tony Fallon Jimmy? I don't know him, do I? Breda asked.

"No mum, he's a good friend of mine, I actually met him in here the first time they banged me up, anyway he's from Liverpool mum, he will be in touch, I will ask him to call you," Jimmy said.

Jimmy would call Fallon tonight and ask him to go and see his mum, take the photos and make them work for him, there was no doubt now that there was someone trying very hard to indicate that Jimmy Walsh was responsible for these two murders, and Jimmy wanted to know who that person was.

The rest of the visit passed quickly as all visits unfortunately do, Jimmy's mum shed her usual few tears, Jimmy held her hand and told her not to worry, everything would be fine, he would just get his head down and the time would pass - slowly - but it would pass.

Breda said a prayer with her son before parting company, holding Jimmy tight as she was about to leave. Jimmy hated seeing his mum so upset every time she came here, but the thought of not seeing her was worse. He wanted to see his mum every bit as much as she wanted to see him, so it was just another price to pay for the life he had chosen, and the lesser of two evils that he had to make the most of.

*****

Jimmy Walsh had grown to trust Tony Fallon as much as he had ever trusted anybody in his life. Fallon had become a close friend and confidant, and Jimmy's go-to guy since his sentencing six months previously. Fallon trusted Jimmy without question.

Jimmy had been sentenced severely for his crimes at the Casbah Club, partly because he would not give up the name of the man that had accompanied him up to the office of Arda Arslan, and the fact that he had destroyed the evidence of the video security tape from the premises, as much to protect his partner in crime as he had to protect himself, this according to prosecution pointed to the fact that his actions had been both well planned and premeditated.

Tony Fallon had also had another big break that day in the Casbah Club that nobody was aware of, even the police. The five-pound note that Fallon had thrown on the bar to pay for their drinks had been *trousered* by the barman. When the police had inquired as to how this mystery man had paid for his drinks and the absence of the note from the till it was explained away as already having been passed onto a customer unknown in the form of change from a ten-pound note. The barman felt it was far better to withhold this information than allow the Arslan family to know he had his fingers in the till. So the opportunity for hard evidence against Tony Fallon in the form of fingerprints was lost.

They had been very careful in the past not to be seen together, the only thing that could connect them was the close friendship they had formed when they were both in Brixton prison when Jimmy was on remand some years back. Fallon had come up with an idea that would keep open the channels of communication without visits, letters or direct phone calls. The plan was that Fallon had a lady friend in Liverpool and that she would take a call from Jimmy every Thursday night between seven and seven-thirty. This way without mentioning Fallon's name messages and information could be passed. This was the method used by Jimmy to ask Fallon to visit his mum in London and retrieve the photographs from her.

Jimmy made the call that night at seven-ten. The call was answered on the third ring.

"Hello love, how are you?" The girl's voice with a strong Liverpool accent said, knowing that it would be Jimmy.

"Yeah, I'm fine thanks how's everything with you? Jimmy answered.

"Can't complain, this is the best job I've ever had" she chuckled.

The girl was Helen Moody, twenty-six years of age and one of Fallon's many female friends. Helen was an old school pal, single mum and part-time exotic dancer, or a stripper as it was more commonly known. The arrangement with Fallon was that he and Jimmy covered her rent and paid her five hundred pounds a month, more than generous for an hour or two's work per month.

Helen was trustworthy and very loyal to Fallon ever since he had come to her aid at the back of the strip joint that she was working at in the centre of Liverpool one night five years ago. Helen had been approached by a man named Benny Fletcher, who had been in the cub all night and had taken an interest in Helen in particular, he was generous with his tips all night, but took offence when Helen refused his offer of a dinner date the next night, he started shouting abuse and threw a glass at Helen that missed her by some distance, but nonetheless, the incident had unnerved and upset her.

Benny Fletcher was frog-marched from the premises by two burly doormen and thrown unceremoniously into the middle of the street, where he narrowly missed being hit by an oncoming car. Of course, Benny was upset and embarrassed by these events and shouted the usual threats and abuse at the doormen from the safety of the opposite side of the street, the doormen paid no heed to him returned inside, and closed the door. Two hours later Helen had finished work and had left the club by the back exit at around two-thirty in the morning. The back entrance led to a side street and down to a taxi rank at the bottom of the narrow passageway. Helen had walked just a few steps when a man stepped out behind her and grabbed her from behind.

"You think your too good for me you fucking slag" Benny hissed in her ear, his arm wrapped around her throat.

Helen started to scream, as she felt Benny's hand slide up her thigh and under her short skirt ripping at her panties. Benny pushed her forward holding her down with a strong hand on the back of her neck, her skirt pulled over her exposed buttocks, the other hand undoing the belt buckle on his trousers, letting them drop down to his knees.

Unfortunately for Benny, he was so intent on having his wicked way with Helen, he hadn't heard the approaching footsteps of Tony Fallon and two of his henchmen. The first blow of the sand and ball-bearing filled cosh caught him clean across the ear. Benny yelped and staggered back looking at his attackers, he turned to run one hand grabbing desperately at the trousers to pull them up, which were now floundering around his ankles. Benny tripped and fell into a row of dustbins sending them scattering along the ground spilling the contents from them. Fallon's men closed in for the kill, blows raining upon the head and body of the would-be-rapist. Benny was dragged to his feet and marched back up the alleyway to where Fallon was comforting the now fully clothed Helen.

"What do you want us to do with him?" Fallon asked Helen.

"Fucking kill him," Helen said as she spat into the face of her attacker.

Fallon's men didn't kill Benny that morning, but they did give him a beating he would never forget as long as he lived, his ribs were broken and he required around twenty stitches to various cuts to his face, he awoke the next morning in a skip on the outskirts of the city, penniless, shoeless and wishing he had never gone to that strip club or met that bitch of a stripper. Needless to say, it was their one and only meeting.

*****

"Yeah good girl, Jimmy said, you're doing a great job for us. I need you to get a message to my friend as soon as possible. He needs to go to London, to my mum's place. She received something in the post that she will pass to him, he needs to get his friend in the press to do something with it, he will understand - that's all ok?

"Ah ok - he knows the address love?" Helen asked.

"Yeah he knows it, but it needs to be quick, it's double urgent, Jimmy said, oh one other thing. I will need to see them too after the press guy. He will know how to arrange that too".

This plan that Jimmy had hatched would be beneficial to him twofold, they could spin the story of the released photographs as, "would anyone ordering the murders of two men aid the police by leaving their initials at the scene of the crimes?". This might just get the tongues in the underworld wagging and they might point to whom it was trying to fit up Jimmy for the murders.

Secondly Fleet Street journalists, and the great British public, lapped up this London gangland crap like a kitten in a saucer of Gold-Top. This would be the biggest story since the Richardson torture trials. Fleet Street paid money for public interest stories and they would pay handsomely for direct quotes or a statement via a solicitor from Crazy Jimmy Walsh, and Jimmy was more than prepared to do this, to cash in on his current notoriety.

Tony Fallon was fully briefed as to the mission he was going to go on down south. Helen had passed on the message almost verbatim. Fallon was now sitting on the train from Liverpool Lime Street to London Euston. He had called Jimmy's mum at just after eight o'clock the previous night to tell her he would be visiting her today. Breda Walsh was very pleased that she would be having a visitor and she would expect Fallon in the afternoon for tea. Bless her Fallon thought, she must be lonely. He was sure he would like Jimmy's mum a lot. She sounded sweet on the phone, she must be missing her only child.

The journey south was uneventful and Fallon got a few hours sleep before the train pulled into London Euston. He quickly went through the ticket barrier and out to the main concourse of the station where he swiftly made his way down an escalator to the underground platform of the Northern line heading southbound to Balham.

Fallon arrived in South London well in time for his two o'clock appointment with Mrs Walsh and so he decided to have a quick drink in The Bedford, a local pub not far from the Walsh home. Fallon had been there before with Jimmy on a couple of occasions.

Fallon sat in The Bedford with a bottle of beer. He was contemplating the best way to play this thing with the photographs and whether or not to give them a direct quote from Jimmy, he would have to make it up of course, but what the fuck, there was money in this he could feel it. After his second bottle of beer, he decided it was best to play the *"a source close to Jimmy Walsh"* says Angle, so he called his press source in Fleet Street and arranged to meet him in a pub on Fleet Street at five o'clock that afternoon.

Ten minutes after leaving The Bedford Fallon was walking up the short pathway to the front door of the home of Breda Walsh. Breda welcomed Fallon to her home with a smile and hug, Fallon, kissing her on the cheek.

"Great to meet you, Mrs Walsh, I hope you are well," Fallon said.

"I'm fine thank you, Tony, and thank you for coming. Jimmy told me you would take those photos from me. I got such a shock when I saw those pictures, it made me quite sick. I can tell you, they left my Jimmy's initials at those crime scenes to make more trouble for him, and him in the jail at that time, who would do such a thing, Tony?"

"Don't worry Mrs Walsh, the old bill knows that Jimmy was banged up at the time. I will get rid of those photos for you and you won't be bothered again if you get any more of those letters again that you don't recognize just let Jimmy know and I will deal with them for you, don't you open them ok, just leave it to me".

"Ah you're a good boy Tony, Jimmy is lucky to have such a good friend, so he is. Come on now I made some sandwiches, let's eat something and I will make a pot of tea. Will you take a small Jameson with me?"

Fallon walked to the dining table, it was laden with plates of ham and cheese salad sandwiches, a Battenberg cake and a Victoria sponge, accepting Breda's invitation to a small whiskey with a smile, he answered.

"Is the Pope a catholic Mrs Walsh?".

Fallon spent a pleasant two hours with Breda Walsh, looking at old photographs of Jimmy schooldays and his earlier life. He knew of the problems Jimmy and his mum had faced with his dad. Fallon felt empathy with their situation having grown up in Liverpool in an Irish family also, and could relate to the environment that a hard-drinking father and submissive mother could create. Fallon genuinely enjoyed the afternoon and could see the pain and loneliness in Breda's eyes, and the happiness and joy that her son Jimmy brought her, she spoke of him with nothing but love and pride. To Breda, Jimmy would never be a cold-blooded murderer as he had been tarnished by the press, the awful things they said about him, and the name they had given him. He would never be *"Crazy Jimmy Walsh"* to her, he would always be just her Jimmy, nothing more and nothing less.

Fallon left the Walsh household at five minutes after four that afternoon and headed towards Balham tube station. He skipped through the barrier using the one-day travel card for access and descended the escalator to the platform, the journey to get to temple station would take around half an hour with a change from the Northern line to the Westbound District line at Monument station.

Fallon arrived at just after four forty-five, he had planned to meet Geoff Jenkins a freelance journalist with major contacts to the national daily newspapers in the Tipperary public house at 66 Fleet Street, just a few minutes' walk down Fleet Street from Temple station. Fallon arrived a few minutes before five. Fallon and Jenkins were not exactly friends; they had met a couple of years earlier when Fallon had been introduced to Jenkins at a party in his home city that was being hosted by a big-time Liverpool gangland figure. Jenkins, being intrigued with gangland things, was only too happy to have made another contact such as Fallon. Jenkins had given Fallon his business card with his details to get in touch if he ever had a story that might be of interest, or if Fallon had a bit of information that he wanted to get out into the public domain. Jenkins could be of help. Jenkins had made a good living with such stories previously showing how his gangland friends were indeed morally upstanding and philanthropic members of their communities who just happened to be misunderstood or were, in fact, being fitted up by the police at every turn while just trying to earn an honest crust.

Jenkins had proved to be useful to people before and had a good reputation among the underworld as an honest reporter, and one with journalistic integrity that would give a story a fair and balanced overview.

The Tipperary was a cosy quaint kind of Irish pub with haunting dark wood panelling and plaid carpet design, it was well known for its lunchtime Irish pub fare and a great pint of Guinness. Jenkins was already at the bar as Fallon approached his hand extended.

"How are you, Geoffrey?" Fallon asked, shaking hands with Jenkins.

"I'm fine thank you, Tony, rather surprised to get your call I must say, very happy but rather surprised, and it's all a bit cloak and dagger I must say" Jenkins replied.

"First things first Geoff, let's get a drink, is the Guinness good?"

"Excellent my friend, let's find a quiet spot shall we?"

Fallon carried the two pints of Guinness to the table and sat down with Jenkins.

"I've got something big for you, but I will tell you first off it won't be cheap, are you interested?" Fallon said.

Jenkins was around forty-five years of age, medium height with grey eyes and thinning brown hair. He arched an eyebrow at the mention of money so early in the conversation, but he knew that Fallon must have something big, he was not the type of man who needed to scam a working journalist out of his hard-earned cash.

"Well I'm always interested Tony, that's why we're here. What do you have for me?"

"Jimmy Walsh - the two boys involved in his trial that turned up dead, one in the pool in Tenerife and the other in Scotland," Fallon said.

"Ah, yes - you have a story about Jimmy Walsh, he's always news Crazy Jimmy - the headline writes itself"

"Drop the *Crazy* shit pal, he's my friend, I just had tea with his mom, she's a lovely lady too"

"No offence intended Tony, just the journalist in me you know how it is with these handles"

"Yeah well - not only a story, I have photos from both crime scenes, and they are not police photos either, they must have been taken by whoever killed them, " Fallon said.

"But - didn't Jimmy have them killed?"

"It serves Jimmy's reputation well to let everyone believe he did, but...no he didn't, and now whoever did kill them is getting a bit too close to home, the photos were sent to Jimmy's mum's home address from Devon". Fallon removed the envelope from his pocket and slid it across the table to Jenkins. Jenkins opened the envelope and removed the photos.

"Fuck - someone is really trying to fit him up. I mean killing these two boys, they were pretty low level in the scheme of things and daubing his initials around the place like that to make the police believe it's him, are you sure he had nothing to do with it? I mean the police obviously don't think he did it, he was banged up at the time, but he could have ordered and paid for it?" Jenkins said.

"I know Jimmy had nothing to do with this, it has nothing to do with him"

"So what do you want from me, apart from a bundle of cash I mean?"

"Jimmy has been questioned as you know, he just wants the publicity for the photos, it might flush someone out or someone might start talking, the details were never released of this crime scene lat alone the photos, so you, my good friend have a world exclusive - and I want twenty grand".

"*Twenty what?*" Jenkins said in disbelief.

Fallon plucked the envelope out of Jenkins's hand.

"Nice seeing you again Geoff, Fallon said rising to leave, this is a seller's market mate, you think I can't get what I want for these from the daily newspapers direct, The News of the World won't even blink at twenty grand".

"Ok no need to be hasty - I was just clarifying what it is you want, I get it, let me make a couple of calls". With that Jenkins disappeared outside to find a phone box for privacy.

Fallon signalled to the barman for another round of drinks. Five minutes later Jenkins returned to the table and sat down with a look of reservation on his face.

"Ok, these are the only photos right Tony? No other copies?"

"On my life Geoff, they have been with Jimmy's mum since they were delivered until I picked them up today".

"I can't get you twenty - fifteen is the best I can do; do we have a deal?"

"We do indeed Geoff, nice one son. Fallon said, beaming from ear to ear.

"Jimmy will be very pleased with you, this will go a long way to taking care of his mum for a while. I didn't think you would get anywhere near twenty".

"Ok, be back here at eight-thirty, can you? I will have the cash for you" Jenkins said, holding out his hand out for the envelope.

"Nice one, I'll see you then, now let's have a drink, cheers," Fallon said.

Fallon left around twenty later minutes later and went to find a bed and breakfast or small hotel for the night. He found a place not far from The Tipperary on Stonecutter Street. He checked in for just the one night, he fully intended to be back in Liverpool tonight, but he hadn't expected to receive the cash from Jenkins so quickly and he wanted to make sure that the money got to Breda Walsh as quickly as it could, he would meet with Jenkins later tonight, have a late dinner and then get some sleep. Tomorrow he would go straight back to Balham and give the fifteen thousand pounds to Breda Walsh, and then onto Euston and home, a good couple of days' work done.

Everything went as planned the night before. Jenkins handed over the cash and told Fallon that he had done a deal with a Sunday national paper to break the story this coming weekend. Fallon had kept to his schedule the following day and had handed Breda Walsh an envelope stuffed with the cash at eleven o'clock that very morning, he had told Breda it was the proceeds from a deal that he and Jimmy had been working on and now it was payday, it was all legit, nothing to worry about. Breda had accepted the money after a little bit of questioning. Fallon had confirmed the money had come from where he said it was from and that it wasn't charity or stolen money, it was Jimmy's cut from the profits.

Fallon was now settled on the train back to Liverpool Lime Street, feeling very pleased with himself and with what his efforts had achieved.

Chapter 15

Parkhurst Prison 1987

Christy Monaghan sat waiting for Jimmy Walsh in the visiting room of Brixton prison, remembering his own time as a prisoner on remand in Mountjoy prison in Dublin on firearm charges that he was later acquitted of. As Jimmy arrived Christy stood up and smiled warmly at him extending his hand.

"So how're things Jimmy, a hell of a thing twenty-two fucking years boy," Christy said.

"What do you want Mr Monaghan, I was surprised you asked to see me?" Jimmy asked.

"Oh straight to the point, the same old Jimmy, well as you are asking son, Mr Riordan would like a favour".

Jimmy laughed loudly.

"Are you fucking sure? He fitted me up and now he wants a favour from me, I did what I did on his order, I kept my mouth shut I never said a word, does that not count for anything, I could have taken a deal like the rest of them, but I didn't?"

"You did the right thing, Jimmy, that's for sure, there's no argument there now is there, but he wants to return the favour so to speak, Billy Kelly gets out in a few days, did you know that?"

"Now he's a fucking grass, not me Mr Monaghan - no I didn't know he was getting out, I try not to think about him, to be honest, it only fucks with my head".

"Well right enough again Jimmy, there's no arguing with your logic today is there" Christy chuckled.

"So what do you want from me, I don't even know where he is, I can't help you," Jimmy said.

"Ah, we know where he is right enough, he's down in Kent on the Isle of Sheppey, I want to know where he might go? Who he knows and the like, friends, relatives, you know the craic so you do Jimmy, for sure he's not coming back to London, am I right?".

"Yeah he's not that stupid, not after what happened to Tommy and Paddy, am I right Mr Monaghan?" Jimmy said, emphasising the words to see if he got a reaction from Christy in regard to the murders of Tommy Callaghan and Paddy Meehan.

"Right again Jimmy, was that not your handy work? What with your initials all over the show?"

"No, I can't claim that, as much as I would like to, I thought it might have been Mr Riordan,"

"Jack Riordan had no beef with those two young fellas, or with you, you just got greedy Jimmy, he understands ambition and he put you in your place - but you still didn't talk, and he respects that so he does - Billy Kelly - well now that fella, he's a different kettle of fish, he's ours Jimmy, whether or not you had anything to do with the other two, Billy Kelly is ours".

Jimmy chose to ignore the last part of Christy's speech.

"You know we didn't run with anyone that wasn't from the manor Mr Monaghan, and Billy doesn't have relatives anywhere else that I know of, so I don't think I can help you even if I wanted to, which I do. I'm not protecting him from anything. I couldn't give a fuck what happens to him" Jimmy said, feeling the anger and bitterness flooding back to him, thinking about Billy's imminent freedom and the years of prison life still ahead of him.

"So nothing then - Ah well I'm setting up a little welcoming committee for him when he gets out, he may not make it out of Kent if you get my meaning…" Jimmy interrupted Christy mid-sentence.

"Hang on, Simone - yeah Simone in Margate, he was seeing her for a few months just before we got nicked," Jimmy said.

"Simone what? Do you remember her surname at all?"

"No, but I do know her address, well her building, she has a beauty salon on the seafront down there on the coast, just along from Dreamland, yeah we were all with him the day he met her, yeah we went for the weekend when I got a not guilty for those *Yardie* mugs, cracking looking sort, yeah Simone, I had her mate that night? Her name was fucking Doris; she was too - boat race like a bulldog".

"Ah I remember that right enough Jimmy, you made a right mess of those two nasty fuckers, so you did, fair play to you," Christy said admiringly, she looked like a bulldog you say, it could have been worse she might have looked like my ex-missus"

Jimmy laughed at Christy's joke.

"Ok, one last thing Jimmy, do you have someone you could trust to put down in Margate at all, just to see if he turns up there, it's not my neck of the woods don't you know, and I think going all the way down to Sheppey will be far enough for the likes of me. I miss London something fierce if I'm away from her for too long so I do, all that fresh air, green fields - makes me shudder" Christy laughed at his own joke, Jimmy smiled politely.

"Yeah I've got someone I will bell him"

"Ok it's just a bit of insurance in case he gives us the slip, you know how it is now, well I'll not take up any more of your time Jimmy, does your mammy need anything, Jimmy? I know things went a bit pear-shaped with us so they did, but she's a good Irish woman, she always was".

"No, I'm taking care of her Mr Monaghan, I still have some friends you know, thanks anyway" Jimmy smiled.

"I'm sure you do Jimmy boy - I'm sure you do".

Christy Monaghan smiled as he stood, tipped his fingers to his brow and was gone.

To be honest, Jimmy felt a bit disappointed, a bit let down. When he had received word a couple of weeks back that Monaghan wanted to see him, Jimmy somehow thought that maybe Jack Riordan had forgiven him, but even if he understood ambition as Christy Monaghan said he did, it seemed that the act of forgiveness was beyond Jack Riordan.

Chapter 16

Swaleside Prison December 1987

Filled with both exhilaration and dread Billy Kelly looked back at the gates of Her Majesty's Prison Swaleside. HMP Swaleside is located close to the village of Eastchurch on the Isle of Sheppey in Kent. Swaleside forms part of the Sheppey prisons cluster, which also includes Her Majesty's prisons Elmley and Stanford Hill.

Billy walked to the nearby line of taxis that were always stationed outside the prison given the amount of business available for them with visitors, staff and legal representatives always needing transport to and from the railway station. Just as he was about to open the door of the first cab in line the driver threw a thumb over his shoulder, directing Billy to the vehicle behind. Billy tried to open the door, the driver pressed the automatic door lock switch and all the doors locked at once. A stern look from the driver did the trick and Billy let go of the door handle and walked to the next taxi in the queue. Billy opened the door to the taxi he was directed to. He looked along the rank, and then around the car park. He noticed a blue Ford Granada with two men inside.

As Billy entered the taxi the driver looked at him in the rearview mirror. The driver was in his mid-thirties Billy thought and looked anything but a taxi driver. His physique told Billy this guy was in good shape and worked out regularly. Billy was not sure what he was but definitely was not a cabbie.

"Good morning Sir, where to?" he inquired.

"Do I have a choice?" Billy asked.

"Of course, I'm just here to drive you in comfort to your chosen destination, that means anywhere on the UK mainland, so if you have a hankering for Scotland, Wales, Cornwall or anywhere else on this fair Island of ours, just say so, your wish will be granted, I'm one of the good guys, I bet your *old april* was going there my son". The driver laughed - Billy didn't.

The driver then removed a fat manila envelope from his inside jacket pocket and threw it on the back seat.

"Passport, driver's license, national insurance card, bank account details, debit card and three large in crisp twenty-pound notes. I'm going to look after you for the next six months. There will be deposits monthly of a further two thousand pounds sterling into that account for the next five months, for a grand total of thirteen thousand pounds to help you get started. The PIN is the first four digits of the account number. You will notice you have a change of name, you are now and always will be henceforth Mr Richard Murray, do you mind if I call you Dick?". The driver laughed-Billy didn't.

"By the way, I'm Detective Constable George Knowles". Knowles said, showing Billy his warrant card.

"Billy Kelly, but I'm sure you know that already".

"No you're not, you're Richard Murray, remember that, it might just keep you alive".

"When the six months are up you are on your own, you know the score, it's all been explained to you, Knowles said, don't get in touch with family or friends, you are on your own. Do not try and rekindle any old romances for whatever reason, you are on your own, make new friends find a nice girl and get on with your life, create a history for Richard Murray and stick to it, better still don't talk about your past at all if you can help it, to anyone. This is for your own safety, you know the people you have aggravated and you know the consequences, you will end up in the ground if you make any mistakes. I will give you a phone number to contact me in case of any emergency situation, it's only for emergencies so don't go calling me because you're bored or need a chat, I'm your handler, not your friend, I'm not your wife or your priest".

Knowles laughed - Billy didn't.

"So my good man where will we be going?" The driver asked. "Cardiff, Swansea, Glasgow-perhaps Edinburgh?" Billy looked at Knowles who was still looking in the rearview mirror while holding the conversation.

"Yeah - I don't think so mate, take me to Sittingbourne railway station please," Billy said.

"Sittingbourne it is then" the driver replied.

As the taxi pulled away from the prison Billy closed his eyes and laid back in the seat. His mind raced with all sorts of thoughts. Would he find Simone in Margate? Would she still be there? It is possible she may have found another guy, what then? Is she married? Does she have children? So many questions…

Sure enough, the suspicious car that Billy had seen at the prison was following them at a distance some five minutes after their journey had begun. It was definitely the same one he had seen at the prison car park. Large Ford Granada, new model, dark blue in colour. There were two occupants in the car, both male heads down, trying to look like they were minding their own business and just waiting for a friend or relative to be released, the same as Billy.

Billy knew he was the only release that day. As he had gone through the process of changing into his own clothes, taking back his personal possessions of his watch, wallet, three hundred and twenty-four pounds and eleven pence in cash the prison officer had encouraged him to *"move it, Kelly, you've got nobody else to wait for you're the only prisoner being released today"*, so the sooner it was done the sooner he was free.

So why now were these two guys following them? They were not the police, that was for sure. Billy didn't get a look at either of them, but that's not to say they were not Jimmy's men. Jimmy was not averse to outsourcing work when necessary, especially if there was a chance the target would know the usual members of the firm.

"I think we have company mate, Billy said to Knowles, blue Granada about a hundred yards back behind the white van, I saw them in the car park back at the prison". Knowles checked the rearview mirror.

"Yeah I see them," Knowles said.

"I'm not being paranoid, it's just that I know that there were no other releases today, and they were a bit conspicuous in the motor back there, trying to hide behind newspapers and that". Billy said.

"In your situation paranoia is good my friend, Knowles said seriously, ok let's try the move, three left turns, then let's see if they are still there with us"

Knowles accelerated the car looking for and anticipating, the next left turn. Two hundred yards further on he took the turn sharply without indicating, the tyres screeched on the asphalt road surface as they gripped the bend. Sure enough, a few seconds later the blue Granada came into sight. Knowles checked the mirror, saw the Granada and gunned the car faster to the next turn, they were travelling at around fifty miles per hour in a built-up leafy avenue, a dangerously high speed in a residential area, and it was making Knowles nervous, a stray dog in the road or God forbid a child, and there were going to be grave consequences.

"I have an idea, but it means dropping you off, you will be on your own, are you ok with that?" Knowles asked Billy.

Billy was more than happy with that arrangement, he didn't want any part of being handled by anyone and had always planned to just disappear when he was released. The cash was a bonus no doubt about that, but he didn't want a phone number, and he didn't need to be in touch with anyone, he would take his chances, as he didn't trust the old bill to keep their mouths shut when someone came asking to buy the information on his whereabouts, his name, address or anything else they had knowledge of and were only too willing to sell.

"Fine by me," Billy answered.

"Right I'm going to stop, if they do the same I'm going to get out and go towards them flashing my warrant card. You get out of the car and stay down, find some cover behind a wall, a car, anything, so they cannot see you" Knowles instructed Billy.

"Got it," Billy answered.

At the next junction, Knowles turned left again, slowed the car to around fifteen miles an hour and crawled at snail pace along the road. The Granada came around the corner and slowed to a crawl when they saw the target car inching along in front of them, following cagily they watched as the target car pulled over to the curb. Billy ducked down in the back of the car as the Granada rolled past, both men straining their necks to get a good look inside. The car pulled over about fifty feet ahead.

"Ok, I'm going over to them, count to twenty then get out. There's a small wall in front of the garages to your left, get out and get behind it, don't try looking to see where I am, I will signal you when I'm back here. Wait until I come back, don't move before I'm back here-you understand? As soon as they follow me let them get out of sight then double back, I'm going to keep heading towards London, go in the opposite direction to the coast, take a few days to work out what you want to do, then call me, here's my number".

Knowles threw a piece of notepaper on the back seat, Billy took it and slipped it into his pocket without looking at it.

"Right good luck, call me in a couple of days".

Knowles got out of the car and walked towards the parked Granada.

Billy slowly counted to twenty then made his move, he opened the door as quietly as he could, as he kept ahold of the handle so as not to let it be seen as open. He slid out on the pavement, came around on his knees and put his hand inside the car, removed the Manila envelope from the back seat and silently closed the door.

He moved in a crouch keeping the car between himself and the Granada. Knowles was leaning on the car window showing the occupants his warrant card. A brief conversation took place, Knowles looked back over his shoulder, and then again - alarm bells went off in Billy's head.

"What the fuck are you playing at you fucking idiot?" the man in the passenger seat said through a two-inch gap at the top of the tinted window.

"He's made you, couldn't you keep back a bit for fuck's sake, you nearly went by us at one point, Knowles protested, listen he's going to hide behind that car over there until I'm gone waiting for you to follow me, he doesn't know the score with me, when I pull away he's yours - don't fuck it up, I'm going to keep going until I'm back in London".

The side passenger window came down silently. Christy Monaghan scowled up at Knowles. And Billy saw him!

Billy's heart almost stopped, Jack Riordan's top man was right across the road, Christy Monaghan, a ruthless ex-IRA killer who Billy hadn't seen since that Sunday in Bradys' at the start of this nightmare, Jimmy wants me dead - now fucking Riordan too.

Knowles checked to see where Billy was - one time too many!

"Fuck, this slag is on Riordan's payroll". Billy said aloud.

Billy crawled out from behind the wall and moved quickly along the front of the garages, there was an alleyway on the right-hand side. Billy climbed the five-foot wall, jumped into the alleyway and started running. A few seconds later he heard some shouting behind him as he ran. The far end of the alleyway was a hundred yards away, Billy's arms pumped the air as he bolted for the safety of the street beyond.

Christy Monaghan screamed at Knowles as he saw Billy making his escape into the alleyway opposite.

"Get him, fucking get him - oh for fuck's sake".

It was too late, Billy was gone clean away and no way to follow unless it's on foot and Christy was not in any shape for running.

As Billy reached the end of the alleyway he heard more shouts but was relieved that he couldn't hear footsteps, so nobody was behind him.

Quickly scanning the area around him he saw opposite a greengrocer shop, a delivery van was being unloaded, a young man of about twenty-five was just throwing his barrow into the back, along with a pile of vegetable sacks. The young man was sporting a shoulder-length mullet that would have been the envy of either Chris Waddle or Suzi Quattro. Billy couldn't decide which of the two the young man reminded him of most.

"Hey mate where are you going?" Billy asked the young man.

"What -? I'm going back to the yard ain't I, got more deliveries to pick up and get out." The young man said.

"I need a lift mate, I'm desperate, where exactly are you going?" Billy said.

"Sorry mate no can do - company vehicle, union rules, health and safety, and I'm not insured to take passengers' besides I'm going to Maidstone now," the young man said.

"I don't care where you're going I need a ride".

Billy fished in his pocket and pulled out a wad of notes, counted one hundred pounds in twenty-pound notes and thrust it into the young man's hand.

The young man looked at Billy in surprise, checking over both shoulders in the process, taking the money from his outstretched hand

"And where exactly in Maidstone would you like to be dropped off squire?" the young man said.

This time Billy did laugh, more from relief than anything else.

After an uneventful journey of just over an hour, the young man dropped Billy off close to Maidstone West railway station. Having thought about his options on the relatively quiet drive to Maidstone, Billy had decided not to take any chances with a train journey. He had already asked to be dropped at Sittingbourne railway station, so he assumed that Knowles would have already given Monaghan that information. They would be scoping out the station and or platforms and also all the trains to go through there. It had also occurred to Billy that his new name of Mr Robert Murray would also be in the public domain, and as such little use to him. However, seeing that the new documents were all bearing that name, Billy was stuck with it.

Seeing a taxi rank outside the station Billy walked over to the line of vehicles.

"Can you take me to Margate mate?" Billy said

"Yeah, no problem, hop in, the taxi driver answered, anywhere in particular in Margate," he asked.

"Just go to the seafront mate, I will let you know when we are there," Billy said.

"Ok chief no problem, on or off?" The taxi driver asked.

"You what?" Billy said, a puzzled look on his face.

"The meter chief, take your chances with the fare with the meter on, or thirty quid with it off?" The taxi driver said.

"Oh ok - thirty seems fair I reckon," Billy said.

All of a sudden Billy felt far more relaxed than he had for the past couple of hours since he'd left the prison. He had hardly closed his eyes the previous night as he excitedly anticipated his release. Billy settled back in the comfortable seat, closed his eyes and drifted off to sleep. A half-hour so later he woke from his slumber. The taxi cab was just pulling off the M20 motorway onto the A28 which would take them through Canterbury and Minster before arriving in Margate.

"You must have been knackered mate, you went out like a light, won't be long we will be there," the taxi driver said.

"Yeah it was a long night" Billy answered. The remainder of the journey continued in silence. As they approached the seafront Billy leaned forward, he fished two twenty pound notes from the wad of money and handed it to the taxi driver.

"Keep the change mate, do you know where the Winter Gardens theatre is?" Billy said.

"Cheers chief, very kind of you, yeah I know it's straight on here" the taxi driver answered.

"Okay, good just drop me there, that will be fine, thanks."

Five minutes later the taxi pulled to the curb outside the Winter Gardens theatre.

The seafront at Margate was bitterly cold. Billy suddenly became aware he was only wearing the suit and shirt he had on the day he was sentenced; it was a scant defence against the winter chill. The biting wind blew in off the English Channel causing Billy to tuck his hands deep inside his pockets and retract his shoulders into his body.

Billy looked around the near-deserted promenade, hoping to find a shop where he could purchase a coat of some description. He walked back up a side street and headed for the town centre shopping area, it was just after midday and there was a fair amount of people around despite the cold weather. Billy found a menswear store selling middle-range clothes and entered. He quickly selected a pack of three white crew-neck t-shirts, a thick black crew neck pullover, a pair of black Levi 501's, a black quilted jacket, assorted socks and boxer shorts, and a pair of black trainers.

As Billy approached the checkout he grabbed a canvas gym bag to complete his purchases.

"Will that be all sir? The salesman asked.

"Yes thanks, but I need to change into these now," Billy said.

Billy selected the jacket, jeans, one of the t-shirts, the pullover and the trainers.

"Throw the rest in the bag please mate, no need to pack them, where's your changing room?" Billy asked.

"Just back there on the left" the salesman pointed to the back of the shop, with his cocked thumb.

Billy picked up the clothes and shoes and headed back to the changing room. He quickly changed into the new gear and returned to the front of the shop, put his suit and shirt into the bag with the rest of the purchases, paid the salesman and quickly left. Billy had also placed the Manila envelope inside the bag too.

He was feeling hungry and walked to a nearby cafe. He ordered a full all-day English breakfast with extra toast and a pot of tea. The next thing he needed was a base. He figured the best option at the moment would be to find a quiet inconspicuous bed and breakfast place. Somewhere off the seafront and one that didn't have a bar so that it would not attract passing trade.

Billy found an ideal place an hour later as he walked along a quiet avenue.

The Seaview guesthouse was a large, but very quaint detached Victorian building, with a red brick exterior. Billy rang the doorbell and waited. He could hear some sounds coming from inside, the usual hustle and bustle of people on the phone, guests chatting together, he assumed the voices were coming from the dining room, perhaps lunch was still being served.

The door was opened by a friendly-looking grey-haired man in his fifties.

"Good afternoon, can I help you?" the man asked Billy.

"Hi, yeah I'm looking for a room for a couple of nights, maybe three or four, not too sure yet," Billy said.

"Well you have come to the right place then, please come in". Th e man said and stepped aside for Billy to enter.

The place was spotlessly clean and tidy, it smelled of citrus air freshener and had a very welcoming ambience. Billy put the bag down and walked to the reception desk.

"Okay, we have a single or double available, what will it be?" asked the man.

"I will take the double please, make it three nights, I should know my plans better by then" Billy answered.

"Ok, that will be seventy-five pounds please Mr ...?" The grey-haired man let the sentence hang in the air.

"Murray - Richard Murray," Billy answered.

"Ok Mr Murray, room seven left at the top of the stairs. The front door is locked at midnight, no exceptions I'm afraid. Room service up until ten o'clock please order before nine-thirty if you need anything, you will find a menu in your room, will you be needing a newspaper for the morning?" The grey-haired man asked.

"No that's fine thank you" Billy replied.

"Breakfast is from seven o'clock until ten-thirty, and dinner is from seven pm until ten, is there anything else I can help you with Mr Murray?" The grey-haired man handed Billy a key with an oversized key fob attached to it.

"No, everything is fine, thanks again" Billy replied.

"In that case, please enjoy your stay with us, if you need anything there is always somebody close to reception".

Billy picked up the gym bag and started up the stairs. Room seven was as clean and well kept as the rest of the building. The bed was freshly made up and the corner of the top quilt turned down. A television, side tables either side of the bed and a small dining table with two chairs completed the furniture. The ensuite bathroom was clean and supplied with the usual complimentary toiletries, of shampoo, shower gel and a small tablet of soap.

Billy threw the bag on the bed, removed his jacket and hung it inside the fitted wardrobe. He lay on the bed, his mind still whirring at the day's events, a surreal quality as if he was a spectator watching the whole episode unfold before his eyes. He knew one thing for certain he had to plan his next move very carefully, he could not put Simone in any danger. His best guess - his only guess, was that Christy Monaghan would still be looking for him and this morning was just the start. Both Paddy and Tommy were dead and Billy believed that Jimmy Walsh had something to do with that. He had sworn revenge on everyone who had testified against him. Billy did not intend to end up the same way, dead at the hands of Jimmy Walsh, of that he was certain.

After another restless night of fitful sleep, Billy knew he had to pluck up the courage to go and see Simone. He had thought of phoning her but didn't want to give her the chance of just hanging up. If that happened, he would not get the opportunity to explain everything to her. The conversation had to be face to face, as much as he was dreading the meeting. He still couldn't quite believe how much he was looking forward to seeing Simone. He had thought about this day ever since the last time he had seen her, he had rehearsed what he would say a hundred times or more since his release yesterday, and today he would finally get to say it, he just hoped and prayed it would be enough.

Billy was up early enough for breakfast and thought about going down to the dining room to eat. He switched on the TV and watched the early morning news, just switching between channels. With hunger finally getting the better of him he decided to go down to the dining room to eat.

The dining room was fairly busy, maybe ten or a dozen people scattered around enjoying their breakfast, reading papers and just chatting to friends or family, there was a radio playing somewhere in the background. *The Pogues* and *Kirsty McCall* singing *A Fairytale of New York*. A large Christmas tree in the bay window of the dining room gave a warm and inviting welcome. This made a pleasant change from the dining room at Swaleside prison that had become Billy's routine over the past eighteen months or so. There was a buffet breakfast table laid out with sliced meats, cheese, tomatoes and cucumbers, yoghurts and the usual tea, coffee and various juices to hand, a bakery table offering different types of bread and pastries completed the spread. A young lady came from the kitchen and greeted Billy warmly as he took a seat. She wore the uniform of an old fashioned tea house waitress, black pinafore dress with a white apron, which was both popular and very smart especially in bed and breakfasts the length and breadth of Britain. She wore her shoulder-length blonde hair pulled back in a ponytail and disarmed Billy with a beautiful smile on her pretty face, showing off perfectly straight white teeth.

"Good morning Sir, would you like the full English breakfast or can I offer you poached eggs with haddock?" the young lady asked.

"As much as I love haddock sweetheart, not even the cats in London eat fish before lunchtime, Billy said, the full English sounds great though, thank you".

Billy took his time over his breakfast, going through the plan in his mind. He would go to the salon and wait for Simone to show up outside, he didn't want to go to her door, not knowing what her domestic situation was at the moment. What if she had a man in her life and he answered the door? What if she didn't live anymore? What if - what if? The same multitude of questions filled Billy's thoughts. There was only one way to find out for sure and that was to go there and front it out.

Billy went back to his room, picked up the bag containing the cash and documents and threw it over his shoulder, he locked the door of his room as left and made his way downstairs stopping to give the key to the same man at the reception desk that he had met yesterday.

"Good morning Mr Murray, how are you today? Will you be wanting lunch or dinner with us today?" The reception man asked.

"Err, I don't think so thank you, I hadn't thought as far ahead as dinner yet, but no lunch for sure thanks again," Billy said as he moved towards the door.

Billy left the guesthouse and walked to the end of the street, it was just before nine o'clock, the morning was dull and grey again with the same bitter wind blowing. Billy carried on walking until he saw a taxi coming towards him, he put out his hand to flag it down and jumped in the backseat after it had come to a stop.

"Where to mate?" the taxi driver asked.

"There's a beauty salon on the seafront not far from Dreamland mate, I need to go there please"

"No problem" the taxi driver answered.

The seafront wasn't far at all from the guesthouse and after about three minutes they were by the Dreamland Amusement Park, the salon was about five hundred yards along the road from there. As they were approaching Billy saw the blue Granada that had followed him yesterday parked outside Simone's place.

"Fuck," Billy said aloud.

"Everything ok mate?" the taxi driver asked.

"Yeah no problem, Billy said, just seen someone I don't want to talk to just keep going please about another five hundred yards will do thanks"

Further along the seafront, the taxi pulled into the curb.

"Ok here mate?"

"Yeah great" Billy answered handing the taxi driver two one-pound notes, keep the change"

"Thanks, mate, good luck"

Billy crossed the road to the beachside of the promenade. He saw a row of coin-operated seaside telescopes mounted on the pavement and fished in his pocket for loose change. He found a ten pence piece and dropped it in the coin box. He spun the telescope around and looked along the promenade.

Billy watched Simone's building through the seafront telescope some five hundred yards away. The blue Granada was definitely the same car that had followed him yesterday. Christy Monaghan wasn't one of the occupants this time. There was a guy he thought he recognised but wasn't sure, he couldn't place him. What the fuck? Riordan really does want me dead Billy thought to himself?

Movement! The door to Simone's flat opened and Simone stepped out into view. Billy caught his breath, she was just as beautiful as he remembered her, even more so. Billy's heart quickened as he stared through the telescope at Simone, her long blond hair partially covered with a light blue beret matching the scarf she was wearing with a knee-length brown leather coat. Simone half crouched back inside the doorway for a split second.

Simone pulled a child's stroller out through the doorway. The child was maybe between nine and fifteen months old, Billy really had no idea, he was useless at guessing ages, especially children. Billy's heart sank, Simone had found somebody new after all. How on earth could he have been so stupid? Why had he not written to her? What on earth possessed him to think this beautiful woman would wait for him after he had just disappeared from her life without a trace. Billy felt the tears burning in his eyes, his throat was dry, the anger he could feel welling up inside was directed at himself and his own stupidity, not at any relationship that Simone might be involved in, she was in no way beholden to Billy since he had done an impersonation of Captain Oates and disappeared from her life.

The door of the blue Granada opened and the two men approached Simone. There was a brief conversation not more than thirty seconds in total. Simone went to leave, one of the men grabbed her arm. Simone jerked free and pulled away. She walked quickly along the promenade. The two men returned to the car and climbed inside. A couple of seconds later it pulled away from the curb in the opposite direction from Simone, right towards Billy.

Billy swivelled around scanning the seemingly endless empty sea through the telescope until the car passed him by. Neither of the occupants had noticed him, and the car was soon out of sight.

Billy had to accept that Simone had a new life now, one that didn't include him. She was a mother of a child, and somewhere there was possibly a husband, but most certainly the child's father. Billy knew he had no right to invade her life now, even without the added complications of her family he knew he would be putting her in danger.

Whoever those people in the blue Granada were, they were working for Riordan and they were not going to give up on coming after him. They were working for Riordan and he would want a result? He knew what he had to do. He had to run far and he had to move fast.

Billy looked up to dark skies sadly, he knew what he had to do, he had to leave Simone. He had to give up the only woman he had ever loved because if he didn't he could be putting her and her child in the gravest of danger.

Billy turned to look in the direction that Simone had taken - but she was gone. There was no sign of her, he wanted to run after her and throw himself at her feet and beg her forgiveness, plead with her to take him back, he would raise the child as if it were his own flesh and blood. He could convince her, he was sure of that, he loved her, and he was sure she still loved him. Billy started to run after Simone. He had only gone about a hundred yards along the promenade when he realized the true horror of what he was about to do. He stopped dead in his tracks, bent over from the exertion of the sprint. Billy fell to his knees, his head bent forward, the silent tears falling from his eyes in a steady drip, all at once he had that crystalline moment of clarity, he could not do this. He was on the run - people wanted to kill him, people wanted him dead, how could he ask Simone to get involved in that life if he truly loved her, it would be a purely self-serving act and nothing more, if he truly loved her - which he did, he had to let her go - he had to leave - and he had to leave now.

Billy rose to his feet, in his haste to run after Simone he realised he had left his bag with everything he owned in the world contained within it on the ground by the telescope. He turned, to his relief the bag was still there. Billy walked briskly back to the telescope where the bag lounged against the metal stand. He picked it up, looked around, wiped both of his eyes with the back of his hands, took a deep breath and walked to the edge of the pavement. Billy looked up and down the road, decided to turn left, as luck would have it a taxi cab was coming in his direction, Billy raised his arm and the taxi pulled into the curb.

"Where are you going, mate?" The taxi driver asked.

"I honestly don't know," Billy replied.

The sound of the music playing on the car radio made Billy fall even deeper into despair if that was at all possible. The sound of The Human League singing their hit song Human filled the car.

"Just take me to Ramsgate please mate - seems as good a place as any right now, but stop by the Seaview Guesthouse first". Billy said.

As Billy made his way towards Ramsgate in the taxi cab, Simone Dawson walked towards the town centre of Margate, her tears fell silently as she walked, the cold wind biting her flushed cheeks. Her eighteen-month-old baby son slept in the stroller she pushed along in front of her.

What did those men want? Why are they bothering her about Billy now? How did they even know about her and Billy? One of the men, the one with the Liverpudlian accent had forced a piece of paper into Simone's hand, he had told her there was a phone number on it, she should call it if she really didn't know where Billy was. She could find out from this phone number. Just call the number, the man who answers the phone will know where Billy is, and what has happened to him. Simone remembered the last thing the man had said to her, as he looked at her baby son in the stroller.

" And when he tells you, you can tell me blondie, we wouldn't want anything happening to the little fella now would we?" He had said to her threateningly.

Simone stopped still in her tracks, her shoulders heaved as she openly sobbed, her head bowed as she remembered the last time she had seen Billy that Sunday morning in October 1983. He had told her he loved her, he had told that he had wanted a life with her, she had been so excited that week waiting for him to return the following Thursday night, she had arranged for them to see the houses she had made appointments with the estate agents - why had he left her - what had she done that was so wrong? Simone knew she had never done anything to hurt Billy, all she ever did was love him - now just when she thought she was over the worst of it these men turned up and brought all these feelings and emotions flooding back to her.

Simone pulled herself together, she looked at her baby boy sleeping peacefully in the stroller, the tears still stinging her eyes.

Deep in her heart, Simone knew that Billy Kelly had loved her, he wasn't that good of an actor so as to make her feel the way he did without meaning it. The way he had looked at her, the memory of the gentleness of his fingers against her cheek or in her hair. The time she awoke to find Billy just staring at her as he leaned on one elbow, the embarrassment she could remember on his face and how his cheeks reddened when she had caught him. Simone knew that something bad had happened to stop Billy's return to her, she had always known that Billy was involved in something dangerous, but she never asked, she really didn't care, just as long as they were together, she would never ask anything about his work. But all at once, it had hit her. The fact that she actually knew nothing at all about Billy. She didn't know his address, she didn't know his home phone number, she knew absolutely nothing about him other than that he lived in London and he had a car, a car to which she didn't even know the registration number, make, or model.

Simone knew that she had to find out what had happened to Billy. As much as she had tried to forget him over the past years, and she had in some ways come to terms with his abandonment and rejection of her, she knew that for the sake of her sanity it was the right thing to do. As much as Simone had lied to herself over the past three years she also knew she still loved Billy more than life itself, and his memory would never leave her - not all the while she had their baby boy to remind her of him.

Chapter 17

Margate 1987

Simone sat on her sofa and stared at the piece of paper with the phone number written on it for the umpteenth time. A London number obviously, given the intercity dialling code. She picked up the phone and dialled the number.

Nearby in the Moses crib, her baby stirred and Simone glanced anxiously at the sleeping child, he just smiled happily in his slumber and settled back down.

A man's voice answered the phone.

"Hello," he said.

Simone stayed quiet, just listening. The voice spoke again.

"Son is that you? the man asked, talk to me Billy - please talk to me please Billy, tell me where you are".

Simone replaced the phone gently in its cradle, shocked at realizing who was on the other end of the line. It must have been Billy's father. She also realized that something must have gone wrong, because Billy had only ever spoken of his father with love and respect, why would Billy's father not know where he was. The other thing that Simone knew she had to do was to call back.

Simone picked up the phone again and re-dialled. The call was answered almost at once.

"Billy, where are you son, tell me?" Michael Kelly asked again.

"Hello, Mr Kelly, Simone said, my name is Simone Dawson, I'm a friend of Billy's. I need to speak to you".

Michael Kelly was surprised by the woman's voice on the line.

"What - who's this? I don't know what you are talking about, who are you? Do you work for the papers? I've told your lot before I don't want anything to do with you". Michael said.

"No Mr Kelly, my name is Simone I need to see Billy, some men came looking for him at my place today, they gave me this number, I was Billy's girlfriend," Simone said.

"I'm sorry I don't know what you are talking about, Billy never mentioned anyone named Simone to me and I haven't seen Billy for quite some time now, so I'm sorry I can't help you, now please don't call here again miss, I can't help you". Michael said.

"Please Mr Kelly I need to meet you; I have to know what happened to Billy - he left me you see - he just left me. I know he loved me - why would he just leave me that way please help me to understand?" Simone said her voice cracking with emotion as she recalled again her last time with Billy.

"He left my flat in Margate on the morning of Sunday, October 14, 1983, and I haven't heard from him since, we were in love Mr Kelly Billy loved me. I know he did and I loved him too. We were going to have a life together; he wouldn't just have left me. Please tell me what happened - I need to know". Simone said, the tears now flowing freely as she spoke.

Something touched the heart of Michael Kelly as he listened to this young lady speak to him with a genuineness of pleading for the truth to be told. He could detect in her soft well-spoken voice that this young lady knew his son and had loved him. Simone was now crying on the other end of the line. Michael wiped a tear from his eye, somebody else had loved his boy too. Why had Billy never mentioned Simone to him? They were close, he could have told me. Michael remembered the date only too well that Simone had mentioned, it was the day that Jimmy Walsh had shot dead those two Turkish men in Islington, the day that Jimmy, Billy and the other boys were arrested, and the start of this nightmare, Michael remembered the day only too well.

"What did you say your name was a miss?" Michael asked, his voice softer now.

"It's Simone Dawson Mr Kelly, I really need to know where Billy is - I know you don't seem to know either, but it's really important he knows I'm still here for him. I still love him - Mr Kelly I don't care what he's done, even if he doesn't want me - I need Billy to tell me himself if he's married I will understand - Simone said. The tears, still falling from her blue eyes, now reddened and puffy from the strain of the day's events.

"No - no Simone - Billy's not married for sure," Michael said.

A gulp and a half laugh emanated from Simone's throat as she heard this statement from Billy's father, a sigh of relief followed, but the tears didn't stop.

"Where did you say you lived, Simone?" Michael asked.

"I live in Margate, I met Billy here in July 1983, he was here for a couple of days celebrating a win or something a friend of his had had. I don't know what he won, his name was Jimmy, he had ginger hair, that's all I remember about him. Billy and I kept on seeing each other after that, he came down here most weekends to see me, but that last time he was here, he said he had an important meeting to go to with Jimmy and some big boss in London. He was supposed to come down here on the following Thursday but I never saw him again. I didn't have a contact number until these two men came by yesterday and started asking me questions about Billy, they said they were friends of his and wanted to catch up with him, I knew that was rubbish, if they were Billy's friends they would know he's not been here" Simone blurted out, hardly stopping to take a breath.

The relief Simone felt was palpable, just speaking with his father somehow made her feel closer to Billy. Simone felt an inner peace she had not felt since the last time she had seen Billy.

Michael Kelly listened intently to Simone and now knew she was not faking the emotional connection she had had with his son. They were after all a kindred spirit, both searching for answers, and both in some way grieving the loss of a loved one. Michael knew that he wanted to meet Simone, she seemed well-spoken, polite and very genuine indeed, he was sure he would like this young lady and was keen to hear of her time with Billy. If Billy had loved her she must be somebody special.

"Could I come down to meet you in Margate Simone?" Michael asked, hoping she would accept his offer.

Simone sobbed again and giggled at the same time. This man was indeed his son's father - Simone could hear the same softness and compassion in his voice.

"We would love to meet you, Mr Kelly," Simone said.

"We - I don't understand Simone," Michael replied.

"Yes we - You have a grandson Mr Kelly - Billy Junior, he looks just like his dad, Simone said, he's eighteen months old now,".

Michael sat down straight into the chair beside the small telephone table, it was now his turn for his eyes to fill with tears. He had a grandson, Billy was a father and knew nothing of it. Simone deserved to know the truth, right from the beginning.

"Oh Dear Lord Simone that's wonderful, Michael said, that's wonderful, eighteen-months old you say…" Michael was doing the mental arithmetic, his heart sank. Billy must have known and had not mentioned anything to his father, what was this? Then he doesn't get in touch with this lovely girl throughout his time in prison.

"Billy didn't know I was pregnant, I was going to tell him on that Thursday night I was expecting him back in Margate, but I never saw him or heard from him again," Simone said sadly.

Michael sighed, his mind racing. He had to get down to Margate as soon as possible to meet his new family. A family he never knew he had, a family that he so desperately needed in his lonely life since his only son had gone away. Michael had a grandson, his heart was so full of love and sorrow for both Simone and his grandson at that precise moment in time. How must Simone have felt during those terrible times when she thought that Billy had abandoned her, had she cried herself to sleep holding Billy's son to her breast? Praying to God that his father would come back to them, or had she cursed his existence and rued the day that their paths had ever crossed. Having spoken with this extraordinary girl on the phone Michael didn't believe that Simone would be able to harbour those feelings against the man she still so clearly cherished, she was just a lonely young girl, a young mother looking for some answers, and Michael would do her the courtesy of providing them.

*****

Billy's father, Michael Kelly, was seventy-four years of age when he had passed a week ago, finally succumbing to a two-year-long fight with lung cancer. Michael had been a smoker since he was a fourteen-year-old boy back in County Limerick in the Republic of Ireland. He had had little schooling choosing to work for a living from an early age to support his mother, and help take care of his sick father, who also died from cancer at a much younger age than his son. His father had been bedridden for the last two years of his life, and with Michael's mother working two jobs to make ends meet, Michael stepped into his father's role helping his mother with his five younger siblings while working as a general labourer at a nearby farm to bring in a much-needed wage. Michael was the eldest of the six, with three sisters and two brothers, he would rise early as his mother was about to leave for her first job of the day at the local bakery.

Michael would prepare his father's breakfast of tea and porridge when he woke, usually before the children were up. The children would then get ready for the school under Michael's supervision. Once the children were ready Michael would then run the mile or so to the local farm to start his day's work. Michael was a happy boy, he didn't see what he was doing as anything other than his duty as a son and elder brother, and enjoyed his life as much as he could. He had left Ireland at the age of nineteen when the children were that much older and could help their mother more, his father had since passed away when Michael was seventeen, two years earlier. Michael kissed his mother, brothers and sisters goodbye that day and had set off to Dublin to catch the boat from Dun Laoghaire to Holyhead on The Isle of Anglesey in Wales, and then to catch the boat train to London, Euston station.

Michael had easily managed to find work with the help of the London Irish communities as a labourer on the many construction and road building sites in and around the capital. Work was plentiful, the wages were good and Michael found digs with an Irish family who had taken him in as one of their own. Michael continued to support his family up until five years later when his mother had died suddenly, this was the only time Michael had ever returned to Ireland. After the funeral and his mother had been laid to rest in the small cemetery next to her husband's plot, Michael left Ireland again this time never to return. He took with him his two brothers and youngest sister. The other two sisters had decided to stay in Ireland as they had lives of their own and romantic ties to pursue. Michael returned to London where he found a small flat to rent for himself and his family. He found work for his brothers in the same construction company, while his sister acted as a surrogate mother to her three elder brothers.

Michael had always been a steady, responsible young man, as his siblings already knew, and they were all very grateful and held great respect for Michael's sacrifices and support over the years. With three wage packets now coming into the household on a weekly basis and with Michaels eye for the future firmly on his family's well being he had started saving money to get the family out of the small dwelling they currently occupied. A year later Michael had achieved his aim, and they were able to move to a rented house with three bedrooms, in a better area of South London. Three years later Michael had saved enough money to put down a deposit on the property and arrange the finance to buy it. This was the house that he had owned all his life and the only home he had known since his return from Ireland, this the same family home bequeathed to his only son Billy in his last will and testament.

*****

Michael Kelly had caught the train to Margate from London Victoria at just after nine o'clock that morning. The train was fast to Bromley South and Chatham and then would call at all stops along the M2 corridor to Ramsgate.

Michael had hardly slept the two nights since his phone conversation with Simone Dawson and the revelations that he has a grandson, the fact that his son Billy was not aware of the child or that he was a father was a source of both sadness and joy to him. The joy part was obviously the fact that Billy did have a son, a son to carry on the family name, the sadness he felt was that given the circumstances Billy might not ever see or hold his son the way Michael had held Billy.

The bag that Michael clutched on his lap contained among other travel necessities a photo album with pictures from Billy's childhood. Photographs of Billy with his mother at the seaside, with his father as he rode a donkey along the beach, birthday parties with friends and relatives, his first communion, his confirmation and of course Christmas at home and many other happy occasions. Michael wanted to give this album to Simone for their son Billy Junior. It seemed the least that he could do, he wanted the little boy to know he had a father, a father who would have loved him the same way his grandfather did - if only he had had that same opportunity.

Inwardly Michael was very nervous about meeting Simone, it was a very surreal experience to have learned the way he did of her existence and that of the child. The nervousness came from knowing that Simone might think that this was the beginning of a great fairy tale, whereby Billy would be coming back into her life and everything would be fine from this point forward. Michael knew in his heart that even if he did know where Billy was he would never tell another living soul. The fact that he didn't know, just made it easier. He dreaded having to tell Simone that Billy could never come back again, that his life was to be that of a fugitive, not from justice, but from the murderous revenge of his boyhood friend Jimmy Walsh. The sickening feelings Michael had felt in his stomach when he had read the accounts of the murders of Tommy Callaghan and Paddy Meehan were horrendous. The lives of those two young men that Michael had known since their childhood days at school with Billy, snuffed out with the most brutal and vicious crimes imaginable, the callousness of the murders made his blood run cold. To think that his son would someday have to face those same consequences was something that he could never come to terms with.

The train slowed to a halt at Chatham station, Michael looked out the window, to his left he could see red painted doors of the fire station beneath the viaduct, the arched tunnel that led directly down to Chatham Town Hall, and the road above that ran towards Rochester and Strood to the North and Gillingham and Rainham to the South.

Michael closed his eyes and said a silent prayer for his son Billy, may the good Lord keep and preserve him. The next time Michael's eyes opened the train was pulling away from Whitstable station, it wouldn't be long now and he would be meeting his grandson and his - what exactly was Simone to Michael? Sure if she had been married to Billy then a daughter-in-law for sure, but this was quite a unique situation. He didn't really care too much for labels, he just thanked God that Simone and Billy Junior had come into his life.

When Michael had asked Simone where he was to meet her, and how he was to recognize her, she had giggled down the phone line to him.

"I will be the blonde with the blue and white striped baby stroller outside Margate station, if there are two by any chance - I will be the happiest one" Simone had said.

That simple statement told Michael a lot about the character of the young lady that was mother to his grandson, she had substance, she genuinely was looking to reconnect with Billy on any level, and Michael knew the truth about his son was going to hurt this poor girl, possibly more than she had ever been hurt before.

The train pulled into Margate station and stopped. Michael climbed from the carriage, slammed the door shut behind and walked to the ticket barrier, he passed through handing the outward bound ticket to the collector.

Michael walked outside the station, his eyes scanning the landscape. There they were, Simone and Billy Junior. Michael looked at Simone, she truly was a beautiful woman. Billy had chosen well.

Michael walked towards them, a smile on his face, Simone's face was lit up with a beaming smile. Michael held out his hand for Simone to shake hands. Simone threw her arms around Michael's neck and held him tight, a small sob of happiness in her throat. Michael shyly embraced her, his hand patting her back to comfort her. For the second time in a few years, a Kelly man had been totally captivated by this beautiful young lady.

After a couple of awkward moments, Michael bent down to the stroller and looked at Billy Junior. He could see his Billy so clearly in the eyes of his grandson. Micahel thoughts drifted back to a time many years before, Billy in the garden, Michael picked him up and kissed his cheek...

He leaned forward and whispered *"Ah Macushla"* in Billy Junior's ear, kissing him on the cheek, he stroked the toddler's face and stood up again. Billy Junior smiled and giggled as he looked at Simone, as he grabbed his grandad's hair.

"He's a fine boy Simone, Michael said, he really is a credit to you, thank you for taking such great care of him".

Simone just smiled instead of speaking any answer, there was no need for words.

Michael, Simone and Billy Junior, now sleeping in his stroller, made their way the short distance to the promenade on Margate seafront to Simone's flat. As they arrived Simone pushed open the door to the salon, she called inside to one of the girls that she would be upstairs if they needed her.

"Do you work here too Simone, that's handy?" Michael asked.

"I'm actually the owner Mr Kelly, the flat and the business, Simone said, I started the salon a couple of years before I met Billy, and it's been quite successful".

"Oh my, that's very impressive Simone, Michael said with a smile, and listen, love, please call me Michael - after all, we are family".

"Ok - Michael" Simone nodded her head shyly.

Simone made tea and sandwiches for a quick lunch, she explained that she had wanted to cook something but didn't want to take a chance that Michael might not like what she would prepare, and decided to play it safe, anyway, she would be happy to cook dinner, and he was very welcome to stay if he was in no rush to get back to London.

Michael accepted her kind invitation and settled back in his seat.

"Simone, I don't know how much you know of Billy's life since you last saw him, I'm guessing you know absolutely nothing," Michael said.

"Nothing at all, I just assumed he didn't want me, Simone lowered her head, I had come to terms with that thought, I knew I was pregnant the morning he left here, but as I told you, I was keeping it as a surprise for when he came back the following Thursday. I had cooked a meal and I wanted to tell him so bad - but I never got the chance" Simone said sadly.

"Ok love - this is not going to be easy to tell you, you seem such a lovely girl. I hate to hurt you the way I know I'm going to have to when I tell you the story of why Billy had to disappear, and why I never want to see him in London again" Michael said.

Michael began to tell Simone of the terrible events that had led to Billy being jailed as a conspirator to the two murders of Arda Arslan and Hamza Yilmaz, albeit on a reduced sentence for turning Queen's evidence against his friend Jimmy Walsh. The threats Jimmy had made as he was sentenced to twenty-two years in prison at the Old Bailey, the subsequent murders of Tommy Callaghan and Paddy Meehan, one carried out in Scotland and the other as far away as Tenerife, in the Canary Islands off the coast of West Africa. How Michael had walked away from Billy that day in the cells at the Old Bailey, telling him to keep moving, to never come back to London because Jimmy would have him killed. He told her how the police would not even tell him where Billy was serving his sentence and that he wouldn't be able to visit him, and Billy wouldn't be able to even call him. Michael was told to trust nobody, he needed to be alert all the time, even if Billy wrote to him he was to burn the letters after he had read them, for fear of someone finding them. In short, there would not be any further contact with his son Billy ever again.

Simone sat transfixed as she listened to Michael tell the tale, occasionally tears would fill her eyes, but she didn't let them fall, she would just dab at her eyes with the corner of a handkerchief. Simone realized that the further Michael went with this story that Billy could never come back home to see his father, he could never come to Margate to see her. Billy just had to disappear and that's what he had done. The men that came here were proof enough that they were still looking for him, and if further proof was needed of what they intended to do to him, then you needed to look no further than the murders of Tommy Callaghan and Paddy Meehan.

As Michael finished telling the story to Simone he looked deep into her tear-filled eyes, she looked broken and lost. Any hope she may have held that meeting Michael was the first step to her finding Billy and being reunited with him had been torn away. She knew now in her heart of hearts that she was never going to see Billy again, and Billy Junior was never going to have the opportunity to meet his father.

"I just love him so much you know, Simone said, I was angry for a long time, but I never stopped loving Billy".

"I know you do Simone, Michael said with sadness and hurt in his eyes, so do I, we just have to be strong, you especially for the beautiful little lad".

"Oh Michael, Simone said getting up from her seat and going to him and taking his hands, you must miss him so much too,".

"I do, Michael said as they hugged each other and wept, but I have you two now, and we will make the best of it, I'm here for you both as long as you need me"

"Yes, Simone said, we are family after all".

Chapter 18

As the taxi arrived at the port of Ramsgate Billy didn't know what it was he wanted to do, or indeed where he wanted to go. He had passed by the Seaview Guesthouse and picked up the rest of his possessions, such as they were and placed them into the sports bag.

He looked around at the options open to him. France and the continent of Europe were just a few hours or less away depending on his choice of destination, he had a passport, was that a realistic option though? The thought of having to learn a new language was quite daunting to him if he went abroad, but then again it would be the same if he decided to head up north!

Billy waited a few minutes more just gathering his thoughts, stark reality struck him now that he really was alone in the world, there was nobody around to ask advice and nobody to share an opinion with. Concentrating on the positives, he really could please himself and move to wherever he felt comfortable and safe. He could move at his own pace.

Billy knew that going to the continent was not really a viable option, but given his geographical situation right now the only way he could travel anywhere else other than going west was by going back to London or taking a major detour all along the coast on a boat. The most realistic option would mean travelling by bus or train. Going back to London was not something he could consider so the only real plan of action was to move carefully and think this thing through thoroughly.

The bus plan looked the best bet. Billy went to the bus station and booked a ticket along the coast to Brighton in Sussex, after that he planned to get a bus or train to Southampton in Hampshire and then further west into Exeter or possibly Plymouth which were both in Devon.

The next few weeks saw Billy continue his quest towards the West Country. He stayed at a number of bed and breakfast places and gradually thought about settling somewhere, the money was not going to last forever and he had gone through a fair amount of the cash he was given. He knew he really needed to find a room or a small flat to rent and start to live as normal a life as was possible. The drain on the cash resources was compounded by eating all his meals in cafes or in the bed and breakfast accommodations, he knew also that he needed employment.

Billy had stopped in Plymouth and had been there for the past six days. Plymouth was a traditional naval and dockyard town steeped in maritime history. Plymouth is also where the Mayflower had set sail for New World in 1620 and this historical event has been commemorated by the Mayflower Steps. Billy quite liked the Barbican district with its quaint narrow cobbled streets and the Sutton Harbour area with its modern marinas, fresh sea breezes and fish markets, the smell of which reminded him of Billingsgate, but that apart, it was all a far cry from the concrete and carbon monoxide of South London.

All in all, Billy had taken a real liking to Plymouth, he decided to stay a while longer, he was sure he could get used to the strange accents after a while, now he just needed to find a job. Having a new identity and a clean driving licence, and given Billy's lack of qualifications, work as a driver seemed to be the obvious and least difficult option.

He had moved around from job to job at first, a couple of months here a couple of months there, he worked any number of places to make rent money, a delivery driver for a supermarket, security guard, short-order cook in a pub in The Barbican district but he never settled anywhere. Always looking over his shoulder, he could never fully trust anyone, he became paranoid and reclusive, he drank too much, didn't eat right and put on weight, in short, he was a mess.

He lived this way for a number of years, but Plymouth had become his home, and he was content being there. He was living in a house that could only be described as one level better than a doss house. Shared accommodation with other like-minded drunks and assorted addicts, he had his own room and bathroom in the modified house that had been split into five flats. Life on the run wasn't easy, and unless he changed things quickly, it was only going to go one way - downwards.

He wanted so much to contact his dad, one of only two people in the world that he cared about, Simone being the other. The loneliness and isolation he felt at times were the single hardest thing to come to terms with. His solitary existence in a world he never expected to inhabit was so alien to him that he wondered if sometimes it was all just a nightmare that he would someday awaken from.

Then out of the blue one day whilst walking past a gym Billy suddenly felt the urge to get his life back into some semblance of order. He went inside, took out a monthly membership and worked hard to get himself back into shape. After three months he had succeeded. He had stopped smoking, he wasn't drinking, he was eating well. Ten pounds lighter and hard muscle now replacing soft flab Billy felt he needed to get a proper job. He had been talking to a couple of cab drivers at the gym who had offered him an opportunity to start working with the minicab firm they owned.

Billy jumped at the opportunity and took to the day to day task of chauffeuring the good people of Plymouth around with a renewed energy and zest for life. As the years passed by Billy came to believe that this was as good as life was ever going to get for him, he made casual friends, he had casual relationships with women, nothing ever lasted, he still loved Simone and nobody was ever going to replace her. Nothing he felt for any other woman would ever change those feelings. He still believed in the miracle that one day this self-imposed exile would end and that he would return to a normal life where he would win back Simone from whomever he had to win her back from and live happily ever after. No doubt after giving the villain of the piece a damn good thrashing and riding off into the sunset on a white charger. Those thoughts never lasted long. The realist in Billy was far stronger than the fantasist, he embraced the futility of his dreams as one would a constant and irritating internal guide. The guidance far outweighed the irritation, and as such offered the better advice and had to be obeyed.

This wasn't the life Billy Kelly had envisaged for himself on that bright autumn morning in Margate back in 1983 as he waved goodbye to Simone, for what turned out to be the last time. He had replayed his life many times through the video recorder of his mind.

The poor choices he had made and wished he could delete. The happy times to which he wished he could rewind, and what of the uncertainty of his future? The finger of his minds-eye was always hovering, trembling above the fast forward button of his life, but never engaged the control that he knew could spin him off his axis.

He had wondered in those pre-epiphany darkest times of his alcohol sodden life if these thoughts were suicidal tendencies. He had to wonder because he had never consciously or seriously contemplated committing suicide.

When the alcohol-induced demons surfaced when his skin felt like it was crawling alive with the infestation of insects. When his hands were swiping the air to fend off imaginary attacks from invisible winged invaders that buzzed in his ears. When the lizards and other reptilian creatures appeared, darting across the walls and floors just enough for him to glimpse them in his peripheral vision, but never lingering long enough for him to catch them.

They would all lay in wait for him, to ambush him and torment him in the silent hours when the night terrors would take over. The paralysis that gripped him as he watched the door slowly opening to the intruder that never showed himself, the voice in his head that screamed at him while his own screams of anguish died an embryonic death in his throat, never to be heard by any potential saviour.

Salvation would come eventually, in the form of daybreak. His tormentors would retreat from the light to whence they came. He would awake with a start, sweat and piss soaked sheets and the delirium tremens wracking his body as he struggled to control his emotions. He catches sight of his reflection in the mirror and wonders if he knows the wretch staring back at him, the pale skin, the unshaven face and unkempt hair, he looks familiar like someone he used to know, but he's not sure if this is the same man he thought it was. This cycle wouldn't break; it would be the same again today. One drink was too many, twenty-one was never enough.

He often wondered if the constant self-abuse he inflicted upon his body through the plethora of bad habits he was addicted to were just an ongoing punishment in lieu of that final act of suicide. The ceaseless consumption of alcohol, the smoking and the junk food binges, then the days that sometimes turned into a week without eating anything at all. Combining all this behaviour with the self-loathing and guilt that inevitably followed, were they, in fact, nothing more than the external manifestations of his own internal conflict? Was he just too afraid to end his own miserable existence?

What Billy had discovered that morning of his epiphany when he had decided to change his life for the better, was that all these feelings were relevant, or totally irrelevant, depending on your state of mind. If you looked good, felt good and were healthy the world was a better place, a positive frame of mind was the compulsory accessory that accompanied this mindset. Whereas the polar opposites when applied, would give you a negative outlook on the same surroundings that would blind you to the good around you, and the opportunity to be at peace with yourself.

Billy knew at that juncture of his life, he had to choose one of two paths. Path one was the life he wanted to discipline himself to adhere to. Eating properly and sleeping well, working out to maintain a healthy lifestyle and to prolong his own good health and sanity. The other path was one of self-destruction, a path he knew only too well and wanted to get off, the path of self-pity and what would be his own choice to submerge himself into negativity and fear. This could only result in an endless inner struggle against the demons he had fought and lost to so many times before. He knew if he worked hard to overcome and vanquish them he would succeed, he needed to find the man he once was. The first step to redemption was to admit what he was and that he needed help.

That was the day that Billy realized that his spiritual health was as important as his physical and mental health. His Roman Catholic upbringing had in many ways stifled his spirituality as well as nurtured it.

The stringent Catechism classes of his junior school had robotically and systematically instilled into him the doctrine of The Holy Catholic Church. For two hours every afternoon the whole class would repeat parrot fashion, and out loud as one, the same sentences that had just been read to them by the teacher. This duty however, more often than not, was handed over to a classmate, no doubt the reason being that the teacher realised her job description didn't include cascading this mind-numbing brainwashing experience upon the minds of any unsuspecting ten-year-old child. Plus, the added bonus for the teacher was being able to immerse herself in the latest *Mills & Boon*, another type of, but no less painful form of mind control.

Just three words formed the opening question of the little green book.

"Who made you?"

The assembled class would answer.

"God made me"

The Catechism then built up the length and complexities of the questions as the book progressed, thus enhancing boredom and taking repetitive teaching to a whole new level. In later years the Catholic Church opened their eyes to the falling numbers of attendees at mass, and the rising number of lapsed Catholics, and somebody, thank God Almighty, saw the correlation of this way of teaching their beliefs to children and the downward spiral in the numbers of the Faithful. Of course, this would never be admitted, but Billy knew it, and still bore the mental scars of his childhood indoctrination.

Billy, in his later years had likened these afternoon sessions to what he assumed it had been like for the Chinese children of the day when being taught the musings of *Mao Tse-tung* and his *Little Red Book*.

However deep those mental scars were ingrained into the psyche of Billy Kelly, it wasn't enough for him to resist returning to the church and to start practicing his faith again. A spiritual calling stirred deep within him, so much so, that he started to attend mass on a regular basis of two to three times a week. He prayed more often, gave thanks for the blessings he had and turned back to God, when, like so many others before him, he realised there was nobody and nothing else to turn to.

This renaissance of his beliefs wasn't so much that he had never believed in God before. There was no flash of lightning or clap of thunder heralding a new dawn of praise and worship, it was simply a conscious decision of a man that didn't want to be alone in the world any longer and needed to believe that there was something more, a higher authority, a greater presence - a more powerful entity - one of compassion and empathy to believe in - anything other than what this earthly realm had to offer.

Now forty-six years of age his mind was far more content with his renewed beliefs, safe in the knowledge that he could now speak to someone when he was in need of spiritual direction, it somehow made the decisions he had to make in his everyday life all that much easier. He viewed the world with a less cynical eye, he tended to look for the good first in everything, maybe he had just gotten older and softer, as the ageing process tends to do to everyone, another debate no doubt for the men of science and the men of faith.

Somehow he knew that his childhood friend Father Danny Gallagher would have been pleased with this shift back towards the church, but that was something they never discussed in their brief monthly conversations.

*****

Father Danny Gallagher was an old school friend. He had not seen or spoken to Billy, at any great length, since Billy had reached out to him from Swaleside prison. Danny had been only too happy to receive the call from Billy and had arranged to see him a week later. Billy had been in prison for around three months and had subsequently learned of the deaths of his friends Tommy Callaghan and Paddy Meehan.

Billy had asked Father Danny to hear his confession. He had asked certain searching questions as to the sanctity of the confessional, and how if there were things that Billy wanted to tell him, or ask him to do, would he indeed hold those confessions or requests within the sanctity of his vows.

Father Danny had considered this and answered him truthfully. Anything that Billy told him, requested of him or confessed to him within the confessional was witnessed only by those present and God Almighty. Father Danny couldn't and wouldn't betray the sanctity of the confessional. With this knowledge, Billy made a request that he wanted Father Danny to be his only point of contact when he was released from prison. The reason for this was that after what had happened to Tommy and Paddy, Billy was convinced he was going to be killed the same way by the same people and he couldn't risk being around his father and putting him in danger.

Billy told Father Danny that he was going to disappear when he was released, that he was never going to return to London but for one thing, and that was to pay his last respects to his father if he indeed succeeded to outlive him. Billy didn't want to know anything else when he called. He would call the parish church of St. Michael's once a month around a week into each month. The call would be very short consisting of Billy asking just one question.

"Is my father still alive?"

To which Father Danny would reply just yes or no. Billy didn't want to know about anything else, it didn't matter what it was, illness, times of trouble or threats to his father's life. The best way for both of them to stay alive was for Billy to stay out of his life forever, this was not an easy decision to make, he loved his father immensely but he wouldn't put his life in danger just to see him or to try and have a long-distance relationship with him that would only endanger them both, and if Billy knew what was going on at all times he would not be able to stay away from London.

This arrangement had worked perfectly for many years; Danny had moved parishes twice in that time but the relationship carried on with the briefest of conversations updating Billy with a new contact number. That was until last week when Billy asked the question.

"Is my father still alive?"

This time the answer was different, just a solitary word as always, but in the negative.

"No" Father Danny's answer came back.

Billy's heart froze in his chest; he knew he hadn't misunderstood the answer but he asked again anyway.

"Danny is my father still alive?" Billy pleaded.

"I'm sorry Billy, he died about nine days ago, he was buried yesterday" Father Danny answered.

Billy's knees had turned to jelly, he leaned back against the glass and metal phone box wall for support. He knew this day would have to have come sometime, he just wasn't ready for it today, would he have ever been ready to accept his father had gone forever? Billy didn't think so, but now he knew he had to go back to London, go back and face whatever there was there waiting for him.

"Danny, was he alone when he died?" Billy asked.

"No Billy, I was there, I gave him the last rites" Father Danny answered.

"Thank you for that, Father," Billy said, reverting to Father Danny's title.

"He must have been so lonely in that house, I'm sorry Danny, I should have been there. I shouldn't have left him alone all those years," Billy said, his voice low now and choking back the tears.

"Billy, he wasn't in the house alone, he didn't die in London, his body was brought back from the south coast to London. He was in a private care home there, he was well looked after, as well as he could have been in the circumstances" Father Danny said.

"I don't understand Danny, what was he doing in a care home on the south coast, where on the south coast exactly? Billy asked, concerned and confused.

"It was just outside Margate, your cousin was paying for his care there, she and her son were always there for him Billy, he wasn't alone," Father Danny said.

"Danny, I don't have any cousins on the south coast, who is this woman, why was she paying for my dad's care? Billy asked.

"Your cousin Simone - Simone Dawson and her son, the boy's name is Billy too. Simone told me that she named him after you because you were so close at one time, you must know them, Billy, he's the spitting image of you…"

Father Danny audibly gasped in the realisation of the truth, the boy was Billy's son - and Billy had never known that truth.

Chapter 19

South London 2004

Jimmy Walsh had become less of a prominent figure in the London underworld since his release from prison some years ago now, he was still respected and held in high esteem by those in the London old school criminal fraternity, but things had changed in South London, and not for the better. Jimmy was living a fairly quiet life in South West London in a moderately small apartment in Battersea. Jimmy Walsh was no longer a major player. He was still a well-known face, but not actively involved in any type of criminal activity that would warrant police interest.

Jimmy was still involved in business with his good friend Tony Fallon. Fallon had stood by Jimmy throughout the sixteen years Jimmy had spent in prison, with good reason, the extra quarter of a million pounds had funded business deals that put Tony Fallon at the pinnacle of the Liverpool crime scene. It was Tony Fallon that Jimmy had turned to nine years ago when his beloved mother had died, it was Tony Fallon who had arranged everything for Jimmy, the funeral, the service and the reception afterwards. Tony Fallon had made a name for himself, enhanced his business and reputation in Liverpool and now also had some property interests in London. In the years that had passed since the Jack Riordan era, there had been a power struggle in South London, up and coming firms couldn't believe their luck back in 1983 when literally overnight, the Jack Riordan and Jimmy Walsh firm had disappeared without a trace. This left the inevitable power vacuum in the lucrative drugs, gambling and entertainment enterprises in the immediate areas that were once controlled and ruled with an iron fist by Jack Riordan, his lieutenant Christy Monaghan and the Walsh firm.

Jimmy had been allowed to attend his mother's funeral flanked by and shackled to two prison officers and guarded by six heavily armed police officers. Jimmy was allowed a brief moment with his escort at the graveside, before being swept back into the armoured prison van and taken back to Parkhurst prison, to where he had been transferred after several violent altercations in Brixton prison that had seen Jimmy put in solitary confinement for much of his time there. It was also Tony Fallon that without fail had made sure that Jimmy's mum had been looked after and he had also made sure that wherever Jimmy was being held, that transportation and accommodation were available for Mrs Walsh to be able to travel and visit her son in five-star comfort.

Tony Fallon had, in essence, become and replaced what Billy Kelly had once been, he was Jimmy's only true friend and the man he trusted with his life.

Jimmy had attended only last week the funeral of Michael Kelly, he wasn't surprised when he didn't see Billy there but he knew he would be coming soon enough. Billy wouldn't stay away, he adored his old man, he would surface and when he did, Jimmy intended to be there to greet him. Jimmy didn't know how Billy had managed to disappear so well, he wondered who had helped him. Christy Monaghan had missed his chance to kill him when Billy was released back in the late eighties, but since then he was off everyone's radar. The Old bill must have helped him, Jimmy assumed.

There were a lot of faces Jimmy recognized at the funeral of Michael Kelly. He was well-liked and respected, a solid upstanding man, who Jimmy himself had always held in the highest regard. The Kelly's were the kindest people Jimmy had ever known. He remembered attending the funeral of Mrs Kelly when she passed. Billy had been just sixteen at the time. He recalled Mr Kelly spoke very eloquently and with such love for his wife at the funeral service, he held himself with such dignity that day openly and outwardly holding Billy close to him, a protective arm around his son whenever it was required. Jimmy thought how the events of the past twenty or so years must have affected Michael Kelly, the son he loved so much ripped from his life much more cruelly than his wife had been, it must have been hard to bear. Well never mind Jimmy thought to himself, I will send him your way soon enough.

What Jimmy had seen and had taken him very much by surprise was a beautiful blonde lady accompanied by a tall young man. The young man had borne a remarkable resemblance to a young Billy Kelly.

Further enquiries had revealed that the lady was Simone Dawson and the young man her son, William Dawson-Kelly, the son of Billy Kelly and grandson of the deceased. Jimmy had immediately been able to connect the dots mentally as his mind went back to that summer in Margate in 1983, the beautiful blonde in the underground dive bar.

So Billy had missed not only his father all these years, but he had had a son by Simone that he was either unaware of, or he knew of and was just keeping away from them. Jimmy had found out further information that Simone had lived all her life in Margate, she had never married and had had only fleeting relationships over the years, nothing serious. Her life had revolved around her son and her business, which now consisted of three beauty salons on the south coast. Her son was at Canterbury University studying law. Michael Kelly had visited Simone and his grandson twice a month for the past seventeen years, he never missed the chance to go to the coast and spend time with his family until his illness had incapacitated him and made it impossible for him to travel approximately three years previously.

For the past two years, Michael Kelly had resided in a care home on the South coast. A private facility paid for by Simone Dawson. Simone had visited Michael Kelly at least three times a week at the care home, taking him for days out to her parents' home and the seaside towns along the coast. Michael had finally met Simone's parents some years previously, and despite a frosty start to their relationship in the unique circumstances, they had taken to this softly spoken Irishman and mutual respect and friendship had blossomed. Michael had spent a couple of Christmases over the years as a guest of the Dawson's.

Michael Kelly had become more than just a grandfather to her son, he was also a big part of Simone's life too and filled the void as a father figure to her son, that his own son Billy had never been given the opportunity to fulfil. Simone had never really recovered from losing Billy and the life she thought she would share with him. His father in some way partly made up for that, and she still felt a spiritual connection with Billy through his father. Watching her son grow as the years went by, and the fact that he was so like his father in appearance also made Simone feel that in a strange sort of way she had never really lost Billy at all, and that he was always with her, right there by her side, living alongside her and their son in a virtual parallel existence.

Jimmy had long lost the desire for revenge on anything or anyone connected to Billy Kelly, but his need to keep his reputation intact, and the still deeply rooted sense of betrayal dictated that he sought out and executed appropriate retribution on Billy himself. The murders of both Tommy Callaghan and Paddy Meehan were still unsolved. The rumours and whispers of Jimmy's involvement had never dissipated despite his numerous denials in national newspaper stories, and one television interview given in 1992 on a popular real crime series aired on all the ITV regional channels.

The income gained from this line of passive employment helped Jimmy to look after his mother until she had died. Tony Fallon had become like a brother to Jimmy, straight, honest and dependable virtues that Jimmy believed in and held close. Tony had made sure that Jimmy's mum had had everything she could have needed to keep her comfortable in her last days, even hiring a home care professional to stay with her and tend to her every need during the day. At night a security firm called her every two hours until midnight. They also made a call to her home at seven o'clock every morning to check on her well being. These were all the things that Jimmy had learned upon his release from prison and the odd phone call to his mum from prison during her illness.

Chapter 20

Plymouth - London 2004

Billy boarded the train at Plymouth station to London Paddington, the journey would take approximately four hours thirty minutes including one change at Bristol Parkway.

The news of his father's death had hit him hard. The feelings of guilt and the emptiness he felt were only compounded by the news that Father Danny had given him about Simone. Could Simone's son really be his child? He was sure Simone wouldn't lie about that, but Father Danny was only assuming, Simone hadn't actually said that the boy was Billy's son.

The memory of seeing Simone that last time in Margate on the morning he had disappeared now tormented his already confused and troubled mind. He had so many questions running through his mind. If Simone was pregnant with his child, why hadn't she tried to find him, why? She was with his father when he died, how? Why was she paying for his care home?

Billy couldn't make sense of any of it. But he had a plan. When he got to London, he would meet with Father Danny, pay his respects to his father and then he was going to find Simone. He had to find out what had happened in the preceding years. Right now he couldn't care less about Jimmy Walsh, Christy Monaghan, Jack Riordan or anyone else for that matter who wanted him dead, there were questions he needed answers to and he was going to find them.

Billy changed trains at Bristol Parkway and waited the twenty or so minutes for the connection to London Paddington. He threw his brown overnight bag onto the overhead luggage rack and settled into a four-seat booth with a table.

The train was very quiet, there was just one elderly lady sitting in the booth opposite Billy, he smiled at her and nodded as he sat down. The lady had a pleasant smile on her face as she silently returned his acknowledgement.

Billy's mind drifted as the journey progressed, the rhythmic sound and motion of the train lulling him into that state of half-consciousness that everyone has experienced while riding the rails.

In his half-dream world, he could see a wedding party, a bride and groom dancing alone on the dancefloor to music being played by a silent band on a raised stage. People were standing around watching, their smiling faces enjoying the first dance of the happy newlyweds. His mother and father were there watching too, holding hands. He remembered this wedding, it was the niece of his mother's friend, they had been invited to the reception at the local Irish community centre.

A man was on the stage now, he took the microphone from the lead singer of the band as the bride and groom shyly kissed as the assembled friends and relatives applauded. He could hear what was being said now.

"Thank you guys, that was a lovely song. I would also like to thank everyone here today for helping my lovely wife and I celebrate the marriage of our beautiful daughter Veronica".

The attendees clapped and cheered loudly again.

"Most of you here know my good friend Michael Kelly over there, I'm going to surprise him, and no doubt embarrass him by asking him to sing a song for us tonight, come on up here Michael would you?"

The crowd clapped and cheered even more. Billy's mum pushed his dad forward as men slapped him on the back as he made his way to the stage, clearly embarrassed by the attention, but it didn't look like he had any fear of singing a song. Billy thought this strange - he had never heard his dad sing before.

Billy was right about his memory of this wedding now, as he appeared in his own dream standing next to his mum. His dad was on the stage now and took the microphone in one hand as he shook his friend's hand with the other. His mum looked so proud as the band played the first bar of the Old Irish ballad Carrickfergus. Billy's dad started to sing.

"I wish I was in Carrickfergus
Only for nights in Ballygran
I would swim over the deepest ocean
To be by your side"

Billy couldn't believe the voice of this man singing on stage belonged to his father, he was - superb. The soft Irish lilt of his singing voice captivated the audience who stood spellbound as Billy himself was.

"But the sea is wide and I cannot swim over
And neither have I the wings to fly
If I could find me a handy boatman
To ferry me over my love and I"

"My childhood days bring back sad reflection
Of happy times there spent so long ago
My boyhood friends and my own relations
Have all past on now with the melting snow"

Tommy Callaghan and Paddy Meehan joined Billy as he stood by his mum, both smiling as they listened to Billy's dad singing - as silently as they had arrived, they turned and walked away, waving to Billy as they left...

"Where did you go Tommy, Paddy, wait don't leave again - don't go, we never got to say goodbye…."

"So I'll spend my days in this endless roving
Soft is the grass, my bed is free
Oh to be home now in Carrickfergus
On the long road down to the salty sea"

"Now in Kilkenny it is reported
On marble stone there as black as ink
With gold and silver, I would support her
But I'll sing no more now till I get a drink"

The boys had disappeared. Billy's dad kept singing, a small tear trickled down the face of his mum as she dabbed at her eye with the corner of a handkerchief. Billy took his mum's hand.

The man who had introduced Billy's dad walked onto the stage and handed him a large glass of Jameson Irish Whiskey in readiness for the next verse. The crowd cheered loudly as he accepted the drink and continued on. The men in the audience brought the noise levels up by some decibels as they joined in the next two lines of the song trailing off...

"For I'm drunk today and I'm rarely sober
A handsome rover from town to town"

...leaving Billy's dad to sing out a solo ending...

"Ah but I'm sick now my days are numbered
So come all me young men and lay me down"

Billy looked puzzled as his mum let go of his hand as the crowd, clapped, cheered and wolf-whistled their appreciation for the performance. She bent forward, kissed his forehead. Turning from him, she walked away - a few footsteps and she was gone…

"Mum, don't go dad's coming back now…" but she was nowhere to be seen.

Billy's father raised his glass from the stage to the audience...

"Slàinte," he said to a cheering crowd, bowing from the waist.

Raised glasses were held aloft as the crowd roared back as one.

"Slàinte"

Turning he looked directly at Billy, he smiled.

"Goodbye Macushla," he said. He turned to walk off stage, a few footsteps and he faded from sight…

"Dad, dad wait…" Billy begged.

Billy awoke with a start. He was embarrassed to realise tears were falling from his eyes. The elderly lady looked at him, her eyes full of compassion and understanding.

Billy sat upright wiping the back of his hands across his face.

"You're a tormented soul son, she said in a soft Irish accent, whatever it is that troubles you so, it will pass so it will, you'll see mark my words you just keep your faith".

Her accent surprised Billy, but it somehow felt right at that moment.

"Yes mam, thank you, Billy replied, I will, I'm sorry it's been a long week".

"No need for apologies son. You're from an Irish family, am I right?" The lady asked.

"I am; how did you know? My parents were from Limerick" Billy said.

"Ah sure don't I have the gift, I can see things you know," the lady said.

"Ah ok - "Billy said, a little taken aback.

The lady laughed out loud.

"I'm *codding* you on son, you were talking in your sleep son, even I can guess when someone is dreaming and humming Carrickfergus and muttering Macushla there's a fair chance he's Irish, is that what your mammy called you?"

"No, it was my dad that called me by that name, he died last week - I only found out yesterday. I'm going to pay my respects". Billy could see the quizzical look on the lady's face.

"It's a really long story mam," he said, by way of an explanation.

"Not my business son, you seem like a good boy. You know son, whatever happened to part you from your daddy I'm sure he loved you, I'm sure he missed you. You know going back sometimes causes more problems than it solves - in life I mean. Don't you know, to let sleeping dogs lie as they say, in my experience no good comes from opening old wounds, especially those that never heal anyways" she said.

"You might be right there mam, but I need to make sense of some things. But thank you I appreciate your advice and concern. Thank you," Billy said.

"I will remember you in my prayers, and your daddy, may he Rest In Peace," the lady said.

The train pulled into London Paddington an hour later.

Billy leapt from the train as it slowed to a stop and hurried towards the exit barrier. He had arranged to meet Father Danny at St. Joseph's church in Colliers Wood in South West London, where Danny was now the parish priest.

Billy walked across the concourse breathing in the London air for the first time in many years, he felt a nostalgic yearning for bygone days of his youth, as he made his way to the escalator leading down to the southbound platform of the Bakerloo line on the underground. From there he boarded the train to Charing Cross and changed to the southbound train on the Northern line; he arrived at Colliers Wood station approximately forty-five minutes later.

Billy climbed the stairs to street level two at a time, it was as if he were to see a London street for the first time, hear the noises and smell the aromas, he was a Londoner and he was finally home after all those years in exile, this was his city, this was his manor.

Billy decided at that moment he was never going to be forced to leave London again. Whatever lay ahead he had to face it from a position of strength and running and hiding was not going to do it for him this time around. Billy felt liberated as he looked around him, the Red London buses, the London Evening papers on sale, the accents of the people on the streets, the smell of the street food, it was London, it was home, and he was home at last. He had missed this London life.

Nostalgia, Billy thought was all well and good, but as reality dawned on him again it forced him to concentrate on the matters at hand. He looked across at Wandle Park before turning right to walk the short distance to St. Joseph's Church on Park Lane.

As he arrived at the red brick fronted church, he felt nervous about meeting Father Danny after so long, this man had been his only contact with his former life and Billy had trusted him to keep his secret but had also bound him by his own vows not to speak of anything that was happening in his father's life. Father Danny had kept his word, he had been as loyal and honest as Billy could have expected, even when for six months in his darkest days Billy seemed to have disappeared without a trace, there were no phone calls in those times to ask of his father's well-being as agreed. When Billy had surfaced, there was no judgement, there was no scolding or chastisement for his disappearance and lack of communication. Father Danny just picked up their calls again as normal, only enquiring as to Billy's own health and well-being.

Billy walked to the side entrance of the church and rang the doorbell. The door was answered by an elderly lady in her seventies who Billy recognized in an instant. Mrs Dooley was a widow of some thirty years now and had dedicated her life to God and the church since her husband had passed away. Mrs. Dooley had been the housekeeper for the old parish church of St. Michael's back in the day.

"Hello young man, what can I do for you?" Mrs. Dooley asked.

"Hello, Mrs Dooley I'm here to see Danny - Father Gallagher I mean" Billy answered.

Mrs Dooley looked at Billy, searching her memory to make a connection and put a name to his face, she thought she knew him from somewhere but couldn't quite place him.

"Is he expecting you, who should I say is calling?" she asked.

"Yes he's expecting me, can you tell him it's Billy?"

The penny dropped, Billy Kelly - as large as life standing at the door of the church looking for the priest.

"Come to confess, have you?" she said snidely as she turned away.

Billy couldn't help but smile.

"It's a little late for that I think Mrs Dooley".

"Indeed it is" she muttered as she walked away to find Father Danny.

Father Danny Gallagher appeared and greeted Billy with a handshake. Billy pulled him close in a hug.

"Mrs Dooley is not a fan I take it Billy" Father Danny quipped.

"Yeah, she never was Danny, I think her daughter Moira might have something to do with that…". Billy didn't finish the sentence given where he was and who he was speaking with, he didn't think he should explain the cryptic reference to Mrs Dooley and her errant daughter any further.

"Thanks for everything you did over the years Danny, I know it can't have been easy. And I appreciate you taking time to see my dad when he was ill" Billy said.

"All part of the service - I'm sure you have a lot of questions Billy and as much as I can I will answer them".

"You could say that yeah - Simone? She was with my dad when he died, I don't get it, how did they meet?

"Well I had a long conversation with Simone, she told me everything from the day you met right up until the day you left and didn't return as promised. Simone thought you were just another flash London git who had dumped one girl for another. She really believed that you had changed your mind about her and didn't want her. She knew nothing about you, other than you lived in London, and her pride was hurt, that's why she never looked for you".

"But she was pregnant at that time? She never mentioned that to me, I honestly didn't know, I would never have left her Danny, you've got to believe me"

"Yes I know, Simone told me the same thing, Billy. I'm not judging you, I know you didn't know, given the circumstances perhaps that was the best thing. You know Simone really loved your father Billy, and that was because she loved you - and she has done a great job raising your son Billy, he's a real credit to her - and to you, he's a real smart boy you know".

"So the boy really is my son then Danny?"

"Yes there are no doubts there"

Billy hung his head, not so much in shame but in an act of pure frustration. His elbows resting on his knees, his fingers interwoven the knuckles turning white as he wrung his hands and bunched his fists.

"Billy - there is nothing you can do about the past, it's gone, but in the future, you have to consider what is the right thing to do. You have to find out what the right thing to do is, not what you want to do - what is the right thing to do - for everyone Billy".

Billy learned everything of the story of Simone and his son meeting and his father. How Simone had called his father the day after a visit from some men that came to

Margate looking for Billy. Simone had explained to him the situation regarding their relationship with her and that she was the mother to your son.

"You know something, Danny? I was there that day. The day they came to Simone's place. I was going to see her, and as she came out of the shop those two guys approached her. They got out of the same car that had followed me and that bent copper who was driving me from Swaleside prison. Christy Monaghan was in that car that day, blue Granada. I saw Simone, and the baby - I just thought she was involved with someone else, maybe married, so I left. I didn't want to give her any trouble. I wanted her but I was frightened that if I was with her that Jimmy, Riordan or Monaghan would keep looking, I'm sure they did. So I just left, I never forgot the last I saw her walking away, the blue and white baby stroller, and Simone's blue beret and scarf, almost matching it - always such class that girl showed, looked like a model even pushing a baby in buggy… Billy smiled and let the thought disappear.

As the conversation continued Father Danny learned how Billy's father had visited Margate on many occasions. At least once a month for the years leading up to his illness, and how Simone, who was a successful business owner had moved him to the coast to be looked after and cared for in a professional care home.

Simone had cared for Michael Kelly as if he were her own father, and his grandson had given him as much pleasure as any child had ever given any grandparent. The unlikely family dynamic they had created seemed to provide great comfort in the roles they all played in each other's lives, somehow living vicariously through each other, to fill the voids left in their day to day existence by Billy's absence.

Billy was satisfied he was now clearly in the picture as to how things had evolved over the years. There were just a couple of questions that he needed to understand the answers to before he could move on and decide his best course of action.

"Has Simone married Danny?"

"No she never married, never came anywhere near getting married as far as I know".

"She is still living on the coast I assume?"

Father Danny looked a little uncomfortable for a second or two before answering.

"Yes, she's still on the coast Billy, still living in Margate. She didn't want your son growing up in London and mixing with the likes of - well the likes of you I guess, sorry there's no other way to put it".

Billy gave a small chuckle and stood up.

"Yeah, that's a fair one I reckon Father. One last question Danny".

"What's on your mind?"

"Jimmy, have you seen him at all?" Billy asked.

"I did see him a couple of Christmases ago, he came to the early mass at St. Michael's, but not since. I hear he's living over in Battersea now, Jimmy will never change, you know that don't you?"

"Yeah, unfortunately, I do know that Danny".

Billy stood up to leave, shaking hands again with Father Danny.

"I have one last thing for you Billy, Father Danny said, throwing a bunch of keys in his direction. I think you'll find your room exactly as you left it. Simone had the rest of the house cleared out some time ago. Your dad wouldn't sell it, he always knew you would come home someday, and that you would need it - to shelter from the storm he said".

Billy caught the keys.

"Thank you, how long has it been empty?"

"About nine months I think, no more than a year for sure".

Billy left and hailed a taxi, the emotions of the day had proved a little overwhelming, he sat in the back of the cab, the driver asked him where he wanted to go. Billy didn't reply.

"Oi mate, where to? I ain't got all night you know".

"Yeah sorry, I need a drink mate, anywhere you'd recommend?"

"You want to go up West or somewhere local?"

"I'll tell you what mate, take me to The Old Kent Road, The Green Man".

The driver looked at Billy as if he'd gone mad…

"You a Millwall boy then…?

"No Palace actually" Billy replied.

Yeah right, that's going to go down well with the natives in there, it's your funeral then mate".

Billy smiled and settled back in the seat.

Billy had no intention of going into the *Green Man* at all and had also thought better of his decision to have a drink. It had been seven years since he had taken a drink, he didn't need it now. He needed a clear head. He would walk the twenty minutes to his father's house when the taxi dropped him off. He just needed to pick a couple of things up first.

Thirty minutes later Billy found himself in a local express supermarket, he picked up two pre-packed sandwiches, two bags of cheese and onion crisps, two one-pint cartons of full cream milk, a small towel and a flashlight with batteries. He threw everything inside his bag and carried on towards his father's house.

As he approached the house he decided to go via the back garden, checking the keys he was pretty sure that the bunch contained both the back garden gate key and the back door key. He turned right just before the row of houses that his parents' house was situated in and crossed the road, he slipped up the back alleyway leading to the back gate. The garden was only about sixty feet in length and given the cover of darkness, he should have no problem going in undetected.

Billy slipped the key into the lock and turned the key, it opened effortlessly. He made his way quickly and quietly up the back garden path to the back door where he stopped and removed the flashlight from the bag. Billy had already inserted the batteries and tested the flashlight at the shop he flicked on the switch. The immediate area was illuminated with light. Billy placed the flashlight on the floor and found the right key for the door, he opened it and stepped inside. Picking up his bag and flashlight, he made his way silently through the house to the stairs and headed up to his old bedroom.

Billy opened the door and was immediately transported back in time as the light filled the room. It was exactly as he had remembered it, the same wallpaper, the same lights. The bed had been stripped to the mattress, with two pillows at the headboard, as he opened the wardrobe he was surprised to find it was still full of his clothes, now somewhat dated but they were still there. Billy checked in the chest of drawers next to the wardrobe and found clean sheets and pillowcases. On the top of the chest of drawers lay an envelope with the single word "*BILLY*" written on it in blue biro ink.

He looked at the envelope unsure if he should open it. Billy sat on the edge of the bed Opening the bag, he realized how hungry he was, he hadn't eaten since breakfast. The envelope was still lying beside him unopened, curiosity or hunger he wasn't sure which would win this battle. Billy stood up and walked to the bathroom, he turned the cold tap on the sink and thankfully water spilt from it, still not sure what to do first, eat something or read the letter he decided to freshen up. He walked back to the bedroom and removed the towel from the bag.

After he rinsed his face and hair with water he sat on the bed again - he unwrapped the cheese sandwich and opened a carton of milk. As he stared around the room he could remember the noises of the house all those years ago, the strained opening bars of the theme tune of Coronation Street, his mum sitting in her armchair waiting for the latest instalment of life in the grim north, the cat creeping across the roof. Billy remembered the smell of home cooking that used to fill the house and how he had such happy memories here of his childhood, he certainly had been blessed with parents that had loved and cared for him.

His curiosity could be restrained no longer, he ripped the envelope open and removed one sheet of folded paper and two photographs. The first photograph was of Simone holding Billy Junior in her arms. The second of Simone, Billy Junior, now maybe five or six years old, with his grandfather in a garden somewhere. Their smiling faces radiant with joy, they looked so happy together, it made Billy regret all the more the bad choices he made in his life and the things he missed that would never be replaced.

He unfolded the letter and read it.

My Dearest Billy,

It is impossible to put into words the regrets I have for us not being able to spend our lives with you. I have missed you and loved you every day of my life since you left.

If I had known anything about your life back at that time I would never have let you go to London that morning, I would never have let you leave. I should have told you I was expecting your baby, and I regret the day I made the decision to try and surprise you with that news when you were due to return to Margate.

I can't explain in this short letter all the things I want to and need to tell you. Your son has always been a constant reminder to me of you, his father, and a comfort to me when I missed you most. I will never tell him anything but good things about you because, in truth, that's all I know.

I understand that you could never have come back and that what you did when you left for good was as much for your family and our safety as it was for yourself and your own.

I don't know if you will ever read this letter but I hope you do, and if you do, I hope you will understand when I tell you that we cannot turn the clock back, we cannot be together. Because as much as I had hoped and prayed that one day we could be, I can't expose our son to your world and put his life at risk for my own wishes.

So please Billy, if you ever loved me, and I know that you did, please don't try to find us. To have to tell you to leave would break my heart again, I couldn't take that.

Your father was a great man and a great grandfather, he loved Billy Junior as much as he loved you, he missed you too. I often saw his eyes fill with tears when he looked at or held Billy Junior in his arms, I knew that he was remembering and imagining it was you.

So please take care,

God bless,

Always yours,

Simone.

Billy read the letter twice more before he put it down on the bed thinking of how Simone must have felt all those years - he was shaken out of his thoughts by a loud knock on the front door.

Billy went downstairs not sure whether to answer the door. After checking from the window he could see there was a police car outside. Mr Roberts, the next-door neighbour was standing by the car pointing up to the bedroom window. The bedroom was only minutely illuminated by the flashlight, he couldn't believe his neighbour had noticed it, the nosy bastard.

He really didn't have a choice, he would have to open the door and explain his presence. It shouldn't be hard given that Mr Roberts would know him, and the police should be satisfied, after all, he hadn't committed any crime, he just didn't want to broadcast his presence.

"Good evening Sir," the police officer said as Billy opened the door.

"Hi, what's up, can I help you?"

"Yes sir, do you live here sir at this property, are you the owner?"

"Well, yes I am I guess, I've been away awhile you see"

Having overheard the conversation Mr Roberts shouted out to the police officer at the door.

"Don't take any notice of him, officer, he's not the owner. Mr Kelly is the owner and the poor man passed away just very recently, he has no business here".

Billy had no choice but to respond.

"Mr Roberts, it's me - Billy Kelly"

Mr Roberts walked a few steps forward to get a better look at him.

"Billy - is that you?" Roberts said as he moved up the garden path to the front door. Recognising Billy he put his hands to his head.

"Billy, it is you, I'm sorry I thought someone had broken into the house and was inside".

"It's ok Mr Roberts, no harm done".

"So you know this man Mr Roberts, you can vouch for him?" The police officer asked.

"Yes, yes this is Billy Kelly - he's the owners' son, how long has it been Billy?"

"Nearly twenty years now in all, I only learned about dad two days ago, that's why I wasn't at the funeral," Billy said almost apologetically.

"Ok good no need for us then, could I just see some ID Sir? Just to verify your credentials, and we can call it a night" the police officer asked.

"Well - yeah sure, can you come in for a minute, Mr Roberts I will catch up with you sometime, nice to see you".

"Ok Billy, I look forward to it," Roberts answered as he walked back up towards the police car.

Billy fished in his back pocket and pulled out a wallet.

"Listen - this is going to sound a bit strange, this is my official ID, Billy said, as he handed the police officer his driver's license"

Billy's photo sure enough, but the name read Richard Murray.

"Well now this is a bit unusual sir, what's the meaning of your official ID?"

"I changed my name by deed poll to Richard Murray, that's why I have been away. I had a big barney with the old man over the name change thing, you know how it is, family name and all that".

"I see, well Mr Roberts seems to know you and he's verified that much to us, you showed us a valid ID albeit in a diffcrent name than that of which the neighbour knows you by. I just need to put it all in the report, you will be here if we need you?".

"Ok no problem, Billy said, I will be here tomorrow yes, well I'm going out around seven in the morning. I will be back by nine, I'm just going up to West Norwood Cemetery to pay my respects to my father".

"That's ok, no problem, I don't think we will need to bother you, so good night sir, sorry to have disturbed you," the officer said as he turned and left.

"Yeah, good night" Billy answered.

Billy went upstairs to the bedroom, decided he had more than enough excitement for one day, he threw a sheet on the bed and settled down to sleep.

Sitting in the police car still at the curb outside, the officer was calling in the PNC check on Billy. The radio report came back as no outstanding warrants on either William Kelly or Richard Murray at that address.

Sitting nearby in the police control room, quite by chance and listening to this conversation was another face from Billy's past, the police driver that had tried to set up Billy the day he was released from Swaleside prison and who had tried to deliver him into the hands of Christy Monaghan. The interested police officer's name was none other than Detective Sergeant George Knowles.

Knowles picked up the phone on his desk and dialled a number.

"Hello," the voice answered.

"I have some good news for you. Your friend is back in town, staying at his old man's place" Knowles said.

"Are you sure, one hundred per cent sure?" Jimmy Walsh asked.

"Yes, no doubt whatsoever, I'm on early shift tomorrow I can keep an eye on him for you from about six. I will bell you if he moves before nine" Knowles said.

"Nice one, I will talk to you tomorrow George".

The following morning as promised George Knowles was sat in his car fifty yards from Billy's Father house with a thermos of coffee and the Daily Mirror. His task was simply to wait for Billy Kelly to move and call Jimmy Walsh as soon as he left the house.

Knowles was on his third cup of coffee at just after seven o'clock when Billy emerged from the house, pushing the front door to ensure it was locked behind him - an old habit now. Billy walked quickly along the road, and his hands thrust deep into the pockets of his grey Crombie overcoat. Knowles removed a Motorola RAZR V3 flip phone from his pocket, keeping Billy firmly in his sight.

Jimmy Walsh answered the call on the third ring.

"Hello".

"Jimmy, its George, he's on the move, I will call you when I know where he's going"

"Good boy George, I'll be waiting"

Billy carried on walking at a brisk pace. Knowles pulled the car away from the curb and crawled behind, keeping his distance. Billy ducked into the same supermarket that he had used last night, picking up two bunches of flowers from the bucket display outside. Two minutes later he was back again walking in the same direction.

Billy stopped and looked over his shoulder. Knowles thought he had been tumbled and pulled into the curb, but it appeared Billy hadn't seen him, he was looking for something else, and there it was - a taxi. Knowles breathed a sigh of relief.

"Too early for a date, too early for visiting a hospital - he's going to the cemetery - definitely makes sense his old man just died," Knowles said to himself.

Billy jumped into the taxi cab and it pulled away into the morning traffic, Knowles not far behind.

"West Norwood Cemetery please mate" Billy said.

The early morning traffic moved swiftly along the route and fifteen minutes later Billy was climbing out of the cab and walking through the gates of West Norwood Cemetery. He waited for the taxi to pull away, before moving.

Billy pulled a flat cap from his pocket and settled it on his head, he undid the top button of the overcoat to reveal the Roman collar of a catholic priest.

He quickly found the plot and bent down to place the floral tributes with the others still piled there. The morning was bitterly cold and damp, drizzle swirled around.

Knowles smiled and muttered.

"Have a look, it's Father Kelly...". The flip phone appeared again and he placed another call to Jimmy Walsh.

"You're not going to believe this Jimmy; he's only dressed up like a priest ain't he"

Jimmy laughed at the other end of the line.

"Yeah, maybe he can give himself the last rites, I'm leaving now," he said.

Chapter 21

South London 2004

His name was Rrok Belushi. He had been born and raised dirt poor in a slum in the backstreets of Tirana, Albania. One of only two children, his father was a cobbler, his mother a seamstress. Rrok Belushi didn't like being poor, he didn't like the life he had endured as he was growing up, hardly ever going to school, helping his father out in the two small cramped rooms that doubled as a workshop and the family accommodation. It had always been a struggle for his family, his mother, his father and younger brother alike. Never enough money in the house, never enough food, second-hand clothes and hand me down shoes repaired by his father. But that was then - and this was now. He had sworn that all that would change when he was old enough to make decisions for himself.

Rrok Belushi was now at the top of his profession' a true master of his craft. He looked out across the river Thames from his luxury London Docklands apartment balcony that cold January morning and breathed in the fresh air. He had always wanted to join the army from an early age, he had wanted to learn to fight, he wanted to look smart in the uniform, but most of all from that early age he had known what he really wanted to do and that it was just something that he knew he was born to do, and that was - he just wanted to kill.

Rrok Belushi was a hitman. A cold-blooded assassin who commanded and got, upwards of one hundred thousand pounds sterling for his elite services, any time they were needed, and they were needed more and more in this troubled and turbulent materialistic world. His family now lived like kings in his native country, and Rrok Belushi had the respect of everyone.

Rrok Belushi had joined the Albania army just as soon as he was old enough at nineteen. He had become a skilled hand to hand combat expert, excelled at close quarter knife attack techniques, and had reached the zenith of his skills with a handgun and sniper rifle. He had been an elite soldier and now he was an elite killer.

Rrok Belushi had achieved all he had wanted too and more, more than he could ever have imagined. Money, power, and respect. He lived a life of freedom to choose what he did, and whom he did it for. He was the master of his own destiny and he loved his life. He had chosen this way of life, it wasn't something he had to do, it wasn't something he needed to do, it was something he loved doing, and he was the best he could be at it. He was physically fit and worked out six days a week, taking Sunday's off for muscle recovery time, as he was taught in the army. His body was impressively sculpted by various calisthenics, weight and resistance training, yoga and swimming, his hand to hand combat skills still as sharp as they were on the day he had left the army and his weapons knowledge and firearms training had continued to this very day unabated to the point of fanaticism.

His work came via recommendations and word of mouth. A two-tier security checking system that kept Rrok Belushi as far under the client and authorities radar as he could possibly be. His only contact with his client being a one-off meeting at the outset for the sole purpose of looking into his, or her eyes when he asked for his fee to be transferred via a laptop computer straight into his numbered Swiss bank account. Only when that transaction completed, did Rrok accept the assignment, with a guarantee of success!

Rrok had had such a meeting a week previously in North London. The meeting had been with Mr Mehmet Arslan, the head of the feared Turkish crime family. Mehmet was dying from lung cancer and wanted the murder of his son Arda, nearly twenty years earlier avenged, and he wanted it avenged before he died. The fee agreed was two hundred and fifty thousand pounds. The fee had as always been deposited in the account of Rrok Belushi and the agreement made. This assignment was different in only one way from his other previous jobs. There were two targets, these two targets were numbers three and four of five, one and two had already been taken care of. These targets were - Jimmy Walsh and Billy Kelly.

Mehmet Arslan had lain in what he was sure was to be his deathbed. Rrok Belushi swore to him he would not fail in his mission to avenge his son. Mehmet had used Rrok Belushi previously, he knew he was a man of his word. Mehmet Arslan had explained to Rrok Belushi, anger burning in his tear-filled eyes, that he had only waited this long for revenge because he wanted the two men to die together, he knew that there was only a small chance that this would ever happen, but he had waited and he had prayed. He had wanted to kill Jimmy Walsh some years ago when he was released from prison, but the problem was that Billy Kelly had disappeared right after he was released from prison in 987. His inquiries led him to believe that Jimmy Walsh had unsuccessfully tried to find

Billy Kelly to kill him also and that he had been trying to track him down all that time, with not a single lead.

Rumour also had it that the other two members of their firm at the time of his son's death, Tommy Callaghan and Paddy Meehan were also killed by Jimmy Walsh, one in Scotland the other in Tenerife. This, of course, could not be proved, and rumours were not always to be believed. The break Mehmet Arslan had been waiting for had come three days ago.

His people had found out that the father of Billy Kelly had died, and that Jimmy Walsh was sure that this was his opportunity to finally catch up with the man who had betrayed him, he was sure Billy Kelly would come to London at some time soon. So it would appear it was just a waiting game.

"If you stick with Jimmy Walsh, he will eventually lead you to Billy Kelly and both will be together, and I will then be able to accept my death as a contented man". Mehmet Arslan had said.

Rrok Belushi had also hired through Mehmet Arslans' contacts a team of discreet private security experts to carry out a twenty-four-hour surveillance programme on Jimmy Walsh. They had rolling teams covering six in the morning until two in the afternoon, a middle shift from two in the afternoon until ten in the evening and the graveyard shift from ten in the evening until six in the morning. The teams were made up of ex-professionals, mainly military and police, and were considered the best in the business. Rrok Belushi was ready and waiting. Jimmy Walsh and Billy Kelly had both been living on borrowed time, that time was about to run out.

Rrok Belushi was a perfectionist. He did everything methodically, he left nothing to chance. The fact he had to hire security people made him nervous. Although he had not, and never would meet or speak to any of the security teams, the fact that other people were aware of Jimmy Walsh being under surveillance was a breach of his own stringent security protocols that he was not comfortable with. Jimmy Walsh would be spotted and Jimmy Walsh would be taken out. The plan was that if within the next seven days there was no sign of Billy Kelly, then the hit on Jimmy Walsh would proceed by default. Mehmet Arslan would at least know that the man who had shot his son down like a dog in cold blood had paid with his own life, and the life of his son Arda would have been avenged.

Rrok Belushi was aware that Billy Kelly was now using the alias of Richard Murray. This information had been of little use to him, he hadn't had any luck in tracking down any financial information such as bank accounts or credit card transactions that gave him any leads as to the whereabouts of Billy Kelly that interested him. A common enough name but easy enough to eliminate ninety-five per cent of the men with that name without having to move from the comfort of your own home. The electoral roll was a very informative tool for the public to take advantage of and was awash with the type of personal details tailor-made for eliminating those of no interest. Age, address and family members made it an easy task for someone as diligent as Rrok Belushi.

The big break that Mehmet Arslan had been waiting for came the morning after Billy Kelly had arrived in London. A faint light was seen through the window of his father's house by a next-door neighbour the previous evening. The dutiful do-gooder called the police and reported a possible break in or maybe, God forbid, squatters. The police had arrived at the scene and carried out a PNC check on one William Kelly and the name Richard Murray at the address of the house. Although this came back as clear, it set in motion a chain of events that would lead Rrok Belushi directly to Jimmy Walsh and Billy Kelly.

Mehmet Arslan received a call that Jimmy Walsh had just arrived at West Norwood Cemetery. He had made his way to the graveside of Billy Kelly's father and was at that moment holding a man at gunpoint, they were almost one hundred per cent sure the man was - Billy Kelly.

Mehmet Arslan felt his pulse quicken as he called for a telephone. He made a call to Rrok Belushi and gave him the go-ahead, even if it turned out not to be Billy Kelly, to take Jimmy Walsh out anyway.

Rrok Belushi gave Mehmet Arslan his solemn word that one way or another his son's death would be avenged that day. He hung up the phone and prepared to leave. He took with him a specially made protective metal case, that housed a broken down R93 Tactical sniper rifle. Rrok Belushi left the luxury apartment at Surrey Quays and hurried to the lifts. Once inside he pushed the B2 button for the second level of the basement parking.

Lifting the seat of the gleaming chrome and black Suzuki Intruder 1400, he dropped the case inside, the cavity the perfect dimensions to hold the case firmly in place. The machine purred into life. Rrok Belushi gave the throttle a couple of revs before gliding up the ramp and into the London morning, en-route to West Norwood Cemetery.

Chapter 22
South London 2004

And so it came to pass on that bitter cold and damp South London morning in January 2004 that Billy Kelly finally emerged from the shadows of his past, to face the ghosts that had haunted him for nearly twenty years. The biting wind cut his face deep to the bone with an icy chill. He walked briskly through the cemetery to find his father's grave.

*****

As Rrok Belushi arrived at West Norwood Cemetery, he moved through the main gate and turned in the opposite direction of the location he was given for the grave of Michael Kelly. The engine of the Suzuki Intruder a low near-silent throb as he made his way some six hundred meters away from where Jimmy and Billy were standing at the graveside. Rrok Belushi dismounted quickly and removed the crash helmet with full face visor and laid it next to the motorcycle. He removed the case and assembled the R93 Tactical sniper rifle in less than twenty seconds.

The R93 Tactical is a sniper rifle designed by German company Blaser Jagdwaffen. It has a detachable magazine, muzzle brake and fully adjustable stock. The R93 Tactical is used by a number of militaries, special forces and law enforcement agencies worldwide, including Germany, Australia, Brazil, France, The Netherlands, Poland, Ukraine and the United Kingdom.

The Blaser R93 Tactical is a bolt-action rifle; it has a 600 mm (23.6") barrel. The weapon is fed from detachable 5-round capacity magazines, there are also optional 10-round capacity magazines.

This version of the R93 had a lightweight stock with fully-adjustable cheek piece. This weapon had a vertical pistol grip. There is an inbuilt provision to mount a mono or bipod option for steadying accuracy.

The R93 Tactical sniper rifle is extremely accurate. It can deliver small groups with sub 0.25 MOA (Minute of Accuracy). This weapon has an effective kill shot range of around 800 meters.

The last piece of specialist equipment he fixed to the rifle was a screw-on, eight-inch long silencer, fixed to the end of the barrel. This would reduce and muffle the gunshot to mere a hiss when fired.

Rrok Belushi now moved stealthily into his firing position, scoping and surveying the graveyard with the expert eye of a predator. He looked directly at Jimmy and Billy through the AR15 sixteen graticule sight. He had a clear and unimpeded line of sight to his targets. The cemetery was extremely quiet this morning, no funerals to worry about and at present, it was even too early for visitors, this was as good as Rrok Belushi could have hoped for, no members of the public to worry about, no unnecessary interruptions or pain in the arse nosy parkers.

Rrok Belushi watched his prey as they stood by the open grave. Jimmy Walsh directly behind Billy Kelly, handgun by his side. They seemed to be having a conversation, what the hell, let them enjoy a few moments more, it would be their last. Revenge is sweet. Unfortunately for Jimmy Walsh, he wasn't going to get to experience that sensation of having killed the man who had betrayed him, righting a terrible wrong was not to be for Jimmy Walsh.

Jimmy Walsh had lived far too long on the reputation of Rrok Belushi, letting the world believe that it was he that had taken the lives of Tommy Callaghan and Paddy Meehan. Or at least letting the world believe it was he who had ordered the hits on them, not that it mattered today, all that mattered right now was that both these men would draw their last breaths at the hands Rrok Belushi on the orders of Mehmet Arslan in the memory of his son Arda, as had the two before them.

*****

Jimmy had arrived some five minutes before the arrival of Rrok Belushi. Billy had been too immersed in his personal grief to notice him slip quietly along the narrow pathway between the graves.

*****

Jimmy's voice was high pitched with emotion, and that made Billy even more nervous. The wind felt colder now, Billy was sure it wasn't colder, but the biting gusts forced his shoulders to retract uncontrollably into his body. He knew he was going to die. He knew that Jimmy never gave anyone a second chance. He had pleaded his case earlier but knew that would not have impressed Jimmy. Billy knew that Jimmy had found him guilty of the worst crime he could have committed, he had turned informant and Billy knew that too. He had taken the plea bargain. Four years of soft time in an open prison, new identity and some cash, not a lot just enough to get started again.

Billy realized all at once just how tired he was, it was a sort of release he might actually want all this to end, even right now at the hands of his childhood friend. He was so tired he didn't care anymore.

"I still can't believe you're a grass Billy, you of all people I trusted you with my life, I never wanted to believe it, even in court I never thought you would offer Riordan up, I ought to fucking kill you right now."

Jimmy's hand was raising the gun - he stopped.

"Just fucking do it, Jimmy, I'm sick of hearing you whine like an old lady, get on with t" Billy goaded him, all thoughts of fear had evaporated in that single moment of knowing you were past the point of no return.

"Don't rush me, Billy I might be enjoying myself, you got brave all of a sudden? Why un in the first place if you're not scared of dying?"

"I'm just tired of all of this, it's been twenty years, do what you need to do and have done with it. I'm sick of running and I'm not leaving London again. So you better kill me or your killer reputation will be gone. I mean the Turks, Paddy and Tommy - and fuck knows how many others".

"I didn't kill Paddy and Tommy - I never claimed to have killed them, I just let everyone believe it was me"

Billy wasn't sure what to make of this, he wasn't even sure if he believed him.

"So who did then - Riordan?"

"No it wasn't Riordan, he thought it was me too, I told Monaghan it wasn't me when he came to see me. Monaghan told me Riordan had no interest in Tommy or Paddy, but you were different, he was on you like a fly on shit as soon as he got the chance".

"I just want to live a quiet life Jimmy, that's what I have been doing all these years, why can't you let this go, hasn't there been enough killing?"

"Oh, you're going to get back with Simone and your boy are you? Yeah I know all about that, I saw them at the funeral".

"No I'm not getting back with Simone, she made that very clear in a letter I found at my dad's place, she wasn't sure I would ever read it, but there you go she still makes it easy to understand. It never really was much, just those few months, but I was going to ask her to marry me you know, I was going to go and buy a ring on the Monday - never got that far though. I was leaving Jimmy, I was going to give up this London life and go and live on the coast, all the things we were involved in, I'm surprised we are even here now".

"Yeah well, we all missed out on a lot, you seem to think that if I let you go then you are free to live your life again Billy, what about Riordan? As soon as he knows you're on the manor Monaghan and a few of his finest ex-Provo boys will be looking for you".

"Yeah well, why don't you just let me worry about that?"

"Turn around Billy," Jimmy said.

Billy turned as he was asked to do. Jimmy didn't look much different from when he had seen him last, a bit heavier for sure, but not that different.

"Why didn't you just stay gone, Billy? Jimmy asked as he raised the gun to Billy's forehead, you've made me do this".

Billy smiled…

*****

Rrok Belushi watched Jimmy raise the gun through the sight. Jimmy was dead centre in the middle of his crosshairs. The trigger finger poised to squeeze - Rrok Belushi checked through the sight and squeezed the first shot off, the rifle hissed spitting silent death. Bolt back, bullet engaged in the chamber, trigger squeezed - the second bullet took flight on invisible wings of death. The targets were struck - both men fell into the open grave - dead

Billy had looked down as Jimmy levelled the gun at his forehead. He then lifted his eyes just in time to see Jimmy's head explode - the bullet had struck him between his temple and the corner of his right eye. Billy's face was covered in a mess of blood, hair and brain matter - less than two seconds later before Billy had had time to realise what had happened he too was hit by the second shot. The bullet smashed through his face just above his nose.

*****

Billy had grabbed Jimmy as he fell. The two men, who were once as close as childhood friends could be, clung to each other in mid-air, falling towards an open grave in a pitiful dance of death. Jimmy Walsh and Billy Kelly both died instantly. As they fell Jimmy hit the side of the open grave as he went, which spun him around, onto his back. They lay in the mud, their bodies intertwined on the bottom of a freshly dug grave as if the grave had been prepared for them. It was as if this was how it was meant to be, to end today on a cold grey London morning, nearly twenty years - and a lifetime after it had begun. Two troubled men, who had been the best of friends and the worst of enemies, who had laughed and cried together, who had won and lost together, and had now drawn their final breaths as one.

*****

Rrok Belushi broke down the sniper rifle as quickly as he had assembled it. The case was repacked and put under the seat in the storage space. He replaced his helmet and pulled down the visor. The Suzuki Intruder hummed into life and he was gone.

Thirty minutes later he was safe inside his apartment. The phone rang and he answered it.

"It is done," he said softly.

"This is excellent news, please make your travel arrangements," Mehmet Arslan said.

"Yes Sir - I will be on a flight to Spain tomorrow"

*****

Mehmet Arslan smiled and closed his eyes. Four of the five men involved in his son's murder were now dead. Very soon the fifth would also die.

*****

News of the deaths of Jimmy Walsh and Billy Kelly soon emerged as a labourer who worked digging graves found them less than two hours later. They had died together that day, their lives entwined in death as they had been in life, their bodies lying in a grave staring up at the sky wide-eyed and lifeless. Their legend and that of the Walsh firm would live long in the memories of the criminal underworld of London.

*****

Father Danny Gallagher called Simone and broke the news of Billy's murder. Simone immediately thought that Jimmy Walsh was responsible and was shocked to learn that Jimmy was also killed with Billy.

Father Danny told her the police believed that it was a professional hit and that Jack Riordan was the prime suspect in the murders.

Simone wept quietly as she asked if Father Danny had known if Billy had found the letter she had left in his father's house. Father Danny had told her that he had no idea, as he had not seen Billy since he had given him the keys yesterday.

Simone felt guilty now and wondered if all the things that had been said, and those that were left unsaid in their short tragic relationship could have changed the outcome of this pointless waste of lives spanning two decades. If she had told Billy that she was expecting their child that Sunday morning long ago, would he have even left her side that day? Could that one simple statement of truth and joy have changed the course of their lives forever? Could it have prevented the pointless deaths of six men, and the pain caused to so many others having to continue in a life lived without their loved ones? Michael Kelly and Breda Walsh had lost their son's so many years before, as had the parents of Tommy Callaghan and Paddy Meehan. Billy Junior had been robbed of the chance to ever meet his father. And Simone had lost the only man she had ever loved. The two Turkish men had also been killed, but Simone had never known their names, bu she knew now how their families must have grieved.

Billy Junior appeared at the doorway, as Simone wept uncontrollably now.

"What's happened Mum, what is it?" he asked.

"Oh Billy, your father is dead, he was shot and killed in London this morning".

Billy Junior went to his mother's side and held her. He had always lived with the hope that he would meet his father one day, it would appear that this would now never happen. Billy felt he had been robbed of the opportunity to know his father and his mother had been robbed of the opportunity to be with the only man she had ever loved.

"It's ok Mum, he's at peace now," Billy Junior said.

Billy Juniors eyes burned with tears that would never fall. He held his mother to his chest and felt her body shake as the sobs wracked through her. He always knew it was going to end this way, he had always known.

The next morning Billy Junior decided what he had to do. He dropped out from his position at Canterbury University.

*****

One week after Billy Kelly had been murdered, a young man walked into an Army recruitment centre in London. He was tall, with brown hair and green eyes. He sat and waited for the Sergeant to call him to the booth where he would be interviewed.

As the young man made his way into the booth the recruitment Sergeant stood up and extended his hand to him, they shook hands and the young man took a seat.

"So you want to join the Army young man?"

"I do"

"And what do you want to learn in the Army, it's not all fun and exotic locations you know" the Sergeant said with a smile.

"I want to learn hand to hand combat, I want to be a weapons and munitions expert, I want to be the best recruit from my year, and I want to be the ultimate soldier"

The Sergeant laughed.

"Well at least you know what you want, what about a career after the Army, you think those skills will be useful to you?"

"Those skills will be most useful to me after the Army Sir"

The Sergeant wasn't quite sure what to make of that response but pressed on with the formalities. The young man seemed bright, well-spoken and clean cut, but there something about his answers - and he had a look of something sinister in his eyes.

"Ok then – what's your name son?"

"William – William Kelly Junior…

The End.

Printed in Great Britain
by Amazon

62775053R00123